D1568926

THE NARCISSISM OF
SMALL DIFFERENCES

A Noir Detective Novel

DENNIS DORGAN

ISBN: 978-1-09839-227-7 (softcover)
ISBN: 978-1-09839-228-4 (eBook)

ACKNOWLEDGEMENTS

My heartfelt thanks go to the following; without their help this book would never have been completed: Dexter Westrum, whose example, encouragement and humor were the initial inspiration for this work. Cecilia MacDonald, who read one page and insisted on editing the whole thing. Doug Watts, whose careful and encouraging developmental edit transformed the earlier drafts into something resembling a novel. Jody Beaulieu, a wise Ojibwe grandmother who made sure the sections of the book dealing with Ojibwe characters and culture never rang false. Fred Staff, whose westerns have captured the imagination of thousands of readers and who helped mold the final shape of this story . The readers whose serious critiques and support were the finest expressions of friendship anyone could hope for: Beth Wickum, Ron Ausan, Bruce Durand, Doug German, Karen Carr, Carol Jackson, Derek Hughes, Peg Halseth and Bob Frey. Special thanks go to Don and Verla Richardson, teachers who never stopped learning. Finally, there is Debra, the center that holds.

CONTENTS

THE NARCISSISM OF SMALL DIFFERENCES

The narcissism of small differences: it is precisely the little dissimilarities in persons who are otherwise alike that arouse feelings of strangeness and enmity between them.

—*Sigmund Freud*

Light is the left hand of darkness and darkness the right hand of light.

—*Ursula La Guin*

All differences in this world are of degree, and not of kind, because oneness is the secret of everything.

—*Swami Vivekananda*

... ineluctable duality of the indivisible.

—*Dante Connacht*

PROLOGUE

He came into the doublewide like a bear ambling into its winter cave. "Grandmother, I heard Henri's back. Is he here?"

"No, Eli, he's still with the Winnebago family in St. Paul. They will send him back when they clear up this confusion. You just gotta be patient."

"I'm doin' that, but it's hard, Grandmother. Who is this kid?" He sat heavily in the chair across the kitchen table from me. "He ain't Ojibwe, so what's he doin' here?"

Grandmother Raven set a mug of coffee in front of him. "He's ten years old, same as Henri. The state people will say they made a mistake, got them mixed up, but I think Manitou brought him here."

Eli studied my face without looking into my eyes. I knew he must be, like the old woman, an American Indian – high, hard cheekbones, a long, single braid, dark complexion and piercing dark eyes. I wondered if he would scalp me. I didn't care one way or the other, I just wondered.

"His face, it looks like an owl and them big grey eyes, they got mysteries in 'em, don't they? But what's wrong with him?" he finally asked.

"Something scared him, scared him real bad. He has not said nothing since he came here two days ago. He just sits and stares at Gichi-Gami with those big owl eyes. I don't know his story yet."

"What you gonna do, Grandmother?" Eli asked. "Shouldn't you send him back?"

"I told you, Manitou brought him here. Why do you think he is here?"

He looked at me again and, after a brief moment, said, "You a lucky kid, Owl Eyes, Grandmother Raven is a Midewikwe with great powers." He stood and turned to Grandmother Raven. "If you gonna conduct a sweat for this kid you want me to build the lodge?" He paused and frowned. "That's why I came here, isn't it?"

Grandmother Raven raised one eyebrow and nodded toward the door.

As he left, she shifted her gaze to me. Sitting where Eli Bouchard had been only seconds before, she regarded me intently, staring fixedly, until all I could see were her deep brown eyes framed by a profound darkness, nothing else, not even her face. I heard her voice, strong and clear, saying, "I must learn your story. When I ask a question and your answer is 'yes', you will blink once. OK?"

I felt my eyelids, without my conscious consent, blink. Once.

"If your answer is 'no' you will blink twice. Go ahead, do that." And my eyelids, despite my resistance, once again bent to her will. She then ordered me to blink three times if the answer were something other than yes or no; like 'maybe' or 'I don't know.'

We sat like that for what could have been two or three hours, or days, or just minutes; I don't know. Time became elusive, like a shadow in twilight. She quickly asked question after question, with my eyes blinking rapid-fire responses. I don't remember the questions or much of anything else other than those eyes. With them she drew out the memories of my young life and began pulling me back from the beckoning abyss of despair.

My story: I was born as a craniopagus twin, conjoined at the skull with my brother Cody.. Surgeons separated Cody and me in our tenth year. I survived the procedure, he did not. Or so it seemed.

The car bomb that killed my parents exploded just four months after that procedure. It left me in a state of wild, manic fear, intensified by soul numbing grief.

My mother was a Belfast attorney who acted as a mediator during the Irish troubles of the '70s. We were in Minnesota to have the operation at Mayo clinic. She also had speaking engagements and meetings with the Irish community in St. Paul.

There were fanatics on both sides of that endless Irish civil war who wanted her dead. Her success at getting Protestant and Catholic women to talk with each other posed too great a threat to some ideal future of Ireland, so they turned to their dark side, as zealots must.

The three of us stopped at Mancini's Restaurant in St. Paul on the way to the airport for our return flight to Belfast. That's when the bomb was planted.

I learned later that a cop plucked me from the burning wreckage of the rental car and rushed me to Phelan Hospital. A week later a bureaucratic snafu kept Henri Bouchard in a foster home in St. Paul and delivered me to Grand Portage Indian Reservation and Grandmother Raven.

I felt my brother's death even more keenly than that of my parents. Known only to the two of us, our physical condition led to our two streams of consciousness becoming intertwined. As a result, we knew each other's every thought and even watched each other's dreams. In the years we were bound together we also never felt what I came to know as the quintessential human experiences of loneliness and alienation. Later in life I sometimes wondered if we were the only human beings to ever have escaped those conditions.

When Cody died, followed so quickly by the violent death of our parents, my universe shattered. Now I knew loneliness, and alienation virtually defined my mental state.

It may have been days, but it seemed like only a few minutes after Grandmother Raven finished her interrogation, that Eli Bouchard returned to announce the readiness of the sweat lodge. It was now dark and a hard wind full of snow and cold was howling across the big lake and shaking the doublewide trailer. Grandmother Raven glanced at Eli and nodded to the doorway.

As he left she moved to the center of the kitchen. She closed her eyes and slowly raised her hands. The wind howled louder; the trailer convulsed and trembled. As she lowered her arms, three wizened old Indian men marched in and stood on each side and behind me. We seemed to glide out of the shuddering trailer and were met by four other old men. We were encased in an invisible wind and snow-free bubble. The eight of us slid smoothly into the sweat lodge. It was far larger inside than out and seemed immune to the wind raging outside. When we sat at the base of the circular lodge, I saw there were about a dozen others waiting for us. Near the entrance three men were beating on a circular drum and chanting in a strange language. The heat generated by the steam boiling off a mound of hot rocks in the center of the lodge was almost unbearable. Sweat immediately began seeping from every pore in my body.

Beside the drummers, there were two elderly women who shook some kind of rattles that had black bird wings attached to them. They rattled these intermittently, sometimes directly in someone's face.

Every so often a man or woman in the group would stand and speak, always in that strange tongue. They would go on for, what seemed to me, a long time, but I didn't mind. Time and place were no longer important to me. Then Grandmother Raven appeared.

Now covered with black feathers, she was bobbing and nodding with the rhythm of the drums. She and the drummers abruptly stopped on the same beat. With her eyes closed, she opened her feathery arms and issued a piercing, high-pitched keen that descended into a pulsating discordant canticle. Despite the heat, a shiver dashed up my spine.

The drummers soon began again and joined in her song, as a large open window appeared on one side of the sweat lodge. Through it I could see the naked back of a boy seated cross-legged on a sunny patch of grass. The old men who had escorted me into the lodge then stood and, one by one stepped through the window to speak to the boy. The first one laid a small fur parcel in front of him as he spoke: "I give you this gift – Wisdom. May you use it to guide all you do and use it to benefit all people."

The second man did as the first had done, and said, "I give you this gift – Love. May you be devoted to all creation and share your love for it with all humankind."

The third: "I give you this gift – Respect. May you treat all humanity with reverence and respect all who cross your path."

The fourth: "I give you this gift – Courage. May you be brave enough to do good things even in the most difficult times."

The fifth:, "I give you this gift – Honesty. May you be a person of integrity and truly honest in every deed and way."

The sixth: "I give you this gift – Humility. From it may you know that you are not greater than, nor lesser than, but equal with everyone else."

The seventh: "I give you this gift – Truth. May you always value authenticity, speak the truth and be true in all that you do."

After each grandfather had presented his gift he returned to be seated near me. After all seven had returned, Grandmother Raven's refrain intensified, the drumming grew louder and the light from the window grew brighter. The boy turned to look around the lodge and finally caught my eye.

Cody.

His window went black, then everything else did.

"Ms. Raven," I muttered as I looked around for her. It was morning and I was back at the kitchen table. The hard sunlight glancing off the Lake Superior ice caused me to finally look around Grandmother Raven's home.

"Now you may call me Grandmother, Conor." she replied. She was at the stove, frying eggs. She smiled when she said, "And maybe I will call you Owl Eyes. Do you know why you got them eyes?

"No."

"With them, you can see into the dark. You see as easily in the dark places as you do in the light. That is a great gift, but one you will not always like."

"Why not?" Hearing no reply, I asked, "Where is Cody?"

"Your brother? Where do you think he is?"

"I don't know. I thought he was dead."

"How many eggs?"

"Is he here somewhere?"

Her eyes bored into mine once again. I could hear her voice, although her lips were not moving, "He is your other soul. He lives where the second souls of all people dwell, in another universe, a universe of dreams. It is similar to ours, but it has different laws. He sleeps when you are awake and when you sleep he awakens and travels in his world. He will show you stories of those who inhabit that place and speak to you through them. They are sometimes hard to understand. The dream souls speak in a way we do not always readily grasp, but you must always respect them and work to understand the meaning and importance of what your brother brings to you."

When I was older and adept at hypnosis myself, I questioned whether it was Cody I was communicating with, or my own subconscious. I finally decided it didn't matter. Given how close we were, they could well be the same thing.

Her eyes released mine and she said, "I'm giving you two eggs. All this talk of yours needs nourishment."

She set a plate of two eggs and two pieces of toast in front of me. I was surprised at how hungry I felt and how quickly I polished it off. Grandmother Raven sat across from me again. "Somebody from the State is bringing Henri Bouchard here today and taking you back to St. Paul."

"Can't I stay here?"

"Your destiny lies elsewhere. But I have something for you." She set a small bundle of fur in front of me.

"Is this a gift like the ones Cody got?"

"No, you already have those. We all do. They are given to us at birth and they are ours to nurture or squander. This gift is different. It has medicine that you will need one day. You will know when you need it, and you should not open it before that time. This is otter skin and is precious to you. Take care of it and do not let it be taken from you. You understand?"

"I think so. Thank you, Grandmother Raven."

"I'm going to fix you two more eggs. You can eat them, can't you?"

For the first time in weeks, I smiled. "Yes, yes I can."

It wasn't long after that that the driver from the State showed up, along with Henri Bouchard. Henri looked like a darker and taller version of Cody. After greeting Grandmother Raven, he came over to me. "You Conor? They told me about you and them owl eyes you got. Did Grandmother Raven heal you?"

"Maybe. I mean, I think so."

The driver cleared his throat. It was the signal for me to leave. I said thank you to Grandmother Raven and followed the driver out to the car. I saw Eli Bouchard lumbering toward Grandmother's trailer as we were pulling away. He smiled broadly and waved to me.

We drove down highway 61 and as we left the Reservation I spotted a large black bird on the low branch of a white pine. It cawed at the car and flew back into Grand Portage. That was the last time I saw Grandmother Raven, until many years later.

MONDAY

Cities are murky places--hatching grounds for monsters.

—*John Geddes*

All cities are mad: but the madness is gallant. All cities are beautiful, but the beauty is grim.

—*Christopher Morley*

Cities, like dreams, are made of desires and fears, even if the thread of their discourse is secret, their rules are absurd, their perspectives deceitful, and everything conceals something else."

—*Italo Calvino*

St. Paul is a stupefyingly boring city.

—*Vladimir Nabokov*

1

MOSTLY NOTHING

"What do you mean?"

"I mean their throats were ripped out and an apple shoved in there, sort of where their Adam's apple would be. Here, have a look." He spread the pictures on the table.

Conor Delaney glanced at them and swallowed back something black and foul. "You should warn someone before tossing those things around."

Detective Roland Gadsen, Big Gad, sighed and said quietly, "I tried, but there really isn't a way to get somebody ready for this, is there?"

Delaney stared at him in mild reproach and turned back to the photos. He felt vaguely guilty that he was fascinated by the idea of the creature now loose in his city.

"We were hoping you could help us find whoever did this."

"You've already ruled out the possibility it might have been an animal?"

"We don't think an animal would have left an apple."

Delaney smiled briefly and continued to gaze at the slaughter. Two men and one woman. Ragged scoops of flesh torn from the throats of the first two. Traces of windpipe, esophagus, muscle, arteries and veins dangling in the cavities and a small green apple set neatly in the midst of the butchery. Delaney's conjecture: some savagely sharp claw had ripped and torn out their throats, before an apple was delicately placed, just so. A psychopath.

The third victim, a husky male with his face and neck torn and shredded, exposing a cheek bone, teeth, gums and the sinews along the jaw line. An apple grasped in his right hand, a bite taken out of it.

Delaney turned the pictures over and asked, "What have you got so far?"

Big Gad's voice became tense. "Not much, not much at all. They were found on a path at Riverrun Park, down by the river. They were all within about fifty feet of each other. It's an area where gay guys go to hook-up after dark. Maybe you remember that politician that got shot there about fifteen years ago? Same area. They were all killed late at night. The first vic was killed on April 18, the second on April 30 and the last one two nights ago, on May 2. He was Danny Fortuno, a cop until about two, three years ago, my former partner."

"Your partner?"

Big Gad's voice slid into an edgier tone. "He left the force to set up his own security and private eye firm. After the woman was killed he called and said he might have a lead for me on her killer. We were going to meet up yesterday, but that didn't work out. Obviously."

"He didn't tell you anything over the phone? Just said he wanted to meet?"

"He said he had a couple of leads he still wanted to follow up and he'd have more solid information when we met. He sort of indicated he knew who the killer was and just needed a little time to put it all together. He seemed pretty confident about it."

Delaney, about to ask another question, paused, staring at Gadsen, who looked down at the file lying in front of him before he mumbled, "I was hoping we'd have more in this file than the pictures and the Med Ex reports. We really have nothing on these cases."

Delaney knew he was lying, knew it with a certainty born of years spent studying kinesics – the art of reading the eighty-five percent of human communication that is non-verbal. He would say that a close analysis of someone's standing and sitting posture, body, arm, hand, facial and eye movements, would communicate more than an individual's spoken words.

Delaney was still an adolescent when ideas about non-verbal communication first grabbed his attention. He read voraciously on the subject and spent an incalculable number of hours watching people in all kinds of circumstances and situations. It was how he sharpened his skill.

He never told anyone that he was, in effect, a human lie detector. Like his equally guarded, secret talent for hypnosis, he used his kinesics' skill instinctively. It was now a part of him, a measure of who he was.

Staring at Gadsen's eyes for a millisecond longer than was socially acceptable, he said, "Fortuno really told you nothing at all?"

"Fuck's sake, do I have to repeat everything for you?" Gadsen's voice was on the rise. "I told you he just said he wanted to meet up. Nothing, no goddamn nothing else at all." That's when he broke down, huge sobs wracking the six-foot, three-inch, two-hundred-thirty-pound frame of the Big Gad.

This was a first for Delaney, watching a cop break down. That it was a veteran of the size and reputation of the Big Gad made it almost unnerving. That, and the room. A police interrogation room is purposefully claustrophobic. The pale green walls, the two-way mirror, the metal table and chairs taking up most of the space, the way sound caroms off the walls; it creates a mood, a real shitty mood. For a suspect being grilled, it feels like the world is closing in. But Roland Gadsen wasn't a suspect. The room was just the only space available for their early morning meeting.

It was in keeping with the rest of Delaney's morning. He had nicked himself while shaving and later had to adjust his tie three times before it finally hung as it should from its full Windsor knot, descending just far enough to cover his belt buckle. The gloomy room and sad, recalcitrant cop added to the sense that this was a particularly lousy Monday. Now his cell phone was vibrating with an incoming call. He was sure the voice mail would convey some kind of bad news. The universe was that much against him this morning. He wondered if, in a parallel universe, his counterpart was having a better day.

Nearly thirty seconds passed before Big Gad breathed deeply and, with eyes red and glistening, in a hoarse voice, said, "Danny was my ex-partner and we were close friends, so I'm off the case. I have to brief you and whoever takes over for me. I hope we can nail the animal that did this."

Delaney felt a surge of pity for the big man. His grief was genuine. "You don't have to do this now. I need to ask you some more questions, but they can wait."

Gadsen looked away before saying, "Thanks, but I can do it now. I gotta do something."

"Then tell me about your partner. What was he like?"

Gadsen snorted. "He was a character. His nickname was 'Dollar Danny' because he was always coming up with some crazy money-making scheme. Like he wanted a bunch of us cops to incorporate as a security firm to, you know, provide bouncers to restaurants and bars. He said we'd corner the market with 'Professional Police Protection.' He had lots of ideas like that, but no one in the department took any of it seriously. He was a good detective though, and had the highest case-closure rate in the department. He got pissed and left when he didn't get chief of detectives. That, and he thought he had a winner with his latest business scheme."

"What did you find at the crime scenes besides the bodies?"

Big Gad was more relaxed now, his voice more even: "Nothing. And I do mean nothing. The lab guys are thorough, and they found nothing more than we did, at least not at the scene. It's a walking path, so there can be a fair amount of traffic some days, but there was nothing unusual. No extraordinary tracks, no real disturbance of the vegetation around the scenes. I mean there was absolutely nothing."

Delaney constrained himself. Hadn't Gadsen heard? There can be no nothing. It's an existential impossibility. Instead, he said, "Blood? Flesh?"

"Blood, yes, but no meat. Just the vics' blood."

"What did the medical examiner say?"

"He doesn't know anything either, at least not yet. Him and the lab guys have come up with squat. Talk to them. You'll see."

"The scenes are taped off?"

"Just the last two. The other one was a couple weeks old and we didn't know there'd be more."

"What's the plan now?"

"The chief wants to do a big sweep of the area, using dogs, uniforms and auxiliary. He's bringing you in to consult on these cases, assigning two new detectives and making these cases the department's top priority. He put your buddy Thorogood in charge."

"Anything else?"

"Not that I know, but I'm out of it now. Personally, I think we're looking at one of these guys hears voices in his head, know what I mean?"

"I guess so. So, what do you think we need to do?"

"Fuck all if I know. The sweep could turn up something. I heard you were good. You closed the cases on that crazy woman and the carney barker. Maybe you'll figure something out."

"I'm only doing some preliminary research. I won't be working on the case beyond that. But let me ask again, what do you think? I want to look at the files on any cops tagged for excessive violence, on or off the job, including domestics."

Gadsen flinched, "I never thought, do you think . . ."

"No, I don't. I'm just covering the bases. Fortuno, he must have pissed off some guys in the department, created some enemies?"

"Sure he did, but I don't think enough for any of them to kill a brother cop. Especially since Danny's been out of the force for so long."

"I'm going to ask someone to comb the files for all the murders in this and adjoining states where the throats were stabbed or slit, over the last ten years or so. That sound right to you?"

"You think it's somebody internal, don't you?"

"Detective, I don't think anything at this point. But we have to, as a practical matter, look here, too. If we find out anything, anything at all that in any way implicates somebody internal, we need to know it before the press does. And by the way, the media has been frantic on these killings. What has actually been released to the press?"

"If you're looking internal, you're looking at me, aren't you?

"Wouldn't you look at you if you were me?" The Gad nodded with a resigned sigh. "Now, what about the press, what do they know and not know?"

"Only that three bodies were found, with the necks mutilated. Nothing about the apples in the official reports, yet. We might not be able to keep that detail out much longer. The media think it's probably some anti-gay freak. And they are going to freak if the apple detail does come out."

"You don't think it's an anti-gay nut?"

"It could be, but those types usually let you know why they're killing 'em, don't they? And the woman? Danny? Doesn't add up to any kind of gay-hater I know."

"I think I'm going to need to talk with you some more later. Can you help me out on an on-call basis?"

"Anything you need, just whistle. I want this bastard bad. Christ, I haven't slept since I saw those first two bodies and Danny's only made it worse. Know what I mean?"

"Yeah, I do." And Delaney did. It wasn't the bloody, gutted throats or the apples jammed into them. It was the faces. They were calm, peaceful, even serene, like a trio of westernized Buddhas.

2

CAMILLE

As Big Gad left, Delaney checked his voicemail. It was Camille.

They first met at Gene Swearingen's annual holiday party. It was one of those events where there are lots of people in a big house, so you have choices. If you're feeling anti-social you can put in an appearance and leave early. You won't be missed, unless someone is looking for you. On the other hand, if you want to talk with friends or make new acquaintances, you can do that, too. Delaney was feeling social with his second glass of wine and in conversation with Charles Finch when she walked across the room. She looped her arm around Finch's and smiled, "You're Conor Delaney."

Delaney, with mock seriousness, replied, "And you are, let me hazard a wild guess here, uhm, Camille Bennett?"

Beautiful, brilliant Camille Bennett. She had been second chair on several of Gene Swearingen's trials before she left to join the City's largest law firm where she could engage her real legal talent for corporate law. Most lawyers and judges thought Swearingen was the best lawyer in the state. The smart ones thought Camille Bennett was not far behind him. The Neanderthals among them refused to believe an African-American woman was that smart.

They seemed an odd couple. An attorney with the Swearingen firm, Finch was British and had an easy way with conversation. An upper-class intonation lent his every utterance an unqualified note of authority to American ears, despite his short and rotund figure. Camille was at least four inches taller than Finch and about fifteen or twenty years his junior. With her height, easy smile, and arresting gray eyes set against her dark complexion, she drew admiring glances and gazes wherever she went.

"My God, I've never seen anything like it." Finch was genuinely startled.

"What's that, my love?" Camille smiled down at him.

"The two of you, darling." He stepped away from her and motioned with his hands for them to stand next to each other. "I've never seen anything like it. Your eyes. The same color and oh, so very striking. It's almost eerie, you know. And you're the same height. You can actually look into each other's eyes without. . ."

Camille laughed. "Slow down, Finch; I'm wearing three-inch heels."

Delaney, with a grin, said, "Why, Miss Bennett, what lovely eyes you have."

"And your eyes, Mr. Delaney, make you look like an owl. An attractive owl, to be sure, but still, an owl. Gene Swearingen tells me, " she said, changing the subject, "that you are a, let me see if I can remember the word, ah yes, he said you were a *brilliant* detective.

"But I disagree." Seeing Delaney's smile, she continued, "The word is you are not, and never have been, a boozer. Nor are you a womanizer, a veteran, a former cop or a loner. You don't own a gun and apparently have never been the target of either criminal or police intimidation."

"You've done your homework."

"I just remember what Gene, my uncle Mel and a few other well-informed friends have said. Totally unsolicited, I might add."

"I'm almost afraid to ask what else you might know."

"Just this, and this is what makes me very, very suspicious of you. Everybody likes you – your clients, your employees and your friends. Even Chief McArdle. And I hear that you have a long-time friendship with Mackey Stately. Tell me, how is someone friends with Mel Thorogood *and* Mackey Stately?

"I have a feeling, Mr. Delaney, that you'll never make it big as a pulp fiction detective."

"I'm not a detective."

"Because you're the head of Delphi Investigations and Research? Stripped of all the pretense wrapped up in that fancy name and address, you and your cohorts really are detectives. Pretty good detectives, but nonetheless…"

"Ms. Bennett, you are every bit as shy as I have heard. Think you'll ever get over it?"

"Is this verbal jousting a private affair or can anyone join in," Finch said as he slipped in between them.

The course of their banter shifted and Delaney found the two of them to be great conversation partners. Both were informed, intelligent, not overly opinionated and they listened as well as they spoke. When Finch excused himself, Camille and Delaney talked on; about socialism in northern Europe, the growing economic power of the Far East, race and class in twenty-first century America, the admirable sanity of Canadians and, finally, the threats to humanity posed by the creation of artificial intelligence.

Finch rejoined them during the second wave of guest departures. Delaney took it as his cue to excuse himself. "Are you sure you have to leave so early?" Finch said.

Camille smiled. "He has someone waiting for him, don't you?"

He said no, wishing he had that excuse, but it was simply that he'd been up early that morning, after too few hours of sleep and, with any more wine, he was going to fall asleep right in front of them, great conversation notwithstanding.

Camille said now that she had finally met *the* Conor Delaney that Gene Swearingen spoke so highly of, she hoped she would see him again sometime soon. Of course, he replied, he'd be delighted to see them again.

In truth, weariness had nothing to do with his need to leave. It was her. Her statuesque beauty, calm demeanor, voice, and easy-going wit and laugh. She was entirely too charming, too mysterious, and Delaney thought it best not to be too frankly admiring. He understood the invitation to meet again "sometime soon" would soon be forgotten by all three of them. But it wasn't.

She called a week later to say she would be working late tonight, but needed a break for dinner. Would he like to meet her at Matteo's?

Matteo's was known for plants and food. During daytime hours the sunlight glowing in through the almost floor-to-ceiling windows drew out the colors of the plants that were spread throughout the restaurant's three rooms. Matteo Benelli was fond of saying Giulia would plant everything from A to Zinnia, if he allowed it. The candles and subdued light of the evening hours gave Matteo's a decidedly romantic glow. But it was still the food that made it the most popular spot in downtown St. Paul.

She had the house-made gnocchi with asparagus and truffles and Delaney indulged in his favorite, Matteo's linguini pescatore. Finch, where was Mister Finch, he wanted to know. She had no idea and hoped he hadn't gotten the impression that they were a couple. He had, of course.

Charles Finch was the gay male friend every woman wished she had, according to Camille. He was also a convenient shield, she said, keeping Delaney at a safe distance. Delaney smiled and, despite her objections, insisted they share what he called Matteo's World-Famous Cannoli. She loved it. Everyone did. She knew the Delphi offices were upstairs and asked if she could have a tour.

Delaney thought he knew why all the warning bells started clanging, but what did warning bells know, and anyway, what was he supposed to say? "No" would have sounded churlish.

They kissed at a window overlooking the river. It was electric and imprisoned them in a long and intense moment. And in that moment they both instinctively understood, but just as instinctively denied, an inexorable truth about their shared future – it was not going to end well.

Despite this unshakable feeling, together they gave in to a blissful acceptance of the inevitable, separately and silently vowing to make the best of their time together.

So began their romance. They fell in love far more easily than either could have anticipated. Falling out of love was harder.

Delaney was about to return her call when Mel Thorogood peered into the interrogation room.

3

A LESS THAN ONE-PERCENT SOLUTION

"Conor, what are you doing here?" There was surprise in his voice.

"Mel, I thought I'd see you earlier. Just finished an interview with Gadsen. Poor guy is in a bad way. And what do you mean what am I doing here? You called me, remember?"

"No, no, I didn't," Assistant Chief Thorogood frowned.

"Thoro, you left a voicemail for me late yesterday. I know your voice. Look, I've still got your cell number on my phone. Here, look."

"My cell went missing last week."

They stared at each other for a long moment. Delaney felt something cold dancing on the back of his neck and could almost see the same chill creeping up Thorogood's spine. The two men were silent for another long breath before Thorogood sat. The stillness lingered as they each wondered about the sinister, dark thing invading their lives and their city.

Delaney was not a cop. Never had been, never wanted to be, and his work as an occasional consultant to the St. Paul Police Department was as close to being one that he ever wanted to come. Nothing against cops, he would say, unconvincingly. He claimed to respect them and understood how hazardous their job could be in those tense few moments between long stretches of intense boredom. But he knew every department had its full complement of assholes, and then some. The culture that pervaded them pretty much made him sick. All the macho posturing, racism, professional cynicism and thin-blue-line ass covering, it was not a scene that appealed to Conor Delaney.

Don't get him wrong, he would say again. Every department also had its share of full-fledged, idealistic, creative and dedicated public servants, men and women who saw their job as a kind of higher calling. He would always point to Mel Thorogood as chief among them.

They met as undergrads. That Monday afternoon the English prof was giddy over Saturday's big game. "And I understand we have one of the heroes of that grand conquest in this class. Mel Thorogood?"

The big kid sitting next to Delaney raised his hand and gave a weak smile. Delaney smirked and whispered, "Congratulations."

Thorogood glanced at him and under his breath said, "Shit," with two syllables.

As they walked out after class Thorogood muttered, "Look man, I'm sorry. It's just, you know, I hate football."

"Hey, I'm from St. Paul too. I remember you played for Central. Can I buy you a cup of coffee?"

Over coffee in the student union, they recounted how they each ended up at this small, tony Midwestern college. The clever Delaney rode in on an academic scholarship, the scholar Thorogood had the athletic variety. That pissed him off. Despite his fine mind and academic inclinations, the stubbornly resilient Jim Crow mindset had written him into a role where he was only an injury away from losing it all.

That belied his play. A bull of a running back, Thorogood played with a reckless style that thrived on running into and over opposing players. Delaney wondered if Thorogood was challenging the other team or fate.

A month after they met, the article appeared in the campus newspaper under their joint byline. It bloomed with the full flower of righteousness only the young can muster. Why, wrote the two, did none of the school's Black athletes have academic scholarships, despite having GPAs well above average for the student body?

It led to a quick flurry of academic angst and Thorogood finished his junior and senior years without playing the hated game.

Together they enrolled for graduate school in DC, Thorogood to get an advanced degree in criminal justice, a career-directed complement to his philosophy BA. Delaney studied neuroeconomics, and, as an afterthought and an extra year, an MBA.

Their professional lives veered in different directions after that. Thorogood joined the St. Paul force and quickly, more quickly than anyone in the whole, odd history of the department, worked his way up to the Assistant Chief's position he now held. Most observers thought he would become the city's first African-American chief.

Delaney went to work for a big insurance company in Chicago, ferreting out financial fraud schemes. He also thought the insurance industry had its own full complement of assholes, and then some. But he always knew he would return to St. Paul. He was a child of the City; he understood its culture and history, its odd way of doing business.

Then there was its dark side. To his owl eyes it was transparent and endlessly fascinating. He had no wish to deny the hold it had on him. There were times when he could almost hear it speaking to him. It was his City.

It was also home to his closest friends: Mel Thorogood, Mackey Stately and Henri Bouchard. While he stayed in contact with each of them during his Chicago sojourn, he knew it was not the same as breathing the same city air and having them nearby.

Delaney was brought back to the city by way of a case he was investigating. There were those who considered what he did ethically questionable. He thought it less dubious than the corporate behavior he was exposing. Besides, when there was a clash between ethics and justice, Delaney did his best to come down on the side of what he thought of as justice.

The case began with a call from Marguerite Garza, an accountant with NovaOne Pharmaceuticals, an insurance firm client. Over the past two years more than three hundred people had become seriously ill and another thirty had died; all had been taking a popular NovaOne opioid painkiller. Gene Swearingen was suing the company on behalf of the injured families. In its defense, the company pointed out that it had been manufacturing the painkillers for years in American plants that were regularly inspected and no defective products had ever been found. NovaOne made much of its practice of making all its products in American plants, never importing and selling drugs from other countries and would not, in fact, be covered by its insurance providers if it did.

It was in the midst of the lawsuit that Garza, a long-time employee, discovered the company was actually selling more of its painkiller than it was manufacturing. She was also responsible for payments on a warehouse lease, one with no discernible purpose assigned to it. Delaney recognized the address on the lease as being located in the industrial Midway District of St. Paul.

After six weeks of combing through insurance company and NovaOne policies and records, Delaney met with Swearingen at his firm. In all likelihood, he told the attorney, NovaOne was importing Chinese versions of its painkillers and routing them through a warehouse located in St. Paul.

In the end, he helped Swearingen, Minnesota's preeminent class action attorney, reach an outrageously large settlement. Even without Delaney's help, the company was likely to have been penalized well over $250 million. With his aid, it was rendered bankrupt and was immediately acquired by a Swiss competitor.

Delaney left the insurance company shortly after that to set up Delphi Investigations and Research, his own, now sizable, consulting agency, where Marguerite Garza became the chief of accounting and human resources. Swearingen purchased a thirty-three percent interest in the new enterprise. While still occasionally doing some investigative work for the Swearingen law firm, the Delphi agency also contracted with insurance companies, bank regulators, the IRS, FBI, DEA and, when Thorogood beckoned, the St. Paul Police Department.

The two of them were having an end of the day drink when Thorogood first asked Delaney to look at a murder case. Thorogood thought it was a typical case of domestic violence carried out to its too-logical conclusion. A husband given to abuse when he drank too much. A 911 call from his wife. A warning from the patrols. Another night, another 911, more warnings. And again. In St. Paul, and across the country, this scene plays out so often it seems as if the actors are all reading from the same script: the abuser, his battered spouse, the 911 operators and the patrols. They all act it out like they've rehearsed it a dozen times, and too many of them have.

The problem with this case was that, beyond his history of abuse, there was nothing - not a smidgen of hard evidence - to indicate that Kyle Lilly had killed his wife. The cops had tossed his house and garage looking for the hammer that bludgeoned her. They sweated him in an interrogation room. They talked to neighbors and retraced his steps over the previous two days and nights. Nothing.

Jennifer Lilly had followed her usual evangelical Christian schedule that night and went to the women's Thursday night bible study at church. Delaney recognized the church as a small Pentecostal parish on the edge of downtown. The night before Jennifer had been there for a prayer meeting and Sunday she'd attended both morning and evening services. The husband reported her missing on Friday morning.

Over ninety-nine percent of murders are crimes of passion or greed. The other less than one percent – committed by psychopaths like Jack the Ripper, Ed Gein and Ted Bundy - get all the publicity, but they are rare. A typical murder investigation usually narrows the field of suspects to members of the victim's circle of immediate family and close friends. In this case the answer seemed obvious. The Lillys had a $100,000 insurance policy on each of their lives. Other than that, they had no real money, but chronically unemployed Kyle had a history.

The detectives had talked to everyone who'd attended the bible study that night, all six women and pastor John Diffley. They all agreed that Jennifer Lilly left by herself shortly after nine p.m., as usual.

Having seen first-hand Delaney's knack for interviewing or interrogating witnesses, agents, and adversaries of one sort or another, Thorogood hoped he could draw a confession out of the taciturn Kyle Lilly. It wasn't that Delaney was a particularly aggressive interrogator, although he could be. Rather, what impressed Thorogood and everyone else who watched Delaney in action, was the way he sat, motionless, focusing his full attention, and strange grey eyes, on the person he was interviewing. That concentration, required if he was to apply his kinesics skill, and the occasional odd, seemingly irrelevant, question or biting comment, kept the objects of his inquiry off-balance and often prone to giving more information than they intended.

Delaney thought this case was something too far out of his field, but was easily convinced he had nothing to lose by at least giving it a perfunctory look. The next day he looked through the files and told Thorogood he wanted to meet with Pastor John Diffley, accompanied by his attorney, in an interrogation room. Delaney asked Thorogood to read them their rights before they started.

The attorney was a member of the church, an overweight, jowly estate lawyer with an unruly walrus moustache. He was a stranger to the practice of criminal law and that, thought Delaney, made this unfamiliar job that much easier.

Seated next to Thorogood, Delaney started by asking Diffley if he was born again. Did he lead a spirit-filled life? Was he living out God's plan for his life?

The leader of the flock nodded and said, "Yes, of course," to each question and, in exasperation, finally said, "I am a born-again Christian, a minister of the gospel, after all. Why are you asking such ridiculous questions?" His attorney nodded solemnly.

"I just want to be sure of who I'm talking to. You understand, it's important to get everything right in a murder investigation." He turned to the attorney. "You understand that, don't you? And you'll be sure your pastor here understands it too?"

"Oh, yes. Very important," he replied.

Delaney paused and gave a brief glance to each man before continuing. "Now it is also critical that you understand that we are dealing with a closed circle of suspects here. Jennifer had her husband, family and church. Since we've eliminated the husband and the murder took place after a church meeting, well, you understand, don't you?"

They both gave a quizzical nod and frowned as Delaney continued. "I now have, seated before me, two characters who might well be prime suspects in the murder of Jennifer Lilly."

Diffley's eyebrows shot up. "No," he said slowly.

Delaney turned to the lawyer. "Mark Minim, attorney-at-law, a solo practitioner, who never worked in a firm, never had a partner; in fact, never even hired a paralegal. But still, a solid St. Paul real estate practice, specializing in commercial and high-end residential properties. Age fifty-two, never married, never convicted of so much as a traffic ticket. Active in the church. The nights get pretty lonely, don't they, Mark?"

The lawyer frowned, opened his mouth to reply, but didn't, choosing instead to adopt a pose of hostile, stony silence.

"Want to tell us where you were Thursday night?"

"Duluth. Now I demand you ask no further questions until I have an attorney present." His small, ursine eyes contracted as his frown grew deeper. As he pursed his lips, the moustache reached almost to his chin.

"That's OK. I'm done with questioning you, for now. But I do wonder, was that Duluth trip business or pleasure? And who provides your alibi?" Minim clenched his jaw and glanced at his pastor.

Delaney smiled. "Now you, Pastor. Whoever did this, acted like someone who was demon-possessed, wouldn't you agree? I mean, this man, or woman, took a hammer and, with one blow, smashed through Jennifer's skull as if it were an eggshell, sinking the hammer face smack into the gray matter of her brain. Tell me, Pastor, do you have that kind of fury bottled up inside of you?"

A wide-eyed, ashen-faced Diffley replied, "No. Never. I could never . . ."

Delaney gave Thorogood a brief glance and smile before turning back to the two men. "Here's what I know - neither of you killed Jennifer Lilly. But you both have a pretty good idea of which one of your parishioners did. Now tell us, who murdered Jennifer Lilly, murdered her in cold blood?"

Diffley stammered, "No. No one in our congregation would do such a thing. What . . . why would any one of our people want to do such a thing? You're being ridiculous."

"Ridiculous? You've used that word twice now. Tell him we're not being ridiculous, counselor."

Diffley spoke first. "Are you trying to destroy our church? You can't be a Christian. You're not, are you?"

"No, I'm not," he nudged a scowling Thorogood, "but he is. More importantly, the two of you know the killer is a member of your congregation, and you both know who it is."

The attorney started to demur when Delaney cut him off. "Tut, tut. And you, an officer of the court, withholding information. Shame on you."

"I am here as Pastor Diffley's legal counsel . . ."

"No, you're not. You're here because we asked you to be here and if you'd like we'll take you into a separate room. Do you understand?" Delaney knew he was dancing on thin ice, but continued anyway. "From what I hear, Jennifer Lilly was an attractive woman. She was, wasn't she, gentlemen?"

Both men caught themselves nodding before Diffley said, "What are you implying here? Jennifer was a good Christian woman. She loved the Lord."

"Yes, yes, of course she did. But she was also a damsel in distress, wasn't she, Pastor? She was hurting and your church doesn't sanction divorce, does it? She needed help and she used to occasionally touch your arm, or stand a little too close when you talked, didn't she?"

"We never did anything inappropriate. Not ever." He turned to his attorney. "Do we have to sit here and take these insinuations? This is getting ridic . . . uh, more wrong by the minute and I do not like it one bit."

Minim began to reply but Delaney ignored him and continued, "Let me tell you about Jennifer's killer. It's probably a woman. Where Jennifer was attractive, this woman is, in all likelihood, anything but. She's probably anxiety-ridden, socially awkward and has few, if any, friends. But you, Mr. Diffley, you have shown her kindness, maybe just of the professional kind, but still, enough to make her adore you."

Diffley scowled but said nothing. His lawyer's eyes widened.

"So, this woman, unattractive, friendless and lonely, fixates on you. She's active in the church, does things like organizing coffee and food for church events and thinks you walk on water, so to speak. And she watches, watches you and watches Jennifer. She sees the danger. Jennifer, in her eyes, is trying to seduce you; and you, might you finally succumb to her touch? She can't stand the thought. Of course, she can't stand Jennifer either; a woman who seems to be everything she is not. It gnaws on her, this notion of Jennifer as a latter-day Delilah, leading you into temptation. She must stop it, stop it at any cost. So she takes a hammer and crushes Jennifer Lilly's skull, all just to keep you from temptation. Now, gentlemen, tell us, who is this woman?"

They greeted the question with dumb silence until Delaney gave the table a small, almost imperceptible pat, followed immediately by Thorogood slamming his big palm on the metal tabletop and roaring, "Who is it? Speak!"

Diffley blurted, "Maude Gruber," and lapsed into a stunned silence. The attorney scowled at Delaney, but maintained his stoic silence.

Thorogood smiled. "Thank you. Now get out of here before I arrest you both for obstruction of justice."

Diffley's red face betrayed what Delaney thought was about ten percent shame and ninety percent simple embarrassment. The attorney's sneer signaled his loathing of Delaney and the proceedings. Maude Gruber was subsequently determined by the court to be criminally insane and was sentenced to a permanent residency at the St. Peter Security Hospital, Minnesota's prison for, among others, the mentally ill and dangerous.

Word got around in the Department. The cops all thought Delaney was brilliant. He thought he knew just enough about evangelical culture to press the right buttons. Despite his skill at reading their non-verbal clues, he knew he had been lucky and said so. But Mel Thorogood was exultant. He'd brought his friend in and it paid off. But he never countered Delaney's claim of luck. Delaney was, in fact, the luckiest man he'd ever met and over the years he'd come to believe that luck was bred into his DNA. Delaney thought that, since Thorogood was a Baptist, he would have come up with the same line of questioning for the minister and lawyer if his professional training hadn't gotten in the way. But still, he did wonder about Kyle Lilly and that $100,000 life insurance policy.

Since that first case Delaney had been marginally involved in a couple of others, but only one other murder -- until now. And this case had him feeling apprehensive. Whoever made that call from Thorogood's phone knew too much about them both. And he wanted Delaney on the case, wanted him badly enough to have told them something, however slight, about himself.

Delaney wondered, was this one of those less-than-one-percent serial killers, a cold psychopathic monster intent on playing out a protracted and grisly game, leading them on, body after bloody body? Did he want Delaney to hunt him, or was he stalking Delaney? Was he trying to show how easily he could penetrate the police department or was he a cop? Was he someone they both knew? Did his intent go anywhere beyond creating a chilling sense of foreboding and fear?

Fear – the cold, pitiless, vicious and unforgiving thing – he had long ago sworn to never again fall into its grasp. Through his practice of self-hypnosis, he told himself, he now knew how to control it, to even use its presence to give himself a psychic boost in times of crisis.

Still, somewhere in the background, he could hear the derisive laugh of the universe.

Thorogood finally broke the silence and voiced another kind of fear: "Do we have a goddamn serial killer cop? A cop who hears voices in his head?" He was as discomfited as his friend.

Delaney said, "Maybe there's a connection between the three victims. It's possible we've seen the last of the killings."

Thorogood stared blankly for a moment more and then, like the good bureaucrat he was, said, "We need to get with the chief right away."

Meeting with the chief about a cold-blooded serial killer. Now that, thought Delaney, is going to be first-rate entertainment.

4

COUNSEL & GUIDANCE

The Chief, Homer McArdle, was big in a different way from Big Gad. He was big enough, six feet or so and round; too stout for a cop, really. But he was Big because he had what he most loved, what he hoarded like a dragon in a cave hovering over its treasure. Homer McArdle had Big Power.

He was old school, like thirteenth-century old school. A political player and skilled nepotist, he viewed the city as his kingdom and the police department as his army. Like all big men of power, he hated racial integration and affirmative action when they were forced on him by the tides of history and the courts. Faced with the demand that he hire people of color he fell back on the old shopworn lie - it kept him from hiring the best talent available. Or the talent from his East Side home turf, where he handpicked whose white sons, nephews and friends got to join the force. Loudly, brashly and with his one eye flashing, he fought the unnecessary interference with good administration with all the Big Power he could muster. It wasn't that he disliked Blacks, browns, reds, or yellows, of course.

The East Side - there he was still a legend, the tough neighborhood kid who made good, who gave good jobs to good kids from the neighborhood, who knew how to treat those others from that other neighborhood, knew how to keep them in their place.

Only now "they" were on the force, and so were, of all things, women. Almost as bad, all the good neighborhood boys on the force were gone, moved to the suburbs and their houses bought by those others: Blacks, Hmong, Mexicans, Cambodians, Somalis and yuppies.

Still, everyone knew that McArdle was doing his best to hold back the tide. They knew because he still lived in the neighborhood, still ate at local restaurants, went to the funerals, first communions, weddings and anniversary parties. And at every event he was feted and thanked for gracing the occasion with his presence, even if he did have to rush off to attend to his unending duties.

Homer McArdle was everything a local hero could be. Wasn't he a decorated war veteran, losing an eye in a Vietnamese swamp? There were a few voices raised about departmental regulations forbidding the hiring of a one-eyed cop. But weren't his father and four uncles all cops? And didn't he pass his firearms test with a near perfect score? Now he had the eye patch and an overlarge remaining eye as testaments to his patriotic heroism. As a police officer hadn't he won six Commendations, three Medals of Merit and seven (seven!) Medals of Valor? And wasn't he Officer of The Year four times? His dedication to the City and the safety of its citizens was palpable.

Affirmative action was a bitter pill for the Big Chief to gag down, but he did it and then moved out front on it, like the good, big power politician he was. He mastered much of the required politically correct rhetoric and scrambled to meetings with the Urban League, the NAACP, the Summit and Frogtown Community Councils and a half-dozen Black churches to urge their help in recruiting "good" young men to make his force representative of the people he served.

Had his cops been a brutally repressive presence in the Black community? Weren't his personal appearances proof of the dawning of a new day? Promising recruits were soon inducted into St. Paul's "new" police force. Mel Thorogood was the best of them.

McArdle had a nose for talent, especially of the kind that made him look good. He spotted Thorogood right away and put him on a fast track to an Assistant Chief position. In the whole odd history of the force, no one got there quicker than steady Mel. The one-eyed chief never let him, or the entire African American community, forget it.

McArdle's desk held an in-out basket, a picture of him with President George W. Bush - "a guy who looks like he just let a fart and he ain't sure if he should be proud or embarrassed" - a glass paperweight, stapler and computer. Behind him a long credenza held just three short stacks of files. At each end of the credenza stood a flag, to his left the stars and stripes, to his right the Han blue Minnesota banner. On the walls were his degree from the University of Minnesota, but not the one from Princeton, awards from national police organizations, pictures with mayors, governors and other presidents. Nowhere was there evidence of The Agreement that had guided and governed police policy and conduct since 1838.

This morning Homer McArdle was unhappy; unhappy with having to meet with Thorogood and his damned consultant, unhappy with three high profile, unsolved murders and unhappy that Danny Fortuno, one of his handpicked East Side boys, was one of the victims. And he was thoroughly pissed that these two men might give him the worst of news, that a homicidal freak was on the loose in his city.

His bulging eye glared, first at Delaney, then Thorogood. He snorted, "What?"

Thorogood, who knew his chief's tells, said evenly, "Chief, I don't want to move ahead on this case without your counsel and guidance. We need to get your feedback before we proceed."

McArdle chuckled, "Hear that, boy genius? He's smooth, isn't he? He knows I don't buy that horse pucky, but ladles it out anyway. 'Counsel and guidance,' my fat Irish arse. What's up, Mel?"

"There's a couple things about this case you need to know and then you've got to appoint some new lead detectives."

"I *got* to do shit, maestro. Last I checked I was the one in this department who handed out the *got-tos*, even to assistant chiefs." With a broad, one-eyed wink at Delaney, "Sometimes you just gotta keep these uppity guys in their place, know what I mean, Sherlock? Now whadda you guys got for me?"

Delaney smiled. The jibe at Thorogood was typical McArdle and barely masked the deep level of trust and respect the two men had for each other. At

Thorogood's nod, Delaney said, "Yesterday I got a call from Mel asking me to come down and take a look at this case."

McArdle frowned. "Wait. I'm the one who called you."

"Yes, and earlier this morning I had a message from someone who sounded like Mel."

"What do you mean, 'sounded like'?"

Delaney explained the sequence of events, his request for files, and his tentative suspicion there might be a serial-killer officer in the department.

McArdle erupted, "NO! Not in my goddamn department!" His voice dropped. "No, we will not have that, boyos. I won't stand for a public trial with the good name of this department associated with some sick sonofabitch." He sighed heavily. "Ah, Christ. What the hell is going on, boys, what is going on?"

"You have the same facts we do, but we did spend a little time tossing around ideas on how to proceed."

The Chief settled back, drawing a deep breath. "That's good, we need that. Good. You know, we've never had one of those guys that hears the voice of God or the neighbor's dog commanding him to slaughter his fellow citizens. Never. We just cannot have one in the department. But if you do find one, shoot the bastard on sight. So, what are your ideas on this? What?"

He looked at Thorogood, who paused for a few seconds, whether to goad the Chief or calm him, Delaney couldn't tell. "The sweep you ordered for this afternoon should proceed as planned . . . "

"I'm fuckin' glad you approve."

" . . . and you should assign two new detectives right now to replace Gadsen. We need to meet with the medical examiner and the lab guys this afternoon and need the detectives to be there."

"I was going to do that anyway."

Thorogood continued, "One of them should be a woman."

McArdle groaned and glared at Delaney. "This is your idea, isn't it, you liberal twit? I don't know why I even let you enter the hallowed halls of this wonderful Department. We'd be a bunch of sorry-assed pussies if you had your way."

He smiled briefly before he slowly swiveled his big, balding head back to his Assistant Chief, giving him the sort of one-eyed, bug-eyed stare that withered subordinates. He spoke slowly. "I am not going to worry about being shit-faced politically correct. I'm going to appoint the best detectives we have. Do you understand that? The best."

"On this case one of your best will be a woman. One of the victims was a woman and we have no idea what she was doing down at Riverrun Park, by herself or with her killer after dark. It's a place where gay guys hang out, not women. And if it is someone in the department, it will be a guy and he'll have friends here. We're going to need a woman and a woman's perspective to figure out some of the angles here. It's not PC, it's just good police work."

McArdle's lip curled as he said, "I suppose you even know what woman you want on your team?"

"I like Ann O'Leary, don't you?"

The Chief took another deep breath and leaned back, big eye closed, as if in meditation. After several seconds he nodded slowly, eye still closed. "Yeah, yeah. O'Leary's good. She's a dyke, too, so maybe she can help with the queers down there. Yeah, O'Leary's good."

He straightened up. "I suppose you also want to keep this blood-sucking consultant on the case? He's already half as rich as God and I still have to pay him. At his full highway robbery rates, too." He turned to Delaney. "You greedy bastard, can't you give us a goddamned price break? No, of course you won't."

"Sure I will. I'll reduce my fee by the same percent that you reduce your salary. But, I'm not going to be working on this case beyond the preliminary research and investigation you asked for."

Thorogood started. "Stop right there. That was your agreement?" His gaze swung from Delaney to McArdle and back. "Think about this for just a minute. Please." He spoke slowly. "After what this guy just pulled, do you think he'll let you not be on the case? He finds out you're not after him, he's going to do something ugly to suck you back in. Do you really want to find out what that something is?"

"Sorry, Thoro, but Delphi has some thirty-plus active projects and cases right now. Several of them require some of my time, including one right here in St. Paul. I can't drop all that for something that's really not within the realm of my expertise, such as it is. This is a classic cop case and you guys will handle it just fine without me."

Thorogood snorted. "That's not the issue, is it? We've got a sicko who's got you in his sights and wants you hunting him."

McArdle sighed. "OK, kids, break it up. You can't force him to do this, so leave him be. It's the responsibility of this department to catch this pervert, isn't it? Mel, isn't it?"

Thorogood nodded reluctantly and McArdle said, "Damn straight it is. Plus, I don't have to pay him that bullshit consulting fee."

He gave Delaney a brief smile and nod before turning back to Thorogood. "OK, you got everything you wanted so far, except for Sherlock, here. Now you have to give me something."

"Please, Chief, this isn't a negotiation," Thorogood began.

The long-time Chief shot back, "Listen, both of you, every meeting is a negotiation. That's why we have them. Don't forget it. Now I'm appointing the other detective and I don't give a good rat's ass about who you've already decided I *got to* appoint. Last time I checked, my name was still on that door. OK with you guys?"

The Chief, title on the door, they understood would not be pushed further. The subordinate chief softly asked, "And who would that be, sir?"

McArdle smiled, "Puckett. Natalie Puckett. That OK with you?"

Delaney didn't know Puckett, but saw Thorogood fidget uncomfortably. McArdle laughed and said, "You know Puckett? She's an Indian. How's that for a politically correct lead team? Black man, lesbo, Indian maid. Can't get much better than that." He turned to Delaney. "You know why he's squirming?"

McArdle glanced at the troubled Thorogood with a smirk. "He thinks that if they don't crack this right away I'll hold a press conference to slam them and then announce a new team of white guys to take over. Isn't that right, Thoro?"

Thorogood's wan smile affirmed his chief's goad.

"Well, I won't, and that's a promise. Puckett is sharp. Yeah, I know she's just been on the family violence unit, but she's got community connections up the whazoo and you will need those. I also know that she is an extremely talented and competent officer. Besides, the psychology of this freak may not be too far off from most of those wife beaters we occasionally arrest."

In Delaney's eye, Homer McArdle had once again transformed himself from a loud, lewd, politically driven egomaniac into a strategically minded Chief whose counsel and guidance was actually worth something.

The Chief hit his intercom button. "Tell Megan I want her," he grinned at them, "and I do, too."

"She's the department's press liaison," Thorogood explained.

Tall, blond, blue-eyed, Megan Hartley stepped in, as though from a central casting call for a Nordic ice queen.

"Megan, Megan me darlin', please sit. We have to discuss how to handle the media weasels."

She remained standing and a cold stare was the only reply to her boss.

"I have to say something to the weasels about these Riverrun murders, but I want to low-key it. Can you do that?"

"Yes, of course."

"Really? You can, sweetheart? How?"

"There are three other important announcements you can make at the same time to deflect public attention. City Council budget hearings are coming up and you have a new department budget to submit. You want a major increase to be able to add ten new beat officers."

"I do?"

"And you're announcing a new annual department award to the neighbor-hood council that has done the most to reduce crime in its community."

"Really?"

"Finally, you want a new twenty-five dollar filing fee added to every mar-riage license application, with the proceeds dedicated to family violence prevention and prosecution. The funds to be split equally between the department and legal aid."

"I like it, like everything right up to fuckin' legal aid. I know where you're going with this, but shit."

"Look, Chief, if you want to downplay this task force, these are the kind of distractions you need. The press likes staying at city hall, so the budget story will keep them there. They will scramble to start covering neighborhood crime watch stuff and they know you hate legal aid, so that's going to get great play. Of course, you'll have to let legal aid know first."

"You do the talking to them. No, Mel, you talk to your buddies over there, since they got you your job in the first place."

"They won the lawsuit that finally added a little color to your department, but that may be why I shouldn't call. Have Megan do it. It's a woman's thing, after all."

Megan Hartley, ice in her voice, looked down at them. "Gentlemen, this affects everyone, men, women and children alike. Let's not pretend otherwise, but I'll be happy to talk with legal aid. I think they, at least, know what this is about."

The two policemen raised their eyebrows, grinning stupidly at each other. They liked this kind of blowback.

"I'll get the press announcement out right away. You *gentlemen* should probably turn off your phones and watch the evening news to see how it's played."

"Didn't I tell you she was great?" McArdle beamed as she walked out.

It struck Delaney again that the Chief had a remarkable nose for the kind of talent that could make him look good. On the way out after the meeting Delaney stopped by Megan Hartley's desk. The angry press flack cut him off before he could speak. "Karleen Martin is a friend of mine."

"Really? You're a friend of Karleen's? I hope she's well."

"She is, no thanks to men like you."

Karleen Martin was a former Kansas City police sergeant who abruptly left there to take a job with the Boynton Detective Agency in St. Paul. Delaney had met her on two occasions. The first was over lunch at Matteo's. She and an attorney from the Aguilera Perkins law firm immediately laid the surprise on the table. They were, they said, empowered to offer him a very handsome sum to purchase the Delphi agency. Delaney dismissed the offer out of hand, which, more than anything else, seemed to exasperate Karleen Martin.

The second meeting, less than a week after the first, was triggered when Shaun found the Boynton agency trying to probe Delphi's files. Delaney walked over to Boynton's offices and immediately saw a red-faced Karleen Martin talking with two anxious-looking young men. The meeting was short. An angry Delaney ordered Martin and her cohorts to immediately stop trying to hack into Delphi's computer system. After that a letter from Gene Swearingen, followed quickly by a five-figure check from Boynton to Delphi, settled the matter quickly and, thought Delaney, finally. That was three months ago and the last time he saw or heard from Karleen Martin.

Delaney briefly stared back at Megan Hartley. "Like me? I wonder how well you know her? Actually, I don't care what she might have said. I just wanted to say that I thought you did impressive work in the Chief's office."

She gave Delaney the same practiced, icy stare she had given her chief.

5

OF SHEM & SHAUN

Michael Collins, the practical revolutionary, put it bluntly: "The fund-raisers win the wars."

To him there was no mystery, no strategic secret. He simply observed that a well-armed, well-equipped and well-trained army has a clear advantage over a tribe armed only with pikes and fervor. The equation was simple - resources determine the winners.

The St. Paul PD was pouring all it had into the Riverrun case. Thorogood, O'Leary and Puckett were backed up by cops sifting through financial and phone records of the victims, running undercover operations in nighttime Riverrun Park, doing 24-hour surveillance on the victims' homes and offices and checking with the FBI and the rest of their Homeland Security cohorts for evidence of similar crimes.

Homer McArdle sought out Delaney because of the "expansive research capabilities" the Delphi agency could bring to the case. Shem and Shaun were the personification of those "capabilities." Their real names were Shaun Neary and Sheshdhar Shivaji. The plaques on their office doors read *Master of the Mystic Algorithm* and *Lord of the Code Cobra*, titles befitting their extraordinary talents as computer science geeks - and hackers, very, very talented hackers. Their claim was that no one could hide from them. If any government agency, like the bureau of vital statistics, a driver's license department or passport office, had you on file; if you had a credit card, a bank account or school records; if you had bought or sold securities or real property, they claimed they could know everything about you.

Delaney almost believed them. But they hadn't caught him yet. Maybe they would one day, but they hadn't yet. Delaney was good at hiding things he needed to keep hidden.

Shem and Shaun quit MIT in the middle of their sophomore years for the same reason as so many of their computer-head peers – their formal education was stunting their intellectual and economic growth. They went to work for Delaney because he paid them handsomely and they got to do interesting work. Nor did he interfere with their continuing practical education and avocation. That included hacking, but only for good causes. He not only did not interfere, he encouraged them. They'd been inside the network systems of the Pentagon, Goldman Sachs, Altria, CIA, FBI, the Ford Foundation and both political parties, among others. Servers, personal computers or smart phones, even with highly sophisticated encryption codes, posed few challenges to their self-described immense talents. Delaney had only one rule governing their online behavior: if they got caught or their taps got traced back to Delphi, they might have to be disavowed, at least publicly and, with luck, only temporarily.

On this day, Delaney outlined the research McArdle had requested: complete deep backgrounds on the three victims, find out if there was anything that connected them or if they were the random prey of a psychotic serial killer. Later Delaney would have them check on some darker figures.

He also asked for a thorough look at Roland Gadsen. Big Gad wasn't being entirely truthful, that much was clear to Delaney. He didn't think the big detective was a killer. But he was certain Big Gad knew something about who killed Fortuno and that he planned on doing an end run to nail the killer. He was old school enough to think that was what the code, the unspoken, the unending and unbending code, required. Getting information out of him would be hard, but necessary, even if Delaney had to employ some of his own "enhanced capabilities."

Delaney directed them to do a worldwide search on murders involving mutilation of throats or necks and cases where apples might somehow have been in the picture. Then the shots of the corpses came out and Delaney told them to also do a search for gloved or claw-like weapons. After a short glance at the photos Shem said, "I know the weapon that killed them.

"My ancestor invented it and used it to free my people from the Moguls." He smiled hugely.

"Really?" said Delaney. "You mean there is a specific weapon involved here?"

"Oh, yes, and it holds a special place in the history of India. It's called a bagh nakh; tiger's claw to you barbarians. It was first used by my ancestor, the emperor Shivaji, in the seventeenth century. He revolted against the Mogul Khan and after some success suggested a peace parlay. The Khan agreed and the two of them met privately in a tent away from their troops. The bagh nakh is a glove with curled, claw-like steel blades. It was easily hidden while Shivaji's palm was covered by the oversized sleeve of his silk robe. When the two of them embraced, he eviscerated the Khan."

"Gruesome devil, wasn't he?" said the admiring Shaun, "and sneaky."

"He may have been that, but he was also an enlightened ruler as the Maratha emperor. You should read about him someday. You'll be impressed. He fought the British to a standstill. Which, as I recall, your bog-trotting ancestors were not doing at the time."

"You're sure some version of this tiger's claw was used to kill our victims?"

"You can Google it to see what they look like, boss."

"I'm more interested in finding out about what kind of person would use this thing."

"Boss?" Shem hesitated. "Despite the good use Shivaji put it to, the bagh nakh is not a warrior's weapon. It was looked down on as a weapon of thieves, women and assassins. That's why the Mogul emperor was caught so off guard. He would never have expected someone of Shivaji's stature to stoop so low as to use it."

"So, it could be a woman who actually did this?"

"You'd probably have to ask a doctor or other expert about that, but my initial impression is yes, if the blades were sharp enough."

Shaun, his brow furrowed, said, "The numbers don't really work for that, though. Women murderers are just so rare and for a woman to use a weapon like this, and do all this bloody ripping and tearing, I just can't believe it."

"Good point, but let's not rule any possibilities out just yet. And speaking of women, Shaun, have we seen or heard anything lately from Karleen Martin or the Boynton firm?"

"No, but I did a little research on the side, boss. I looked at the usual records and accounts. Then I went to internal police department memos and reports.

"In KC she was quite a successful cop. She moved up quickly and was a founding member of the National Women Police Officer's Association."

"There's the connection to Megan Hartley."

"Huh?"

"It's nothing. Do we know why she left the department?"

"Only that, shortly before resigning, she was assigned to the Vice Squad. I haven't been able to find out yet if the two are related.

"This was two years ago. Last year she was hired by the Boynton Agency here in St. Paul. Want me to keep digging?"

"I don't think so. We've got too much real work confronting us. For now, even though this is a quick and dirty research assignment, make the St. Paul PD research your top priority. Use your instincts to pursue any other avenues on this project that may suggest themselves to you. So, is there anything else I should know? Will the two of you have enough for us to talk about in another 24 hours?"

They both nodded and Shem said, "Yeah, we should have dossiers and background on everybody. If any of this stuff takes some extreme tickling, we'll let you know. And any red flags will get you the immediate call, as usual."

Delaney left with the uneasy feeling that today's unkind universe would deliver more than one red flag.

6

OF POPEYE & OLIVE

Delaney had another resource that was off limits to the rank and file of the city's police force. Mackey Stately was not someone who talked with your everyday cop, except when he chose to.

Mackey was a foster kid, like Delaney, and a school classmate. Polio left him with a stunted and weakened right leg that required a brace and something like a three-inch sole on his right shoe. He never, as a child or adult, sought pity; nor did he ever offer it.

They got to be friends playing baseball as kids. Mackey was in a tussle with Bob Mellinger, the neighborhood bully, who kept shoving him off his precarious balance and yelling, "C'mon cripple. Hit me cripple. Get up, you fuckin' cripple," and more in the same vein. Delaney, his temper roiling, grabbed the bat and, walking up behind Mellinger, slammed it into his ankle. The big kid went down screaming that it was broken.

Delaney nodded at Mackey, who needed no such encouragement, and was quickly all over Mellinger, bloodying his nose and bruising his face. The assemblage thought Mackey was done when he stood and grabbed the bat out of Delaney's hands. He clubbed Mellinger over and over, laying down two cracked ribs, a broken collarbone, a crushed cheekbone and a concussion before the other ball players wrestled him down and took the bat away. It was the last time anyone bullied Mackey and the episode ended all hope that either of the two foster kids would be adopted out of the system.

Mackey was the sort of loner who got a grasp on things ahead of the rest of his adolescent peers. He found Big Al's whorehouses long before his fellows knew what they were and used the bordellos in his first foray into criminal enterprise. Mackey watched the men going into the houses, took down the license plates of likely looking candidates and started blackmailing them. First there were the ridiculously small amounts, just one or two hundred dollars. Gradually he upped the ante into the thousands.

He had them send cash to a post office box. A few, bolder than the others, caught him there but believed his story - he was just the delivery boy for a very big and very bad gangland heavy. Of course, they believed him; after all, he was just a dumb-looking crippled kid, wasn't he?

Then came his big mistake, his big break.

A Cadillac Deville, a great mark, and off went his letter shaking down the customer for $5,000. But when Mackey opened the envelope at the post office there was a note, "Your dead asshole." Outside two guys in long coats were waiting for him.

They took him to the dimly lit basement of a bar and restaurant on West Seventh Street. The guy sitting at the table asked who Mackey worked for. The bold Mackey replied that he was the bagman for a Mr. Big and if this guy knew what was good for him, he'd better let him go. Mr. Big was connected.

The guy laughed and asked Mackey if he knew who he was talking to. Doesn't matter, Mackey told him. "Would the guy you work for be Eddie James?" the guy asked.

"Yeah, and he'll cut your balls off if you don't give me the cash to take to him," Mackey said.

At that the guy laughed again, really laughed, until tears started. Mackey knew then where he was and what could happen to him. Eddie James said, "Kid, you got balls, I give you that. Christ, look at you, you little pissant." And he laughed some more.

"You wanna work for me kid? I mean really?"

"Yes, Mr. James. It would be an honorable." He was respectful, and hopeful, now.

Eddie James laughed again and said, "OK, I can always use a little weasel like you with big balls. Jesus, kid. First, you gotta promise to stop shaking down the customers, OK? That's just bad for business. Can you do that?"

The chastened Mackey gave him a contrite yessir and waited for the hammer to strike a second time.

Eddie James asked how much he made from his shake-down racket and how much he had left. Mackey, in a state of semi-terror did not lie and gave up his remaining $20,000 to Eddie James, who said, "It's really my money, kid. You scared away my customers and it belongs to me." Then he cuffed him hard, knocking him to the floor. "Now go to work, you little shit." He laughed again.

Mackey started out stocking the bar and soon moved on to actually acting as a bag man, making pick-ups and deliveries around the City of St. Paul for Eddie James, who thought a crippled kid was not likely to draw anyone's suspicion.

Years later Mackey made occasional business trips to Reno and Cleveland, and more frequently to Kansas City. But for the most part he stuck to running his multi-faceted business out of his place on West Seventh, Eddie's Bistro & Tavern.

Eddie James' reign as king of the St. Paul underworld ended on a sunny morning when he was riddled with bullets while sitting in a barber's chair. The word was the hit men were from Cleveland.

By this time grown-up Mackey had a barrel chest and huge forearms, although his bad leg meant he still moved with a stiff-legged limp. Only now he was the Mr. Big of St. Paul, with a new nickname - Mackey the Merciless.

The charismatic Mackey showed a natural talent for leading and organizing. Eddie's was the heart of his enterprise, but his tentacles reached into every ward of the city and were felt most strongly in those neighborhoods where desperation was thick in the air and the need for escape, through drugs, gambling or flesh, was highest – West Seventh, the West and East Sides, Summit, Frogtown and the North End.

If you wanted a decent, but not great, meal, Eddie's was an OK place. If you wanted to gamble, score some dope, fence stolen goods, launder some ill-gotten gain, connect with a hooker or arrange a financial deal that no court of law would ever recognize, Eddie's sprawling back room was more than OK.

The bar was devoid of customers when Delaney stopped in that afternoon, but four of Mackey's men were playing cards at a corner table. He caught a rare glimpse of Aloysious "Foxy" Higgs, leaving through a rear exit. Higgs was Mackey's disappearing man, so named for disappearing Mackey's enemies, as well as his seeming ability to appear and disappear at will.

Mackey was behind the bar talking with Butchie, a tiny bald head parked on a massive three-hundred-pound frame of muscle and flab. Butchie's lips were set in a perpetual sneer and he was reputed to have pounded men to death with his huge fists. He rarely spoke, preferring a nod or shake of his bare skull. When he did speak, it was in a squeaky, high pitch that belied his otherwise fearsome appearance. His one apparent concession to human feeling lay in his utter and complete devotion to Mackey. Mackey fed him, housed him, employed him and relieved him of any need to ever make a decision. He did as Mackey instructed, always eagerly and without question. He was dressed in his Mackey-mandated, everyday uniform of light gray suit and bow tie.

Delaney had talked with Butchie once before when Mackey was called away. They had a one-sided conversation, with Delaney doing the talking. Seeing Butchie again reminded him of that time and how incongruously soft Butchie's huge hand had seemed at the time.

A smile spread across Mackey's broad face as he reached across the bar to shake Delaney's hand. His grip was strong. "If it ain't Jesus H. Lucky Christ himself come to slummin' with the common folk. Jameson's Vintage, neat?"

"How are you, Mackey?"

"Still able to sit up and take nourishment. You?"

"Aces over Kings and I'll be even better if you pour some of that mouth wash for yourself, too."

"I'll join you for one, seeing it's you. But I'm guessing this isn't entirely a social call?"

"Not entirely, but it is good to see you again. You're looking prosperous."

"I'm doing OK, as you are. You're here about, let's see, Port Authority bonds? Credit default swaps?"

"Nope. Murder."

"The Riverrun murders? Beautiful. I didn't think you were into that kind of investigation."

"That's what they're calling them, the Riverrun murders?"

He smiled that huge smile again. "Sure. I mean it's pretty hard not to call 'em that, ain't it? But slipping an apple in their throats, that borders on the gruesome, don't it? You have to be a monster to do such things. Right?"

Delaney was hardly surprised Mackey already knew about the murders in some detail. There was little about the dark side of life in St. Paul that Mackey didn't know. He had connections.

"I'm wondering, what's the word on Danny Fortuno? Or his former partner, Gadsen?"

Mackey lifted his bushy brows, smacked his lips and leaned forward on the bar, lowering his voice. "Ah, now there's a pair. As mismatched as my shoes. Danny was a regular here. He liked drink, gambling, nose candy and whores. Very bad habits and he indulged them all in a very foolish way."

Delaney nodded and sipped at his Irish whiskey.

Mackey looked over at the men seated in the corner, winked at Butchie and smiled. "Maybe we should go upstairs and talk about this."

Upstairs was where Mackey entertained visitors and held meetings. It was a huge, rambling apartment that occupied the whole second floor over Eddie's. Evelyn Rose, his business manager, lived upstairs. Mackey also had a room up there, but usually stayed at one of a half-dozen hotel suites he kept around the City. A man in his position could not always afford the luxury of predictably staying at the same place every night.

"How is Evelyn these days?"

"Oh, y'know, she's good, but that agoraphobia, it ain't getting any better. She still can't stand crowds and mostly stays home, but she comes downstairs more often now. She's even gone out to the bank for some meetings. I gotta tell you, she is a genius for business and keeps the books and our investments. We're doin' real well in that department, by the way."

"It's good to know that she's doing well, and that you have someone running the business end of your enterprises."

He gave Delaney a slight frown before saying, "C'mon, let's go upstairs, I know she'll be happy to see you. She likes a little educated conversation now and then."

Mackey moved out from behind the bar and stopped. "Wait, you gotta see this." He called over a short, thin, Black man from the corner table. "Marshall come over here. I want you to meet an old friend. Show him a trick, OK?" Turning to Delaney he smirked. "You know the rest of these guys, don't you?"

"Hate to admit it, but I do."

As the others grinned, Tommy Swenson, the tallest of the group, called out to Mackey, "Business can't be so bad that you're letting Delaney in here. He might give us a reputation."

With a grin and wave of his hand Mackey turned and said, "Marshall, go ahead, show him something quick, we got business to get to."

Marshall Pinckney, in dark blue pinstripes and electric blue tie, smiled and quickly fanned a deck of cards. "Pick a card, any card," he said in a W.C. Fields voice. "Don't show it to me, my little chickadee. Got it memorized? Already? You could be a memory expert, although you look more like a bank dick."

Smiles all around when he plucked the card from Delaney's jacket pocket after Delaney had tucked it back into the deck. "This guy is fabulous, isn't he? You should hear his Trump or Pacino sometime." Mackey laughed. Turning to Delaney, he said, "Let's get upstairs. You know, Evelyn's always happy when a visitor stops by, even if she does argue with all of 'em. She argues with you, doesn't she?"

"Oh, yeah," Delaney muttered as they started up the short stairwell.

Evelyn Rose's fear of the outside world was legendary, as was her business acumen. Some thought Mackey and her a mismatched pair. Evelyn was thin, pale, blue-eyed, dark-haired and stood about two inches taller than the broad, muscular and dark Mackey. Even though she rarely left the apartment, she dressed herself in suits, dresses or formal wear. Her wardrobe colors were always black, gray, white or a combination of the three, usually with a string of pearls and matching earrings. Her long fingers always sported two or more rings besides a huge sapphire Mackey had given her and she made a habit of wearing narrow, elongated heels.

Where Mackey was a hail-fellow-well-met, story-telling kind of extrovert, she had an aloof and distracted manner that made it seem as if conversation was a sideline to her private interior dialogue.

"Look who I dragged in with me," Mackey announced, a little too loudly. As always, the clubroom area was in semi-darkness. She was at the computer and Delaney caught a few bars of Leonard Cohen's "Bird on a Wire" coming out of the speakers before she switched it off.

"Ohhh, you can't drag that man," she said in her little girl voice. "No one could want to hurt that suit. It's a beauty. I don't know about the man inside it, but the suit is beautiful."

Delaney smiled. "You always know how to make a guy feel welcome, Evelyn."

Mackey, big grin flashing, said, "We need some privacy. Gotta talk some business. Mind moving to another room?"

As she left she said, over her shoulder, "You're doing business with Mackey? I'm not sure I believe that."

Mackey sat in one of the half-dozen easy chairs scattered throughout the room. A spacious enclave that was as wide as the entire front of the building and something like twenty-five feet deep, it was filled with leather couches, Turkish rugs, over-sized chairs, ottomans, sculptures and paintings. A small bar occupied one corner and Evelyn's Queen Anne desk enhanced another. Delaney knew the similarity to an Edwardian era clubroom was intentional. Evelyn had that kind of taste.

"Fortuno and Gadsen." Mackey smiled. "Gadsen, you gotta understand, is a boy scout. But a very unpleasant personality. A real prick. He's never taken a taste of nothin' and I respect him for that. But Christ, what an obnoxious prick. Danny was his opposite number. He thought bein' a cop gave him privileges and he took advantage. It was strange how they remained friends after Fortuno left the force. The two of them came here together once in a while. Fortuno, of course, came here a lot without Gadsen."

The intercom buzzed and Evelyn walked in to say they needed Mackey downstairs for a minute. He grinned again as he got up. "Sorry, I really am. You'd think those guys could take care of things without me, wouldn't ya? Evelyn, here's your chance for a higher quality intellectual conversation."

She sat at the other end of the sofa and glanced at Delaney through the dim light for just a moment before speaking. Delaney wondered: was she just perpetually stoned or did she develop the inclination in childhood, this disconcerting habit of either gazing off into the distance or focusing on some object across the room while talking. Only when she was perturbed in some manner would her eyes take on a different cast – wide open, pupils dilated and a laser-like intensity focusing on the object of her ire. Delaney had once asked Shem and Shaun to do a deep background check on Evelyn Amber Rose, but, to their great surprise, just like Delaney, they found nothing.

She opened the conversation in typical Evelyn fashion. "I'm curious about your thoughts regarding government entering into partnership with a criminal enterprise. Ostensibly this partnership is for the benefit of the public. What do you think?"

The object of her current low-intensity stare was Klimt's *Eyes of a Goddess*. Delaney wondered fleetingly if a certain Viennese museum was actually displaying the original. He knew what she was getting at, but paused for a moment, not prepared to broach the real topic yet. "If you're asking do I approve of something like the CIA contracting with the mob to assassinate Fidel Castro, no. What do you think?"

Evelyn licked her lips, furrowed her brow and decided to play along. "I think if you knew that Fidel's death would stop the incipient uprisings and revolutionary communist fervor spreading throughout Latin America, it would be the right thing to do. Would you disagree with me?"

"If you mean was the maintenance of US corporate hegemony in the western hemisphere justification enough for all manner of dirty tricks? No, I don't think so."

"I suppose that from a strict moralist's perspective you have a point. But from the CIA's? No, their interest was entirely in making this country safe and that meant getting rid of Castro, to remove him as a threat to us in the USA. Of course," she smiled, "that goes double for those gentlemen gamblers and pimps who had a good deal going on in Havana before Castro. I have sympathy for them and their losses."

"So, Uncle Sam allied himself with a dictator and the Mob. Makes for great optics, doesn't it? But your original question included benefit to the public, the citizenry of the US. It is almost impossible to spin that plot as benefiting the people of this country. We are despised in Latin America just for this kind of hubris. The rest of the hemisphere isn't that big on the Monroe Doctrine, you know."

Her gaze shifted to a small white onyx sculpture across the room. He recognized it as *The Head of a Girl*, by the Swedish artist, Carl Milles. He found Evelyn's contemplative stare distracting and wondered if she was even conscious of how odd it was. He found her hard to read and wondered if her unconventional body language was intentional.

She glanced briefly at him again and said, "Touché. But you should think more deeply about that notion of 'the public' you're using. If you had taken a poll of the 'public' what do you think the response would have been? I know, and so do you, that overwhelmingly, the great unwashed would have said go for it, assassinate Castro."

"That's valid only if they are in full possession of the facts. And we both know that the people of this country were hardly knowledgeable about the conditions in Cuba or the rest of Latin America at that time. The truth is the CIA was betraying this country's best interests with these kinds of pranks throughout the world."

"Betray." The sarcasm dripped from her voice. She barked a quick laugh. "You're kind of a boy scout yourself, you know. Somebody less thoughtful and articulate would make me sick. But you're evading the real question, aren't you?"

"Nope. Our government entered into a corrupt alliance with avowed criminals and it ended badly."

"Oh, please. You know as well as I do that government-sanctioned criminal enterprises have always existed. The Yakuza, the Mafia, the Triads. They provide control and stability for enterprises that have always, and will always, exist and prosper. Imagine the chaos there would be without them."

"An economist would say they are the source of bad money that drives out good."

"Good, bad? Governments don't operate on that kind of morality, do they? They do what's expedient. They allow a hypocritical society access to the goods and services it can't publicly admit it wants. You think it somehow diminishes life, economy, whatever. I know it keeps it working." She was quiet for a moment then said, "I worry about Mackey sometimes. You don't see him the way I do. He's always happy when you're around. You seem to have some kind of soothing effect on him. Why is that I wonder? Are you some kind of voodoo doctor? Anyway, I do get seriously concerned. Do you ever worry about him like I do?"

"Not much, why?"

"This is a dangerous business, isn't it?" It wasn't a question. "There are people who don't like him, you know?"

"I think that people who want to see him fall neither like nor dislike him. They just want his money and his power. But McArdle likes him and protects him."

"Eddie James was supposed to be protected, too."

"Eddie strayed outside the agreed upon boundaries. Getting involved with the Teamsters was stupid. Mackey isn't going to make that kind of mistake."

"Still, it's a lot of money and power. People kill for a lot less than that, don't they? Like this freak that's killing them down by the river - that's not about money or power, is it? Just the joy of slaughter."

Mackey came through the door and her demeanor changed. "Mackey, you have got to bring this man up here more often. You know how starved I get for a decent conversation. Your boys are all, oh, I don't know, not exactly intellectual stars? And you," she looked at Delaney, starting to move to the other room again, "you should come to dinner sometime. How about Friday night? You could bring a date and we could all discuss John Rawls."

Mackey scowled and said, "Who's John Rawls?"

"Just a guy," Delaney said. "A philosopher and a good guy." But he now claimed to be running late for an appointment and could Mackey walk him to the car? It was clear Evelyn had been listening in and Delaney wanted Mackey alone.

Outside Delaney quietly said, "Malcolm, this is a serious thing. McArdle really has put these murders at the top of the department's list. He is embarrassed by them and he'll tear the town apart to find the killer. You know he wouldn't bring me in otherwise. Is there anything you know that you haven't told me? Anything at all?"

Mackey looked at his feet and then into Delaney's grey eyes. "You're a good friend, always have been. Fortuno played too hard and Gadsen played not at all. But I don't think the kind of freak who'd do this kind of murder would be hangin' out with either cops or crooks, do you? Aren't these kind of guys usually loners listening to something in their heads? Fortuno might have been in hock to some tough boys, but this ain't their style."

Delaney felt his cell phone vibrating, but ignored it and asked, "I don't suppose you want to tell me who these tough guys are?"

"You know I can't do that, not even for you. But here's what I will do. I'll tell them you're on the hunt and better they should not try to dodge you. If you want, I'll set up a pow-wow with them. But just you, no cops. OK?"

"Can you set it up in the next 24 hours?"

"I'll get them here. That's as much as I can do and as much as I know, and that's no shit."

"Thanks, Mack, set up the meeting as quickly as you can, will you? I appreciate what you're doing. Keep me in the loop on anything else you might hear, will you?"

"Of course. You do the same for me?"

"As much as I can. And that's no shit either."

7

THANK YOU, SIR

The Troubles were winding down. No one knew it at the time. Shootings, bombings, sorrow and revenge were still the stuff of life in Northern Ireland. But George Mitchell was leading a diplomatic dance that would finally lead to the Good Friday Agreement and an end to the latest round of hostilities. Nevertheless, on this day Belfast was still a treacherous place. Conor Delaney could smell it in the city's fetid air.

He was twenty-one years old and a newly minted college graduate with a Bachelor of Arts degree. In two months he'd begin studying for his Master's in Washington, DC. But, before that, there was vengeance to be exacted in Belfast.

He had researched the circumstances of his parents' death's. It had not proved difficult to finally identify the zealot who made and planted the car bomb that killed them. He left his signature on each of the fourteen explosives he planted in Ireland and the United States. It was the wires. Instead of the usual red, black or white, his wires were purple and gold. Bright, brazen colors that announced the homicidal explosions as the work of one William Robert "Billy' Pletch.

He and his small circle of military vets were well known in certain dismal precincts of Belfast and even hailed as heroes in a few local pubs. Like dozens of other small coteries of violent, self-styled patriots, they promoted themselves as Belfast's natural defense against "the other."

Delaney first located Billy Pletch's apartment and within the week found him in a neighborhood pub. The man looked older than Delaney had imagined him. With a weathered face and long grey hair pulled back into a ponytail, he looked like a refugee from the nineteen-seventies. Delany followed him for three days before making his move.

Pletch left the pub with two of his mates. They split up after two blocks, Pletch taking a turn to his second-floor apartment just a short walk down the dark street. The dreary block of concrete buildings where he slept were covered with graffiti. The outdoor lighting, mounted as a crime prevention measure, was destroyed the week it was installed.

Delaney waited, looking through the darkness for any sign of a possible witness. Then he moved quickly, tracing his quarry's steps. He pounded loudly on the door. As expected, Billy Pletch angrily jerked it open.

Delaney slammed the Taser into his chest, pushing him back into a dark hallway. The shock left Billy Pletch moaning in pain and anger. In a few short minutes Delaney, taking a roll of duct tape from his backpack, secured Pletch's hands behind his back and taped his mouth shut. He dragged him into the kitchen and turned on the lights.

After lifting and taping him securely into a chair, he looked at the man's eyes and saw anger and fear fighting for dominance. "Do you know who I am?" he snapped. "Just nod if you do."

Pletch grunted, struggling to spit words through the duct tape. Delaney casually swatted him with a well-aimed backhand.

"Here's what we're going to do. If your answer is yes, you will nod once. If your answer is no, you will shake your head. Do you understand?" Seeing him nod, Delaney continued, "Do you know who I am?"

He shook his head.

"You remember being in St. Paul twelve years ago?"

His eyes grew wide.

"Now you know who I am, don't you? And you know why I'm here." Delaney could see fear taking the lead in the battle with anger.

"It's true what they say, you know. Revenge really is a dish best served cold."

He used more tape to fasten Pletch even tighter into his kitchen chair.

"How does it feel, knowing you're going to die in the same way they did? Do you appreciate the justice of that?" Seeing no response, Delaney swatted him again. "Remember our agreement?"

Pletch nodded wildly.

Delaney pulled a length of plastic pipe from his backpack. Purple and gold wires dangled from one end. "You know what this is, don't you? Sure you do. It's a little thing they call an improvised explosive device, a car bomb. It dismembers people; blows them apart. Innocent people who never harmed you or anyone else."

He taped the pipe bomb to the bottom of the chair.

"Now, when we are done with this little exercise, we are finished with each other, aren't we?" He stepped back.

"Aren't we?" he shouted as Pletch nodded frantically.

As he was leaving Delaney said, "I'll be detonating that thing sometime in the next twenty-four hours. Not sure when. Ta ta."

William Robert Pletch pissed himself.

In the morning one of his mates found him on the floor, still bound to the chair. Two hours earlier the pipe bomb had exploded with all the force a small bundle of firecrackers could give it. A purple banner with "BOOM," written in gold letters across its face, popped out, along with a scattering of green, white and orange confetti. It lay crumpled on the floor, just a few feet from the wild eyes of William Pletch. When the tape was torn from his mouth, Pletch laughed hysterically.

Three hours later, on the other side of the city, Delaney was smiling as his taxi made its way to the airport. The trip could hardly have worked out better. He imagined that the man who killed his mother and father had felt the cold hand of death stroking him. Pletch would have felt abandoned by a remorseless universe as he was overcome by mad, irrational fear. And then the full force of a cosmic joke would have drilled itself into every level of his consciousness. The Irish habit of revenge would not be indulged between them. He, Conor Delaney, had decreed that the murderer Billy Pletch could live.

As he indulged this happy fantasy, he was unaware of the black sedan pulling up alongside the taxi until a passenger waved a pistol at the driver, motioning him to pull over. Two big men piled out of the back seat of the sedan and grabbed Delaney. Within the hour he was back on the other side of town in the basement of a small Belfast pub.

Pletch was in the room, seated behind a table next to an older man. Delaney was pushed onto a small wooden chair across from them. The men who brought Delaney in stood in a semi-circle around him. The man next to Pletch had short, steel-grey hair, rigid posture and was clearly in command.

He looked at Delaney's eyes for a short time before speaking. "As far as you are concerned, my name is Major Tom and you look like a bloody owl, don't ya?" He waited for a reply and hearing none raised his voice. "I said, you look like a feckin' owl, don't ya?"

Military, possibly still active, thought Delaney. "So I've been told."

Wrinkling his nose as if a foul odor had just wafted across his nostrils, Major Tom mimicked, "So I've been told."

Delaney grinned and nodded. Billy Pletch giggled.

"Listen up, lad. You are in deep shit. You see what you've done here. This man is one of our best, so the only question is, do we kill you or fuck you up so bad that the rest of your years on this planet are full of unending pain and misery. That is the question, and the only question we are here to settle this morning. So, wipe that shit-eating smirk off your gob. Where's your passport?"

Pletch giggled again as Delaney began reaching into his jacket. The Major held up his hand. "Stop. Tell me or motion to where it is."

After Delaney pointed at his jacket pocket someone behind him ripped it out and passed it to Major Tom.

After seeming to study it for a long minute he looked up. "St. Paul? No shit? We have done business in St. Paul. You know Eddie James?"

"I know Eddie," Pletch snorted between giggles. "He's a raving lunatic."

Delaney waited for the giggles to subside. "I've met him."

"Let me put it another way, does Eddie James know you?"

"No."

"Does anyone in St. Paul know ya? Anyone of importance? Anyone who matters to us?"

"Mackey Stately."

Major Tom's glare kept Billy Pletch from jumping into the conversation again.

"Mackey? That smart little crippled lad? Eddie likes him. You know Mackey? Again, does Mackey know you?"

"Yes, we know each other quite well. We've been friends for many years."

"Does he know you're here?"

"In Ireland, yeah."

"Well now, we'll just see about that." He waved at a phone a few feet away and the passport retriever fetched it for him. Major Tom looked into a small notebook and dialed.

"Yeah, can I talk to Eddie . . . You already know who it is, don't ya?" He rolled his eyes and spoke at Pletch, "As though the dumbfuck hears an Irish accent every day."

He turned his malevolent stare back at Delaney until Eddie James came on the line. They passed a few pleasantries before he said, "I got a guy here, claims to be a friend of Mackey's; name of Conor Delaney. Heard of him? . . . Yeah, he said you wouldn't know him. Listen, Eddie, do ya mind if I talk with Mackey for a minute? I just want to get this guy's bona fides . . . Thanks Eddie."

Still holding the phone, he glared at Delaney until he heard another voice on the line. "Mackey, Eddie told you . . . He is? Well, he kinda fucked up a close friend of mine. . . Don't know about permanent damage. He's OK physically.. . ." The conversation continued for another ten minutes, with Mackey apparently cutting off Major Tom in the middle of most of his sentences.

When the call finally ended, he looked at Delaney. "Christ, are youse homos or something?" Turning, he said, "Sergeant, I hardly know what to think. St. Paul's been good to us and . . ." He let his voice trail off.

Billy beamed. "Let him go. I killed his Ma and Da, didn't I? And didn't he leave me alive, anyway? And I seen the universe. Yeah, he coulda done me lots worse." Now looking to Delaney, he said, "Best favor anyone ever done me, kid. I saw the universe when the bomb went off."

Turning to Major Tom, he drew himself up straight and snapped a salute. "Sir, this universe is beautiful."

The Major looked at the men who brought Delaney in. "Take him to the airport and no harm to him, got it?"

As they turned to go Pletch said, "Eh, just a minute," and took a clumsy swing at Delaney. Delaney easily slipped the punch and grabbed his arm. His grip was a vise the older man couldn't shake.

"This is over, remember? We had an agreement."

The still laughing Pletch groaned, "Let go, ya shite. Jesus, yes, I just wanted a little payback for last night."

As Delaney released him, Major Tom chuckled and barked, "For Christ's sake lads, will ya get him outta here?" Pointing at Delaney he said, "If you ever show up in Belfast again, you'll be a dead man the day you land. Got it?"

Delaney looked back at Major Tom *Why would I, or any other decent human being want to put a foot down in this putrid cesspool of inhumanity?* he thought. But he said, "Thank you, sir."

Half a world away, Mackey Stately mumbled the same three words to Eddie James. But he was thinking, *You're dead, you foul heap of shit*, and in that instant began planning for how he would replace Eddie James as the head of the St. Paul underworld.

Eddie James had just lectured Mackey about how he was not authorized to make deals on behalf of the organization with international clients like the Irish. Eddie would now be forced to take seventy-five percent of the earnings from Mackey's rackets, instead of his customary fifty percent. Mackey should realize, it was something he would do to anyone who stepped out of bounds like this.

"You understand, don't you, kid? This is for your own good. It makes the organization stronger and that's good for all of us, ain't it? You'll thank me for this later. In fact, you should thank me for it now, shouldn't you, kid?"

"Thank you, sir."

8

HOME SWEET HOME

Delaney strode into Thorogood's office and asked, "Anything yet?"

Thorogood nodded, "Yeah, we got your business card. CSI sent me a copy of it."

"I don't have a business card; never have had one."

Thorogood's hand shook as he laid down a page with a business card copied onto it. In the center was the image of a green apple, with Delaney's name and Thorogood's cell phone number embossed over it. "It was in her mouth."

"What? Who? What are you talking about?"

"A package came in this morning addressed to me. After the bomb guys went over it they routed it to CSI. The package had a hat box with the head of a woman in it. Karleen Martin. They said she had been terribly battered and bruised. Someone you knew?"

Delaney, as stunned as Thorogood, sat. Looking past his friend, he slowly shook his head. "I met her, yeah. But I didn't know her. Did you?"

"Only met her once or twice. She was on the Kansas City force. I knew something ugly would happen."

As Delaney demurred, he continued, "Oh, I know, the bastard couldn't have known about our conversation this morning so no need to feel guilty on that count. Can I assume that now you'll come on the case full-time? McArdle already approved it." Delaney nodded reluctantly and, while mentally cursing a hostile universe, replied, "Shem and Shaun should have some stuff for us in a few hours. How soon did your CSI think he'd have anything from . . . ?"

"Karleen Martin? He doesn't know. So far we have an apple in her throat with your card and my phone number in her mouth. Who knows what else we might find tucked away in there? He's running an MRI, tox screen, DNA and some other tests. What was your relationship to this woman?"

"There was no relationship," he replied, then recounted his two meetings with Karleen Martin. "Your Megan Hartley knew her, by the way, apparently quite well. Something else – it may not be important – Karleen Martin apparently told Hartley some story about how I had wronged her. I didn't, but you may want to follow up with her anyway.

"Something else, do you know anything about a Marshall Pinckney?"

"Dude has a small reputation."

"I was just introduced to Mr. Pinckney's skills of impersonation and pres-tidigitation before viewing, uh, . . ."

Thorogood gave him the short bio: Dapper Marsh Pinckney showing up in town a year ago from Kansas City with a short rap sheet. Time spent at Lansing in Leavenworth for dealing and blackmail. Arrested at other times for statutory rape and burglary, none of the charges sticking. There were no arrests after his hard time and the general consensus held he had a connection to the Civella family before moving up to the Land of Ten Thousand Lakes.

"No," Thorogood said, "I didn't know about Pinckney's voice and sleight-of-hand skills. There was a belief about him in the KC department, that he was the fall guy in the blackmail case, that he didn't have the balls or connections to threaten the real perp. That's the rumor anyway. Why? Do you think he's the guy who lifted my phone?"

"I don't know, but Mackey did push him forward for no reason that I could discern. I don't suppose you remember bumping into Pinckney last week?"

"No, and remember, if he was a fall guy once he could be again. About Mackey pushing him forward? Is he the first Black guy he ever hired?

"Yeah. So, you think . . . "

"For some strange reason known only to himself, Mackey cares about what you think and he may have put Pinckney on display because he knew you'd be pleased that he added a little color to his band of outlaws."

Delaney chuckled, "I find it hard to believe that he'd make any personnel decisions based on what I may think. Anyway, I don't know if Pinkney's worth a look or not. He's got light fingers and does broad voice imitations. With some practice he might have you down, especially for a short phone message."

"OK, we can look at him, it would be irresponsible not to. But it's not him. He's a guy that takes orders. This killer is not like that. This guy is a take-charge, take-no-prisoners kind of wild man. Pinckney's too much of a woe-de-doe for this action."

"Maybe he was told to lift the phone and do the voice, in which case he knows the killer. And if he is the fall guy, he works for Mackey and would likely be taking the fall for him or one of his guys. But Mackey? Higgs? This just isn't their style. If they did them, they'd just disappear. Mackey is not one for this kind of extravagant show. Nor are our victims the class of people Mackey offs."

"Let's talk about it at this afternoon's meeting. But I gotta agree with you, it's not Mackey. McArdle would really shit a brick if it was, wouldn't he?"

McArdle would. The practical policeman and consummate politician knew he couldn't stamp out dope dealing, prostitution, gambling, protection rackets, loan sharking, money laundering, fencing and a dozen other enterprises proscribed by the laws he was sworn to uphold. But, like his predecessors he could wall them in, control them, and see that St. Paul neighborhoods didn't collapse under the weight of gangs and crime.

He could keep most of the neighborhoods clean and pristine and make sure his city remained among the nation's most livable; at least as it was ranked by those magazines he never read. That's where Mackey came in.

McArdle favored Mackey as St. Paul's Mr. Big. Mackey could quietly run his businesses with little or no hassle from McArdle's police force. In return, he had to shut down any rivals quietly and, if necessary, with the tacit, but active, help of the cops. He was to inform on anyone not connected to one of his undertakings. If it became necessary for a rival to be eliminated, he was to simply disappear. The word was that no one offed by Mackey's chief enforcer, Aloysius Higgs, had ever been found. No trace, no evidence allowed. No charges ever against Mackey or Higgs.

It also meant that St. Paul was immunized against highly organized crime syndicates like the mafia, Latin American drug cartels and the Russian mob. While they infested cities large and small across the nation, the McArdle/Mackey partnership kept St. Paul impervious to their incursions.

The St. Paul system was elegantly organized; Mackey could be shut down or replaced at any time and there was plausible deniability for everyone on the right side of the law.

This was not a system invented by Homer McArdle. It was just the latest iteration of an agreement extant at the city's founding. Fort Snelling was put up in the early nineteenth century at the confluence of the Minnesota and Mississippi Rivers, both to control the flourishing fur trade and to toss white settlers out of what was then Indian Territory. Indian Territory by treaty, by law. Forever. It was a vast expanse of the northern reaches of the Louisiana Purchase. But of course, there were settlers, and one in particular whom the Fort garrison was happy to have in residence.

Pierre "Pig's Eye" Parrant was a one-eyed bootlegger, gambler, pimp and river pirate. His settlement at Fountain Cave, just a few miles downriver from the Fort, was the precursor to what is now St. Paul and produced the only booze available in the Territory. The Fort's Irish and German immigrant soldiers happily overlooked Pig's Eye's alien status. They bought his booze, fucked his whores and gambled at his tables. And if, on occasion, a few fur trappers disappeared, the soldiers simply chose to believe their canoes had capsized and they were sucked down by the Mississippi's notorious undertow. That Pig's Eye also conducted a side business in the fur trade was no concern of theirs.

Several years after its founding, Father Lucien Galtier came to Pig's Eye's Landing on his never-ending quest to bring the church to frontier Catholics and convert the native pagans to the more refined ways of the white man's religion. Galtier was also the first cartographer in the Territory and thought St. Paul was a more dignified name for the settlement and identified it as such on his maps. The name stuck, but then so did The Agreement devised by Pig's Eye and his partners at the fort.

The system created under terms of The Agreement was publicly visible during the early decades of the twentieth century when Police Chief John J. O'Connor, and his successor Tom Brown, reached their accommodation with high profile gangsters from out of town, like John Dillinger, Alvin Karpis, the Barkers and Homer Van Meter. With Prohibition and banks hated by everyone, the city could wink, not only at bootleggers, but at big-name bank robbers and racketeers - particularly if it meant they wouldn't ply their trade in St. Paul. In that era, it was local fixers like Dapper Dan Hogan, Leon Gleckman, Jack Peifer and Harry Sawyer who shared the role of Mr. Big and supplied the supportive infrastructure that gangsters needed to launder the cash and securities they stole, plan and finance their next ventures, and provide the network of underground connections they needed to continue their work.

A big part of the modern version of The Agreement was that Mackey was to stay away from politicians and unions. In short, for a pure monopoly he submitted to limited regulation, There was not much government interference, just enough to make the City appear to be a law-abiding and respectable sort of place.

Homer McArdle was the inheritor of the culture established by Fort Snelling officers, and refined by O'Connor, Brown and other Chiefs. He saw no reason to change a system that had worked so well for nearly 200 years, especially given the city's theoretically low crime rate and reputation as one of the country's most livable communities. He was happy to do business with the lineal descendent of Pig's Eye Parrant if it meant his City would thrive.

And that's why the whole fabric of the day's events seemed queer to Delaney. Danny Fortuno knew that if you played too hard and slid too far into debt to the wrong people in St. Paul, Mackey, Mackey the Merciless, would have his cold, unforgiving hooks in you. Fortuno, the former cop, knew that he should have been getting his illicit jollies somewhere out of town or in the 'burbs. That he got them in St. Paul meant either that he had somehow lost all sense of perspective and caution or was closer to Mackey's operation than anyone suspected.

Delaney hoped that Shaun would have something from the deep background check that would tell why he strayed so far into forbidden territory.

Then he left a message for Henri Bouchard.

9

THE A TEAM

Within the ranks of cops and prosecutors the medical examiner and crime lab techs hold a place of special regard. They can make or break a case. In St. Paul it was rumored that the medical examiner had even massaged the evidence here and there, but only when it was needed to convict a guilty criminal. He knew they were guilty because the cops said so.

He was Gunnar Thor Olafsson. With snow white hair and neatly trimmed, equally white beard, pale blue eyes, ramrod straight posture and a hint of North Dakota in his always proper and impeccable American English, Delaney thought he was as white as a white man could get. Olafsson was also the founder and chief executive officer of MEDEX, Inc.

Ramsey County was the largest of the four county governments that engaged his firm to act as their medical examiner. A too common practice around the country, this kind of contracting came in for hard criticism. But county commissioners could be stingy bastards and anything that saved taxpayer dollars was a good deal for them, even if it meant lousy service. Who, after all, ever complained about the coroner's office? Contracting with Olafsson meant they paid a flat fee, didn't pay benefits and avoided union hassles. Since he wanted to maximize profits, Olafsson and his fellow practitioners did their work quickly, cheaply and profitably.

The system also made him a toady for the cops. He wanted to keep his contract, so he was eagerly responsive to their demands. He was happy to expedite an autopsy or take other steps to move things along when they just had to have something immediately, if not sooner. With the press he was aloof and dismissive. He was imposing and aggressive enough that they never pushed him very hard.

Then there was the city's crime lab. It was created in 1935, one of the first in the country, when St. Paul was just taking a public peek out from under the rock of the O'Connor system.

Chief John J. O'Connor had declared that gangsters had only to fulfill two requirements to live freely in his city. First, they were to commit no crimes in St. Paul and, second, they were to make a contribution to his widows and orphans fund. In addition, gangsters spent outrageous sums in St Paul's haberdasheries, restaurants and speakeasies. They loved the jazz joints and drew crowds of locals along with them. In native son F. Scott Fitzgerald's Jazz Age, St. Paul was the jazziest city in the US of A.

That all took a left turn in 1935 when, among other temporary reforms, the Crime Scenes Investigations Laboratory came into being. By all accounts, its personnel in those early days were too honest, too straight and too professional to even imagine jerry-rigging forensic evidence. But that was then. Things change. Over the years the lab developed a reputation for shoddy work, a result of its eager compliance with police and prosecutors' demands. Once the tip of the spear for reform, it became a target for legal reformers.

The lab's member of the Thorogood task force was Gunnar Olafsson's polar opposite. Dalton Gettler was short, dark and intense, alert behind his pocket patch and forensic expertise. Thorogood said he was the youngest and smartest of the CSIs, and, as yet, uncorrupted. He was also, like the others assembled there, clearly not comfortable in Delphi's large conference room, which, by the standards of city and county government, was luxurious.

Ann O'Leary, Natalie Puckett, Thorogood and Delaney rounded out the group seated around the table. Marguerite Garza had ordered in soda, coffee and hors de oeuvres from Matteo's Restaurant downstairs.

The group was impressed with the comfortable chairs, the mahogany table, the paintings and sculpture, the forty-eighth-floor view of the river, the food, drink and hospitality. Delaney wanted them out of their usual surroundings, away from what was ordinary, comfortable and mundane. He wanted each of them,

Thorogood included, jarred out of whatever rut of thinking and acting they had fallen into.

Thorogood had his reservations but went along with it. In the whole history of the department, there had never been a meeting like this. While the cops, techs and medical examiner, of necessity, interacted all the time, they never had formal meetings together. This Delaney knew without asking, knowing they all had a strong task orientation and a casual disregard for process.

At the first lull in the get-acquainted chitchat, Gunnar Olafsson looked at Thorogood and said, "This is all very nice. Thank you for bringing us here, but what is the purpose of this gathering? As you might know, we are terribly under-staffed and overworked. I hardly have time for meetings that take me away from our work. You know, we've been accused of doing too few autopsies. With a staff of only three physicians, we can barely keep up with the regular flow of work. This ... this is hardly helpful."

Thorogood picked up the challenge. "We needed to get you away from the immediacy of your work and any surprises or distractions you might have in your offices. By the way, all of you, turn off your cell phones."

He pulled his out and set it on the table. "I want each of you to do what I just did. I need to see they are all turned off. Now pass them over to me." He waited while they all reluctantly complied, then said, "I'm less worried about you getting called than I am about someone listening in."

That drew startled looks from Gettler and Olafsson. It was Delaney's cue. He tossed a half-dime sized disk on the table. "This was found in my office phone just an hour ago, it's a bug." Seeing the startled looks all around and satisfied with their reactions, he continued, "We've had this room and the rest of our offices swept so we can be sure there are no other listening devices."

That wasn't all quite true.

Marguerite walked in with a basket into which Thorogood dumped the cell phones. "We're going to have your phones examined by a technician here to make sure they have not been compromised." That was not the whole truth either.

Thorogood paused and looked around the table. "Last week my cell phone went missing. Yesterday it was used to make a call."

THE NARCISSISM OF SMALL DIFFERENCES

"To me, the guy sounded exactly like Mel, whom I've known for years. I would swear it was him asking me to help on this case."

"A practical joke, perhaps?" Olafsson asked.

"No. The guy knew it was Mel's phone, had it for a week, called me the morning after the last murder, before the press knew about it. And he imitated Mel's voice perfectly. That goes way beyond a practical joke. And then we have this telephone tap."

Ann O'Leary broke in, "You guys think it's someone in the department, don't you?"

"We don't know," Thorogood confessed, "but we can't rule it out. Doesn't it seem like a reasonable suspicion to you? Who else might have access to my phone? Who else would know to call right after the last murder? Who would know to call Delaney?"

"I suppose that means we have to start investigating cops? That's going to make us real popular with our brothers and sisters."

"I've got you covered," Thorogood shot back. "You use my name or McArdle's with any cop you talk to. Or with anyone else where you think it might help."

It was Delaney's opening. "These cases are different. It looks like we may have the first serial killer in the city's history. And yes, it could be someone internal. We may have to break some balls, detective. I don't need to tell you, we have to act on this case with an absolute sense of urgency."

Thorogood leaned forward. "As of today, this case is the department's absolute top priority. McArdle is on the warpath. Whatever we need, we get. O'Leary and Puckett, you have no other assignments. This is it. You break this, your careers are made, just like Woodward and Bernstein. Puckett, you've never worked a murder case. I will tell you, and so will O'Leary, that no one in this department has ever worked a case like this. So don't worry about your lack of experience.

"Because there might be an inside perp, we're consolidating copies of all case files here at Delphi. Whatever is entered at the department will be entered here at the same time." What he didn't say was that entries made on Delaney's computers would not be automatically registered at the department.

Delaney said, "We have another conference room here set aside for just this case. We've got computers set up for your use in there already. Security now is very tight. By 'all of the files,' we also mean the crime lab and MEDEX files. You will each be given key cards and passwords to get in whenever you need to. Just so you know, your comings and goings here will be videoed. We've got cameras and sound recorders in every room, so there will be a complete record of every move any person makes in any room or hallway of this suite of offices." In fact, every move they made from within thirty feet of the building entrance or parking garage would be recorded, but Delaney didn't think they needed to know that.

"To start, as part of my investigation I've made copies of the rather large number of files on reported spousal abuse incidents committed by police officers. You'll find those files on the computers in your conference room."

Thorogood nodded, "Detectives, I think you might want to start there."

Gettler asked, "What do you want me to do?"

"I'd suggest you make copies of your reports and add any additional observations or suspicions you may have. This goes for you, too, Dr. Olafsson. And please look for connections to your past cases. In particular, pay attention to any case where the victim's neck might have been cut, bruised, bitten, sucked or mutilated. It's possible we have a fetishist here. The two of you should also check with your professional networks to see if they have records of anything that involves apples and/or necks anywhere else in the country."

Thorogood added, "You are all being issued another cell phone to be used only in connection with this case. It has the numbers of everyone here already keyed in. Keep this phone with you at all times. If you see, hear or even suspect anything, call one or all of us. Immediately."

Natalie Puckett smiled over at Delaney, "What are you going to do, besides provide computers and feed us? And scout the warpath for Chief McArdle?"

Delaney ignored the dig at his friend Thorogood, and replied, "Detective, do you know why insurance companies hire outside investigators, even though they have their own people and often FBI and local police all working on the same case?"

"They can afford it?"

"It's because they all see things differently. They operate differently. They all have different constraints. They all have different perspectives, different blinders. I'll be doing a parallel investigation to yours. I find something, suspect something, you get that information immediately. You do the same for me, OK?

"And remember, I'm not a cop. There are lots of things I don't have to do and things I can do that you can't. I do not need probable cause, a search warrant or a Miranda card. On the other hand, I don't have your authority, public credibility or legal standing."

Puckett and O'Leary nodded. They got it. And Delaney's reputation within the force and his friendship with Thorogood inclined them both to trust his judgement and capability.

Thorogood said, "We'll meet for the daily debriefing at seven a.m. sharp, right here, seven days a week, starting day after tomorrow. And no, Gunnar, you don't have to be here unless you have something. Gettler, I do want you here.

"And here's the last bit of protocol for all of you." He looked around at everyone, eyes narrowed. "You do not talk to anyone about this case. Not the press, no one in the department, not your spouse, not no one. Nothing goes beyond this group. Nothing. You talk only to the people in this room. Is that clear?

"Break that rule and I will cashier your ass and your pension right now. Got it?" The chronically impatient Thorogood easily slid into the mean bastard role when the occasion called for it.

"Now, let's review what we already know. Victim number one is Graham Byrd, a realtor who handled corporate offices and residences that tend to cluster along Summit Avenue and River Road, as well as downtown. And the guy was popular with a lot of buyers of those 'old' new condos in Summit."

Puckett said, "Chief, we might want to keep in mind that Byrd was an activist in the gay community and a firm believer that everyone needed to come out of the closet. He is rumored to have threatened to out a couple of people if they didn't do it themselves. I'm not sure I believe that, but it's something we may want to investigate."

O'Leary added, "I knew Byrd a little bit and I don't believe he ever outed anyone. He felt strongly about people coming out, but I don't see him as any kind of a blackmailer."

Thorogood nodded. "Follow up on it anyway, would you? The threat of being outed could be a plausible motive. Conor, run over what you've found so far."

"I just found out a little while ago that the female victim is one Suzanne Porter, aptly named given she was secretary to the President of the Port Authority. We know nothing else about her, yet. You already know the third victim is former detective Danny Fortuno. His ex-partner, Roland Gadsen, is also known to all of you. He's pretty broken up, but has accepted that, because of his close friendship with Fortuno, the case has to proceed without him in an official capacity. His story about what happened with Fortuno has a bad odor about it."

Delaney, noticing the two officers and Dalton Gettler nodding, continued. "About two hours ago I was presented with a fourth victim." As he, Thorogood and Gettler went over what little they knew about the life and death of Karleen Martin, the mood in the room shifted from one of untroubled professional confidence to one of quiet dread.

Thorogood brought them back to the practical problems facing them. "Dr. Olafsson, what can you tell us about the cause of death and what or who killed our first victims?"

Olafsson looked around the table with what seemed to Delaney to be a prolonged hesitation, the kind you see from a student who hasn't read the assignment. "Yes, well, uhm, the immediate cause of death for all three was traumatic injury created by some kind of five-pronged instrument that tore out a good deal of flesh from each victim's neck. It must have been a terribly painful way to die."

His hesitation and broad, non-medical description set off alarms for Delaney, but he let it ride for the moment.

Thorogood glanced around the room. "Does anyone else have anything to add?"

O'Leary hunched forward. "Do we have anything that connects the four victims, yet?" Delaney liked her adding the "yet."

"Not yet. That should be one of the first things you two look into. Dalton, you'll be going over the Riverrun crime scene with these three tomorrow morning." He indicated Delaney and the two detectives.

"Gunnar, anything else you can extrapolate from the bodies, well, we need every shred of evidence we can find, so please review and pay special attention to anything that might help. Any little thing at all."

Delaney caught Thorogood's eye before turning to Olafsson. "Those faces, the first three, they're eerily serene. What did the tox screens show?"

The Chief Medical Examiner shifted uncomfortably in his chair. "We are overworked and the cause of death was obvious, so I did not order a tox screen."

Delaney's left eyebrow rose, almost involuntarily. "Isn't that unusual, Doctor?"

"It is my duty to determine the cause of death and I did that. Perhaps you know better than I and the other professionals who work on these things every day, who have years and years of experience and who are terribly overworked every day."

"Are you sure, Doctor? Have you really determined the whole cause of their deaths? Don't you think . . . "

Thorogood cut in, "Dalton, can you still do a screen on the latest victims?"

"The results may be inconclusive, given the time that has elapsed, but yes, it can be done." He looked uneasily at Olafsson. "One is already underway on the remains of Ms. Martin."

"Please do the others right away," Thorogood said briskly. "There's one other character you all should inscribe into your mental hard drive. There's this punk named Marshall Pinckney."

Thorogood had Delaney cover his encounter with Pinckney, before going over the little he knew about the man. "I don't think he's a person of interest, but it's possible he could be involved somehow."

Thorogood stood and, looking around the room, asked, "Any other questions? OK, let's go to work and I'll see you here seven a.m. on Wednesday. You can pick up your phones on the way out and please remember, say nothing to anyone about this case."

Puckett and O'Leary spent the next three hours going over files of cops cited for domestic violence where they might have strangled or otherwise injured their partner's neck. No flags, but there was more to go. Much of any investigation involves this kind of drudgery.

As Delaney walked back into his office Marguerite was on the intercom, "Mr. Stately for you."

"Thanks, Marguerite. You say that name with the disdain one usually reserves for the odor of rotting fish."

"He is a pimp, a pusher and a killer. He is uniquely odious, isn't he? I don't understand how you can even talk to him, much less keep him as a friend."

"We have a history, Marguerite. It goes back a long ways."

Delaney sat before picking up the receiver. That's when he saw him, sitting curled up like a cat in the corner chair. "Higgs, what are you doing here, and how did you get in?"

Aloyisius Higgs, Mackey's notorious disappearing man. He was rarely seen, despite his usually conspicuous appearance. Today it was tan leather pants with a matching vest over a red striped shirt. Half boots, and a short top hat completed the wardrobe. Tufts of ginger hair curled out from under the hat and his deep-set blue eyes were framed by a three-day stubble of pale orange whiskers.

"I here to tell you I got your back. Mr. Mackey, he say, 'you watch over that man. You see nothin' happen to him, Higgs.' Now you know, you got Higgs protection."

"We'll see about that," Delaney turned away as he spoke into the receiver. "Mackey, Higgs is here claiming you sent him."

"He's there right now?"

Delaney looked at the empty chair in the corner. "Was here. Says you ordered him to watch my back."

"That's right. From what I've seen and heard, you need protection. This Riverrun freak seems to have a thing for you."

"I think I can take care of myself and besides, I've got Kyle and the whole damned police department on call."

"Then just consider Higgs an extra layer of protection and quit whinin'. You ain't ever gonna see him anyway. Just be glad he's there."

Delaney, knowing the argument was lost, asked if a meeting had been set up yet.

"Yeah, it's at six today at my place with the guys who floated Fortuno's loans. That work for you?"

"What took you so long? How many guys am I meeting and are you in the meet? Do I know any of them?"

"Three, yes and yes. The one you know is Fat Harry DeGidio. The others are Manny Sanchez and Jimmy Flynn. You heard of 'em?"

"Yeah, but I heard Sanchez was muscle, not a loan shark."

"Mr. Sanchez has been interested in expanding his portfolio and getting into more legitimate work."

Delaney momentarily marveled at the universe where loan sharking was legitimate but knew Wall Street was the home of the biggest and most vicious sharks. Sanchez was just getting into the same business that made Goldman Sachs executives some of the richest men in history.

"Thanks for setting this up. You're going to be in the meeting?"

"Yeah, I'm there as your bona fides. These guys sometimes, you know, they deal in bullshit. If I'm there they'll keep it down."

Delaney suspected it wasn't quite that simple, but said, "You are a prince of a fellow, Mack. I'll stand you to a Jameson's tonight."

He wondered why and how Mackey had arranged the meeting so quickly. He had to have called the sharks right after they talked and used some leverage to get them together in such haste. It struck Delaney as odd. Perhaps, he thought, the universe was even swinging back to his favor.

Shortly after Thorogood called to report that the chief's sweep of the area had yielded nothing, Delaney heard back from Henri Bouchard.

Delaney's friend was now a private investigator of the old school persuasion. He was the founder and head of the Gwayakotam Detective Agency and beloved of divorce lawyers and law enforcement agencies alike. With the attorneys he was famous for his almost otherworldly ability as a shape-shifter. He could, on one evening, appear as a boisterous businessman in an Armani suit, and on the next as a shapely blond in a black dress. Other disguises made him appear to be a construction worker, a teen-age boy, a cop, or almost any other identity that his current assignment might require. He had an uncanny ability to shadow a misbehaving spouse and secure the telltale evidence needed to gain a separation on terms favorable to his clients. Law enforcement agencies liked his talent for tracking and catching terrorists and other violent suspects in situations that almost always guaranteed a conviction.

But Henri Bouchard was different from other detectives in a way that frightened off some prospective clients, and reassured others. Gwayakotum – find the truth – was his credo and he warned his clients that he was committed to that above all. He gained a certain kind of notoriety several years earlier when he took on the task of finding Earl Alonzo's missing wife. Even though Earl was a prominent figure in elite St. Paul social circles, Marsha Alonzo was rarely seen. Shy, and a real homebody, was Earl's usual description of her. Then Henri tracked her down.

She was in a homeless shelter in Phoenix and told Henri she preferred that to spending another night with Alonzo. Then she showed him the picture. It was of her face; bloody, bruised, one eye closed shut and the other bulging. Earl had taken it and every so often pulled it out to show her again what would happen if she didn't "behave herself."

Two months later Earl Alonzo suddenly moved to Milwaukee and Marsha was back in St. Paul with most of Earl's holdings now being transferred to her as part of a pending divorce settlement. Those who saw Earl shortly before his departure described him as distracted and hurried. It was almost as if he were afraid of something.

Delaney loved Henri Bouchard for his many years of unqualified friendship, as well as his professional capabilities and idiosyncrasies. He had tried, on several occasions, to lure him to Delphi as a co-equal ownership partner. Bouchard's response was always that, while he loved his brother Owl Eyes and was happy to contract with Delphi, he liked his independence and was uninterested in joining the firm.

On this day, Delaney's request was a fairly straightforward one. Was Henri available to shadow a small-time gangster, one Marshall Pinckney, an associate of Mackey Stately?

"One of Mackey's men?" There was surprise in his voice. "Can't Mackey help you with this?"

"I'm afraid it's too complicated for that. I'd like you to keep tabs on this guy and let me know who he's coming in contact with every day and night. It will require something like twenty-four-hour surveillance. Can you do it?"

"For you, owl eyes, of course. I assume this needs to start immediately?"

"Yeah. I'll have Marguerite send over a contract and the first week's payment right away. Actually, I suspect you may not need to spend more than a week on this."

"Word is out that you're working on those Riverrun murders. This have anything to do with them?"

Delaney marveled again at how quickly and broadly the word got out in his city.

10

SWIMMING WITH SHARKS

Fat Harry DeGidio stood about five-seven and weighed something south of 130 pounds. His hair was as thin as the lining of his lungs. Harry loved his weeds and insisted that anyone who worked for him also had to smoke. Manny Sanchez was his burley opposite and Jimmy Flynn had the sort of "average" appearance that was easily lost in a crowd of three or more.

They were seated around a circular oak table in one of those upstairs rooms that Delaney had never seen. The fifth member of their entourage was a surprise. Evelyn sat back, out of the light, and looked as distracted and ethereal as always. Even in this setting she managed an air of indifferent authority. Delaney tried thinking of why she would be there and remembered Mackey's comment that she handled finances and investments. Delaney wondered how much Mackey had sunk into Fortuno. Mackey smiled his big smile as Delaney walked in and introduced him to Flynn and Sanchez, like they were at a cocktail party.

"I'll try not to waste your time," Delaney began. "Here's my reading, and please disabuse me of any misunderstandings I might have. OK?"

Mackey nodded and DeGideo smiled. "I think you, Sanchez, went over your limit on Fortuno so Flynn and Harry had to buy a chunk of Fortuno's debt. You made a rookie mistake. Right?"

Sanchez took a deep breath and looked at Mackey, who said, "Didn't I tell you he was a smart guy? And no, I didn't tell him nothing. Didn't have to, he smells this stuff."

Delaney continued, "So you went deep and had to sell. Knowing Harry to be the smart businessman he is, he got a deep discount. I'm guessing Mr. Flynn did also. So, you're pissed and want a pound of flesh from this overbearing cop."

Sanchez glared and slowly said, "Yeah, I wanted to hurt him. But I didn't. That would be bad for business. He used to be a cop and he still owed me money. A lot of money."

"Yeah, I know. It would make no sense. But you, and you two," Delaney said, looking at DeGidio and Flynn, "know some things about Fortuno that will help solve his murder and I want you to share."

Flynn shook his head and smiled. "Share?"

"Yes, share, because if you do not, Mel Thorogood is going to unleash some of his mean guys to lead each of you away, in cuffs, one by one in front of lots of other upstanding citizens. I wonder what that will do to your business? Oh, and if you think you'll get to call your lawyer and get out within a few hours, forget it. These murders are different and McArdle will not deal in any of that bullshit. You will just be spending three or four days with St. Paul's finest and people will naturally wonder why you're hanging out with them and what you're talking about. You understand these murders have created a different climate and a new set of rules?"

"Fuck, Mackey, you bring us here to get threatened by this cocksucker?" It was Sanchez. Flynn and DeGidio were too smart to talk to Mackey like that.

"Manny!" Mackey snapped the name, much as a dog trainer might have barked, 'sit!' Then he smiled. "Look, Manny, he's only telling you what Thorogood and McArdle will do. He's giving you an opportunity to avoid it. You want to stay in business, I want to stay in business. We all want to stay in business, don't we? So, let's do what it takes to stay in business."

Fat Harry broke his silence. "Whaddya wanna know?"

"What did he want the money for? Why was he so desperate?"

Sanchez nodded, too quickly, and glanced at Mackey before interjecting, "Fortuno liked drink, gambling, nose candy and whores. Very bad habits and he indulged them all in a very bad way." He nodded sagely, throwing another quick glance at Mackey.

Delaney didn't need to look at his friend to know he was embarrassed by Sanchez repeating his own phraseology. Flynn hurriedly jumped in, "That's right, Fortuno was a wild man, outta control and spiraling into the gutter. He was doping and drinking and doing way too much of both. He was on a loser's trail."

"Is that what you think, Harry?"

Fat Harry's eyebrows went up and then he shrugged. His lips curled into something resembling a smile. He was smart enough not to dig the hole any deeper.

"Tell me," Delaney said, looking at Flynn. "If Fortuno was such an apparent loser, 'spiraling into the gutter,' how is it that three smart guys like you are fronting him those kinds of bucks? You just don't put out that kind of long green for that kind of loser. Cop or no cop, you just don't do it. It is bad business and you guys are not that stupid, are you." It was a statement, not a question.

Sanchez and Flynn glanced anxiously around the room, as if searching for a story that would break them free of their own words. Mackey was not smiling. "Maybe we better take a short break. Evelyn, why don't you take him to the club room, pour some of that Jameson's and let the four of us have a little chat?"

As she stood she gave Sanchez and Flynn an intense, hot stare that visibly jolted them, and then nodded at Delaney to follow her. "You presume a great deal," she said after handing him the drink.

"Is that so?" Delaney was in no mood for bullshit. "I think they presume too much. That I'm stupid, that the cops are stupid, that people with twenty-twenty vision are too blind to see them brewing crap right in front of them. Which, by the way, may be what the four of them are up to right now. What do you think?"

"So, you think Mackey is involved?"

"Are you going to insult my intelligence, too? 'Very bad habits and he indulged them all in a very bad way.' Give me a break."

"Oh, he heard Mackey say it, but not as lines to rehearse for a role in a cover-up conspiracy. He just remembered Mackey talking about Fortuno and repeated what he heard. Sanchez is not a guy with a lot of insight into his customers' character."

She paused while pouring herself a Jameson's. Delaney had never seen her drinking anything stronger than wine before and wondered if it meant anything. "You don't trust Mackey, do you?"

"Quite the contrary, Evelyn. I trust him with my life. I also trust that he doesn't always 'share' with me. He may have reasons for concealing some things, and in his eyes the reasons will be good. He wouldn't do anything to hurt me, and I have the same feelings toward him. But we have frequent differences about such things as left and right and right and wrong. Given that we're often heading in completely different directions, that's to be expected, isn't it?"

"You sound so smugly sure that he wouldn't do anything to hurt you. Are you really that certain or do I detect some self-delusional bravado? You know Mackey tells lots of lies, don't you?"

Delaney did know. Mackey was hard to read precisely because he rarely spoke without omitting something or including something that was, at best, a partial truth. Delaney thought Mackey was a bullshit artist of the highest order. To Evelyn he said, "So do I, as you well know. I even lie to Mack on occasion."

"Has he ever caught you at it?"

"I dunno, he plays his cards pretty close to the vest. I doubt even you know all his secrets."

She sighed and nodded; there may have even been a slight shiver. "You're right there. I know a lot, but he can be a secretive man sometimes. Why do you think he's mixed up in the Fortuno murder?"

"I don't."

"Really? You practically accused him a few minutes ago."

"No, I said he may know something, that's all." Delaney didn't like the drift of her conversation; she seemed to be pushing him toward the notion that Mackey had some role in the Fortuno murder. Delaney knew better and changed the subject. "Mackey says you're now handling the firm's finances and investments. Are you playing the stock market?"

She perked up at the question. "Unlike you, I'm not a gambler. Our investments are very conservative. I only invest in health care and pharmaceutical stocks and triple-A rated tax-exempt bonds, the safest thing you can possibly own. I do make the occasional real estate investment in St. Paul, but only very safe ones. I'm doing just fine and haven't lost a dime. The returns on pharmaceuticals are marvelous. The bonds may not be spectacular, but they're safe and I'm making a decent return. Maybe I should have asked you about how to invest? You're some kind of economist, aren't you?"

Delaney snorted. "Some kind, yeah. But you're doing a smart thing. The more money you have, the smarter you are to invest it just as you are. Are you buying any corporate bonds, to go with your municipals and revenue bonds?"

She didn't take the bait. Too obviously didn't take the bait. While throwing a look at the room they had come from, she abruptly said, "I wonder what's taking him so long? You'd think he'd have them straightened out by now, wouldn't you? Maybe I should go back in there and move them along."

Just then Mackey came out and motioned them to come back in. "I think I'll skip the rest of this soiree," Evelyn said. "Looks like he did it without me this time," she whispered to Delaney in passing. Absent from the room, he thought, but listening in.

"Suit yourself," Mackey said over his shoulder. In the room, the three loan sharks were leaning over the table as if ready to pounce.

Jimmy Flynn started, "OK, Fortuno was a wild man, but he didn't borrow to cover gambling debts. He said he needed the money for an 'investment.' He said it was a 'for sure' thing and a guaranteed quick return. He said he'd pay it all back in 60 days, with interest. It was some kind of commercial real estate deal and he put up his house as collateral."

"If it was such a hot deal why didn't you get in on it?"

"I asked, but he said he had a silent partner fronting the deal and couldn't talk about it. We had his house as collateral, so it was a good loan."

"Who was the partner?"

Sanchez shifted uncomfortably and Flynn shrugged. Fat Harry remained a study in silence. Flynn finally said, "All we know is the guy was supposedly a lawyer. Sanchez here wasn't smart enough to get a name as part of the deal and when we got into it," he nodded toward DeGidio, "we were really just buying

Sanchez's paper. The wise guy behind the deal remains a mystery. Did he kill Fortuno? We don't know, but now we have told you what we do know."

Delaney looked at DeGidio. "Harry?"

He nodded.

When Mackey nodded Delaney knew they were done for the evening. But the juxtaposition of this and his conversation with Evelyn about investments began to trouble him. He thought their stories must have a nexus, but he couldn't locate it. Yet.

11

THE CITY

Dreams From My Brother, Monday, May 5

Henri grinned as he reminded me of Grandmother Raven's caution that messages from Cody's universe could be difficult to decipher. Cody's Universe: Grandmother Raven had spoken to a ten-year-old in terms he could understand. As I grew older I came to understand that it was my subconscious mind that was at work. All the dreams and messages I was receiving were being generated by my subconscious, not a deceased brother in another universe.

Of course, that leads inevitably to questions about what the subconscious mind really is. Those are fascinating questions and I hope to explore them more fully at some time in the future. In the meantime, I've dodged those questions by giving my subconscious self a name: Cody.

I am reporting the dream below as if it were a first-person narrative. Dreams don't actually work that way, of course. They are far, far heavier on emotional content than verbal substance. Nonetheless, in recording it, I am forced to reduce it to language, to words. I am quite satisfied that what follows is an accurate account of the feeling and focus of the City in the dream:

I am this idea that lingers in the psychic expanse between your collective unconscious and subconscious minds. I'm here and you almost know that I'm here.

But you just can't quite get a grip on the notion of my existence as a sentient and conscious being, can you.

The conscious Self – you know, the I, the Me, the Id, the I AM – is a story we sentient beings of all kinds tell ourselves. It's a story made up entirely of memories, memories recollected, altered and invented. Thus, we are, on the one hand, a collection of memories, the majority of which may be the output of our imagination. On the other hand, we also have the power of thought; the ability to think about ourselves, about our consciousness, our memories and our Selfhood.

My consciousness is different from yours. It operates on a wavelength something akin to your mind on magic mushrooms. Different, but real. You should keep that in mind.

My Self – that unique sense of identity, dissimilitude and place in the world – was born nearly two hundred years ago on the day Pig's Eye emerged from Fountain Cave, close on the shore of the great river.

On that day Pig's Eye, the one-eyed river pirate, bootlegger, gambler, pimp, thief and murderer, began building his city. Three years later the priest - cartographer Fr. Lucien Galtier, who despised Pig's Eye, christened me The City of St. Paul. It may be a misleading title, but it suits my purposes.

My consciousness emerged like a butterfly from its chrysalis when Pig's Eye stepped into the stark morning light and started construction on his saloon and warehouse. Now I could think, feel, perceive, predict, plan and act on this gift of self-awareness.

Just like you, come to think of it.

My memories of the times before Pig's Eye are all formless: ghostly men chasing great spectral beasts across the ice and snow of the Pleistocene; burial mounds rising on the high bluffs above the eternal river; tribal campfires on the crests of my seven hills. All dim, all without substance, shadows wandering in a void. The light came with Pig's Eye, and he is where my story, my Self, really begins.

It was the river that drew Pig's Eye to this place, just as it had Fort Snelling, the voyageurs and the tribes centuries ago. Gichi-Ziibi, Father of Waters, captured them all with promises of wealth and power.

On the surface the great river looks so placid, flowing serenely out of the north woods of Minnesota down to the Gulf of Mexico. But this quietude hides an inescapable truth – the dark river has a vicious and murderous undertow. He is a remorseless and unrepentant killer. The Mississippi River is my father, whom I deeply love.

Pig's Eye and the priest Galtier hated each other; because of, in spite of, their need, each for the other. The two of them are conjoined like eternally battling Siamese twins in my story, in the DNA of my Self.

The officers at the fort forged an Agreement with Pig's Eye. In the decade that followed their role was taken over by the City's Police Chiefs. The Agreement was a model of simplicity. Pig's Eye and his successors were protected as the sole organizers and controllers of gambling, prostitution, drugs, loan sharking and other illicit services and goods. In return for this monopoly, each succeeding "Mr. Big" was to limit the size and scope of his activities. He was also to quietly eliminate any rivals, with the assistance of the city's police, if necessary.

This system was designed to hem in and prevent the growth of so-called illegitimate ventures that otherwise might spread, discouraging the development of legally sanctioned enterprises. Each successive Chief of Police, through The Agreement, acknowledged the reality and duality of human desire. The Agreement is also locked in my memory; it is integral to my Self. In other universes The Agreement is often different in small ways. In one it is unwritten, in another, it is in force only for a limited time. But always there is an Agreement.

Control, not elimination, was always the guiding credo of this practical City from its founding to this day. Fr. Galtier, of course, was never told about the Agreement, but understood there was something unnatural about his St. Paul, something he couldn't quite see; but his small chapel grew and decades later became the grand Cathedral that now dominates my skyline from the highest of my seven hills.

My story today: Urban experts all agree, I am one of America's Most Livable Cities. I am, by many accounts, the very best place in the nation to live, work, raise a family and die. My school system is excellent and I have several top tier colleges and universities within, or adjacent to, my boundaries. I have world-renowned theaters, museums and other cultural venues. I am possessed of some of the finest health care facilities in the world.

My metro area has the highest number of Fortune 500 corporations per capita in the nation and the level of employment among my residents always, and I do mean always, exceeds the national average. The housing stock, both old and new, is sturdy, has character and can be bought much more cheaply than in other, more heralded cities. The politics here appear to be extraordinarily inclusive and free of the sharp, partisan divisions that wrack the electorate elsewhere. In a word, the political arena is, to all appearances, free of corruption.

My neighborhoods are models of the urban good life. Quiet, with beautiful parks and playgrounds, accessible transportation of all kinds and, most of all, with very few (really, hardly noticeable) exceptions, crime and drug free. Among all the cities of this Great Nation, I am the crown jewel.

In truth, I am so comfortable, so placid, that even Nabokov, who certainly should have known better, was fooled. He said I was a stupefyingly boring city. He just didn't know the real story.

Generations of men come and go, but I remain as a monument to their struggles. During their lifetimes the men fight for the power to control my future. Every generation promises more and better roads, schools and buildings; especially tall, glassy commercial buildings. They outdo each other in their proclamations of devotion to me and to making me even better than I already am. They think they can make me into the manifestation of their sick political ambitions.

They say very little about my father, the one who brought them here in the first place. Is it because they sense his presence and are afraid? Perhaps they can feel the power of the current beneath his placid surface. They know he cannot be controlled. He can be hemmed in by their dams and river walls, but never controlled. He is too wild, too much his own master. His dark power is just so much greater than theirs.

In any event, the whole truth about me, at least in this universe, is that I am my father's child in every respect.

Oh, yes. Yes, I am.

TUESDAY

I do not know much about gods; but I think that the river
Is a strong brown god—sullen, untamed and intractable.

—*T.S. Eliot*

Every river has, nevertheless, its individuality, its great silent
interest. Every river has, moreover, its influence over the
people who pass their lives within sight of its waters

—*H.S. Merriman*

Some sail rivers deep and muddy
some sail rivers clear and cold
But the river that I'm sailin' goes to sea

—*Hoyt Axton*

Eventually, all things merge into one,
and a river runs through it.

—*Norman Maclean*

12

THE RIVER KNOWS YOUR NAME

Delaney was only mildly surprised by the call from Dalton Gettler at seven the next morning. A short time later Gettler was in Delaney's conference room with his and Gunnar Olafsson's photos and paper files. He had started on the tox screens the night before and had already found something. "A rocuronium-like substance showed up in the first three victims. That leads me to believe that, because Ms. Martin's face did not have that same lack of expression, she was not given that substance. I don't know anything beyond that, but I should have more by tomorrow morning. Rocuronium, you may know, is the muscle relaxant most commonly used in death penalty executions.

"I may also have something else." He laid out a set of three photos. "Please tell me if you notice anything unusual."

Delaney did. The photos of the Hidden Falls victims showed the bodies were all on their backs, lying at the same odd angle to the walking path. He asked about what direction their heads pointed to. Gettler said that was the first question that occurred to him, too. North. The bodies were all placed with their heads oriented to the north, their feet to the south.

He said there was one other oddity. The ground around the first victim, Graham Byrd, had been soaked with his blood, same for Danny Fortuno. Not so for Suzanne Porter.

"The obvious conclusion," he said, "is that she was killed somewhere else. That leads us to another conclusion."

Delaney was puzzled and said so.

"The gate to the park," he explained, "is shut and locked at nine o'clock. You can't get a car down there to the parking lot. If you were to physically carry a body, it would be about a half mile down a steep and winding road in pitch blackness. And you'd have to park at least two blocks away off River Road and take a huge risk of being seen carrying a body.

"If you didn't take the road into the park, you'd have to go down an almost vertical incline through thick woods and brush. You'd be in free fall. If anything, it would be even darker that way and no one could do it without breaking a limb or leaving an obvious trail through the vegetation."

"So, she was brought in on the river. Our killer either has a boat, or access to one. Now tell me, is it really normal for Olafsson to not ask for a tox screen?"

Gettler hesitated for a second. "They really are overworked and he said the cause of death was obvious. He has been known to cut corners."

"That's really no excuse for this kind of shoddy work, is it? Did you raise the issue with him?"

"Yes, I did, but he didn't like it. He's very territorial and does not like having his decisions questioned. You may have made an enemy of him."

"In the future, if he gets the least bit intransigent, let Mel Thorogood know. He'll call so Olafsson and his minions will give you whatever you need. We don't have time to screw around with egos or territories. The rest of you have to work with Olafsson day-to-day so Mel will take any heat he might try to put out. It won't matter if he resents an Assistant Chief. Oh, another thing, can you find out how much blood Suzanne Porter lost?"

The light came on. "You think she may have already been dead before her neck was, uhm . . .?"

"It's worth looking into, isn't it? Even if it makes more work for Dr. Olafsson. Could you give him a call on this? You can use the phone in the next office. If he's not in yet, leave him a message."

Delaney saw the lab tech's discomfort with having to even ask Olafsson this simple question, but he nodded and got up. He hesitated for a moment at the door but then apparently thought better of whatever he was going to say.

At Delaney's request, Thorogood left Olafsson a message too. He wanted the Medical Examiner to first deal with Gettler, then if there were problems, him. And Homer McArdle after that, if necessary, all of them delivering the same message - "quit screwing around." Thorogood was with Delaney in wanting the Medical Examiner to know that intransigence would only lead to frustration and yet more work for him and his perpetually overworked staff.

Ann O'Leary and Natalie Puckett walked in immediately on time. Delaney and Gettler filled them in as the four of them rode in the detectives' unmarked car to Hidden Falls. The path was cordoned off with yellow crime scene tape and two uniforms were stationed there to see that there was no tampering.

Gettler gave the tour. Here was the chalk outline of body one. Here's where the others were. Delaney was struck by how close the river ran to the path at this point. It was less than thirty yards away. The Mississippi flowed here between high bluffs to the west and St. Paul on the east. Only the occasional swirl on the calm brown surface hinted at the river's deadly undertow.

Old Fort Snelling peered down solemnly from the west.

Gettler pointed to the silhouettes of the bodies and noted their north-south axes. O'Leary said, "Uh-oh, this means there's some kind of ritual involved in these killings, doesn't it?"

"The Vikings," Puckett said. The other three looked at her, wondering what the football team had to do with this.

"The real Vikings," she said. "The Norsemen whose asses my people whipped while you Europeans were being terrorized. They buried their dead in a north - south orientation."

After a long moment O'Leary, looking sideways at her partner, said, "We'll have to do a database search to find out if this has cropped up somewhere else. Do you have any theories yet?" She looked at Delaney.

"No," the practiced liar replied. "You?"

She laughed. "Sure. The killer is a white male in his twenties to forties. A loner who doesn't draw attention to himself. Possibly active in his church. To all outward appearances a very normal guy. He either lives alone, with his mother, or with a wife and two kids. He has an apple tree in the backyard."

"Except for the apple tree, that's a pretty good take on the standard FBI profile, detective. I foresee a brilliant career for you as a special agent."

"I have another concern," Puckett said. "If this is a Viking fetishist, he might be building up to a performance of the blood-eagle ceremony."

Delaney shuddered inwardly, but said, "And the blood eagle ceremony is . . ."

"It was a religious ceremony and really gruesome. They would cut away the ribs from the spine of their sacrificial victim, which caused the ribs to spring out like a pair of wings. Then they pulled out the lungs, still pumping air in and out. The victim died shortly thereafter."

O'Leary knew the answer, but still had to ask, "They did this to people?"

"Oh, yeah," Puckett replied and hesitated before saying, "Let's talk to him this afternoon."

"You mean Gadsen?" O'Leary said. "I'd rather do it tomorrow. Give him enough time to get nervous, concoct a story and trip himself up when we go at him. We lose some of that edge if we aim for later today. But, we probably don't have the luxury of time, do we?" Delaney admired how neatly O'Leary was training her pupil.

She turned to Gettler, "Do we know anything more about our victims?"

"Only that Suzanne Porter and Danny Fortuno had a kind of muscle relaxant substance in their tissue. Given his facial expressions, Byrd probably had it too, but it's too late for a tox screen on him. Porter was definitely not killed here. She lost lots of blood somewhere else. As for Ms. Martin, her profile is just different from the other three."

O'Leary shook her head, "That's it? Nothing else?"

"I wish there was," he said wistfully.

There was a call from Thorogood just as Delaney got back to the office. Did they see anything at the scene that McArdle's sweep had missed? More importantly, did O'Leary and Puckett find anything in the files they reviewed last night?

"No, nothing in the files, at least not yet. At the scene, maybe something, maybe nothing. The bodies were all laid out in the same direction, pointing due north. Puckett says that's how the old Vikings buried their dead and we're all wondering if it has any significance. Oh, and you know how there was no blood on or near Porter's body? And she had to be taken there after dark when the gate is closed? That means she was probably transported by boat, post mortem. I'll leave you to tease out why the body had to go there and not somewhere else."

"Hmmm. What do you think?"

"I suspect it has something to do with creating a serial killer narrative, but that's just a guess at this point."

"So, you think maybe it's not . . .?"

"I don't know," Delaney cut in. "It's all speculation right now and not yet worth discussing."

"Still, I hope you're right. What are you going to do now?"

"What else in a case like this? I'm off to see Dr. Phil."

13

FRIENDS

There were three calls from Shem and Shaun while Kyle Lilly wove the Prius in and out of the light traffic heading down the Minnesota River valley to St. Peter. Lilly was Delaney's driver, pilot and man Friday. He had been for the last six years, rising like a phoenix out of his perpetual state of drunken stupor.

Delaney had first gone to see Lilly after A Safe Place received an anonymous $100,000 donation, the same amount as the life insurance policy on Jennifer Lilly. A Safe Place in St. Paul was the very first domestic violence shelter in the country. It opened in the mid-seventies when nearly everyone thought the women who started it were bra-burning crazies interfering in what were, after all, private matters. Delaney grudgingly admitted to himself that, since then, some things were actually shifting to a more sane place in the public's perception.

By the time he went to see Kyle Lilly, he knew that the man was a combat pilot in the first gulf war, had suffered the pangs of a guilty conscience and post-traumatic stress disorder, was unable to hold a job longer than two months and medicated his sorrows with Jim Beam, whom he called his best friend. Police reports generated by the domestic calls to the Lilly home always noted that Jennifer did not exhibit bruising or other signs of physical abuse.

When Delaney knocked on Kyle Lilly's door he expected to be confronted by an unshaven, unkempt, drunk and belligerent fat man. He was right on all counts, save the fat and belligerence. The man's eyes were red and hollow, and he appeared to be seriously undernourished. He was apologetic when he spoke. "You must be from the bank?"

"No, Mr. Lilly. In fact, I may be able to help you with the bank. Could I have a word with you?"

"I don't think so. I don't have any money and you'd be wasting your time trying to sell me something. I'm sorry."

They went back and forth for a few more minutes before Delaney was admitted. He expected the rooms to match Lilly's slovenly appearance, but he was wrong again. He thought it almost eerie; no dirt, no dust, no used glasses, cups or dishes. No newspapers, magazines or knick-knacks out of place. Yes, Lilly said, he lived alone. Jennifer would want the house properly kept up.

Lilly said later that he remembered only a few scattered moments from that initial meeting. He was already drunk when he answered the door, but he recalled Delaney shaking his hand in one of those two-handed grips and talking to him, very deliberately, very slowly and rhythmically, in a low voice. He thought he might have passed out while Delaney was talking.

But he did remember Delaney making the offer: Delaney would make his house and utility payments for the next six months. Lilly would have to find the money for food and other expenses. Beyond that, all he had to do was meet with Delaney's friend Fritz Lieberman and work with him during that time.

Fritz was a seventy-one-year-old Austrian émigré who was a fitness instructor at the health club in the same building that housed Delaney's offices and condo. He was also an AA sponsor.

Six months later, Kyle Lilly was a new and different man and he remained on Delaney's payroll after that. He piloted the company jet, drove Delaney when he needed a driver, became the firm's security head and, when Delaney needed one, a bodyguard. He was now as indispensable as Marguerite. And, like Marguerite, he was irrevocably and completely devoted to Delaney, thinking him to be one of the greatest of all living human beings. Didn't Delaney, after all, save him from an existence of nothingness, give him a life and a whole new grip on reality? Didn't he do this out of sheer goodness, expecting nothing in return?

As Lilly drove, Delaney took calls from the office and listened to the voice-mail that came in while he was finishing yesterday's conversation with Mackey. It was from Camille.

Delaney sighed. Camille had turned things upside down. Before her there had been a pattern to his rather sparse history with women. After the first short-lived flashes of fascination, he would settle into a feeling of calm ambivalence. He told himself that it was kinesics that kept any romantic encounter from evolving into something permanent. The ability to catch every emotion, mood, thought or lie doomed his chances for any long-term relationship. Or so he told himself

There was that, and there was the memory of Cody. The two brothers had open borders between their conscious and unconscious selves, sharing immediately every brain wave that was received or transmitted by the other. He knew he shouldn't use that peculiar childhood intimacy as a gold standard against which to measure present-day relationships. But he did.

Thus, it was that Delaney's feelings for the women he dated always regressed into an indulgent and affectionate friendship. He became a master at ending his intermittent romantic affairs. In a couple of unfortunate instances, he even took one of their hands in both of his and spoke quietly in a slow and rhythmic cadence. When he finished, the two of them were now friends. Good friends, but not the kind with benefits.

Camille Bennett was different. With her he felt an immediate bond of affection and thought it might be leading to something more profound. With her, the romance matured and became more interesting just at the point where he usually found it waning. Although not heartbroken when she broke it off, he nonetheless was both surprised and disappointed. Poetic justice, he reflected; it was a fine example of poetic justice that Camille had been the one to devolve their relationship from love to friendship. She didn't say why, and he never asked. He assumed that her Aunt Ida, Mel Thorogood's wife, had something to do with it.

Delaney glanced out the car window at the swiftly flowing springtime Minnesota River. He briefly considered returning her call. But St. Peter was drawing close and he didn't want to delay talking with Dr. Phil.

14

THE CARNEY BARKER

Not that Dr. Phil. Delaney thought of the TV guy as a charlatan. His Dr. Phil was a permanent resident of the St. Peter Treatment Center, Minnesota's prison hospital for, among others, the criminally insane. He was also a brilliant Doctor of Psychology, a Jesuit priest, a convicted serial killer and, thought Delaney, one of the most moral men he knows.

Dr. Phil was sent to St. Peter for a series of murders he committed while working as a barker in a traveling carnival show. His victims were all priests who had a history of molesting children. One of them murdered a six-year-old.

The good Dr. Phil began his career as an intern at Fort Leavenworth federal prison and stayed on as a staff psychologist. He developed a particular interest in the neurology and social origins of psychopathology. What better place to practice and study than a maximum-security federal pen? He loved it there and felt a sense of displacement when Rome called him to a new ministry - reforming and curing pedophile priests.

He hated his new assignment and always claimed the prison psychopaths held themselves to a higher moral standard than the predator priests. But, as a good priest himself, he was obedient and did as he was told, in this case heading up a new retreat center that was supposed to rehabilitate repentant priests and return them to parish work.

Human sexual proclivities, Father Phil insisted in letters to Rome and arguments with bishops, were not a matter of choice and these priests should not be returned to churches, and especially should not be allowed around children. A monastery was the only appropriate place for them. But the pious counterarguments all repeated a mantra about the power of repentance and prayer, and science lost out to superstition once again.

Delaney first met him at a county carnival while on an outing with Camille and her favorite nephew. Somehow the eight-year-old managed to shoot an over-inflated basketball through an undersized hoop three straight times, giving him the joyful possession of a stuffed panda that stood almost as tall as himself.

As they strolled along, every barker in the midway had a free deal to offer. If the kid won the game, he'd get another stuffed toy. If he lost, he gave up the panda. It was almost pitiful, thought Delaney, the hunger in the eyes of these skinny, tired, slick-haired and aggressive carney barkers. The one with the concrete milk bottles that could be knocked over with a hard, well-pitched baseball finally got to the kid. Delaney began to warn him against it, but a wink from his aunt backed him off.

The kid lost and his eyes welled up as he lifted the panda into the waiting hands of the expressionless huckster. Camille hugged the boy and said, "Remember this now. You don't want to make the same mistake again," or something to that effect.

But the barker in the next booth was waiting for them. Unlike the others, he didn't seem to be suffering from the ravages of drink, tobacco, meth or other obvious vice, save, perhaps, for a mild touch of gluttony. He was chubby, neatly dressed and seemed to have a perpetual half-smile glued to his face. He grinned at Delaney and said, "I saw what happened and wonder if your young man might not like to take a few shots at the ducks?" He pointed at a row of moving mechanical ducks with targets painted on them. "Since it is him, we'll give him five shots for fifty cents and if he knocks down three, he'll get another panda. What do you think?"

The pleading eyes shifted between Delaney and Camille. "If you want to do it," she smiled, "sure, we'll do it, won't we?" Delaney saw the barker move something behind the duck display as the kid shot. Four ducks fell and everyone went home happy that evening.

The next morning's news was full of the story of the sixth priest murdered that year in Wisconsin and Minnesota. Same M.O. for all of them, a .38 slug to the heart or head. The story intrigued Delaney enough that he looked up their locations and proximity in time and geography to the carnival as it moved through the Midwest.

The correlation was rough, but real. Each murder occurred during a week of the carnival playing within thirty miles of each priest's home. Delaney thought of the wretched looking carnival barkers and thought that almost any one of them might have been abused enough as a child to turn into a vengeful, cold-eyed killer.

He went back to the carnival that morning, heading straight for the chubby guy.

"Are you a policeman?" the barker asked. "You're carrying yourself like one today. Last night you acted like a doting uncle."

"I'm not a policeman but I have a couple of very cop-like questions to ask, if you don't mind."

He smiled and said he didn't mind at all.

"Have you heard about the priests that have been killed this summer?"

"Oh, yes. I think everyone has." His smile broadened.

"I suspect someone from the carnival, perhaps even one of the barkers here, may be the killer."

"Really? I find that hard to believe, knowing all of them as I do. Whatever drew you to this conclusion?"

"I've examined the route of this carnival and tied it pretty closely to the location and times of the murders. If you've followed the news at all you must know that someone affiliated with this carnival is the killer."

Still smiling, the barker said, "Surely there are other groups, like motorcycle gangs or traveling professionals of one sort or another that have also been in the areas of these terrible murders?"

"The timing, the distances, they all fit this carnival too neatly. Let me ask, if you were to put your finger on the most likely one of your fellows to have committed these murders, who would it be?"

"Without so much as a second's hesitation I would say none of them did such deeds, as I told you earlier. They are all innocent men and women; at least in so far as these crimes are concerned."

Delaney gazed at the dark, wooden cross the man was wearing. The horizontal and vertical arms were of equal length and formed a squat, square shape with an oval in the center. Inscribed in it were the letters IHS. Delaney was visibly jolted and the barker smiled as he touched his cross. Delaney asked, "That's a Jesuit cross, isn't it?"

The man beamed. "You have done a good bit of detective work here. Now you know why I'm so certain it's none of these men. And you say you're not even a policeman?"

"You're the one," Delaney stared at him with something near to disbelief. "A former priest, atoning for the sins of your brethren?"

The man beamed, "Yes, I'm the 'one,' as you choose to refer to me. But no, I can't atone for their sins. I just tried for some measure of justice."

"Would you please come to the St. Paul police headquarters with me?" Delaney surprised himself with the "please."

"I would be delighted to accompany you and I will tell them of your sterling detective work. Quite impressive for an amateur, or even a professional, come to think of it." He was still smiling.

Delaney remembered asking the man he came to know as Dr. Phil, to please be patient as he made a call ahead to Mel Thorogood. The man was cheerful, courteous and talkative the whole trip into the city and the two became friends.

Dr. Phil talked about how disgusted he became with men who not only betrayed the sacred role entrusted to them, but who felt no real remorse over their acts. He was sickened by how they got off on each other's stories in group therapy and how the confessional seemed to become a place more of secret celebration than repentance.

"In my eyes they were all psychopaths and deserved to die. But I gave them all the opportunity to confess and receive last rites. A couple of them did, but the rest were snarling animals, furious that I, a fellow priest, could do such a thing to them. They were quite full of an indignant narcissistic rage. I think the other two were just trying to con me, hoping I'd feel enough pity to let them off. Anyway, I felt no remorse for having rid the earth of them, until the last one. He told me, rather matter-of-factly, that I was no better than them. Who was I to take their lives? Was I better than they? I had to admit, in God's eyes, no. They were simply predators in a predatory universe. I was no better.

"You understand that, don't you? Of course, I couldn't keep living this secret life. Feelings of guilt have begun to plague me and, you know, they do take their toll. I'm glad you came to stop me. Now I can go to confession again. I have missed the feeling of purity that comes from that."

The next day Delaney called Gene Swearingen to see if he could find a competent criminal defense lawyer for Dr. Phil. He did better than that; he got Earl Gray, the state's most notorious, and effective, defense attorney.

At trial Gray brought out all the sordid history of each of Dr. Phil's victims and the jury was sympathetic. The prosecution played on his lack of remorse, claiming Dr. Phil was the real psychopath and should be put away forever.

On the hand, Father Phil, his preferred term of address, said he was happy to have rid humanity of such patently evil men and was doubly sorry his church had been such a grotesque enabler of their depravity.

The jury, in effect, said he met the legal definition of insane and he was sentenced to St. Peter for life. There he quickly became a volunteer consultant and mentor to the in-house psychiatric staff who viewed him as a heaven-sent gift.

Although today's visit had a purpose, Delaney had been there to see him several times before just because he liked his company and his conversation. Dr. Phil knew right away that today's was not entirely a social call.

St. Peter, seventy-five miles south of St. Paul, is one of dozens of small picturesque towns that dot the rolling hills of the Minnesota River valley. It is a pleasant college town and was supposed to have become the state capitol back in 1857. But Joe Rollette, an enterprising St. Paul legislator, stole the only official copy of the enabling bill passed by the legislature. He was chair of the committee that had oversight of the bill, but as a good St. Paulite he did his duty. He took the only copy of the bill and hid out in a St. Paul brothel for a week, by which time, if the governor hadn't signed it, it was dead. Thus, St. Paul remained Minnesota's capitol and St. Peter got the insane asylum. Popular consensus of the time held that St. Peter got the better part of the deal.

Although it housed, among others, the state's most violent mentally ill criminals, the St. Peter campus was a long way from the old stereotype of an asylum. It's situated on nearly six hundred acres of forested land and has ample park-like areas where visitors and non-violent inmates can meet.

As they sat on one of the outdoor benches Dr. Phil said, "You have that policeman look about you today. Must be a serious case?"

"You've heard about that series of murders in St. Paul?"

"Oh my, yes; gruesome affair, isn't it? They were smart to bring you in to solve it, weren't they? I have every confidence you'll catch the killer." He smiled and continued, "You must think this is a psychopathic serial murderer and would like my help in sketching a psychological profile. Am I right, my friend?" He tilted his head and smiled again.

When Delaney nodded he said, "Please tell me what you know about this fiend and spare no detail. This should be interesting."

After Delaney filled him in on the facts, as he knew them, and his conjectures, Dr. Phil sat back, clasped his hands over his ample belly and began his Socratic interrogation.

"You say there is an apple inserted into the throats of three of the victims and the hand of the other grasped one? I think it's safe to assume the intent is not decorative. Apples have so many meanings. In myth they are often symbols of temptation, as in Genesis and numerous Greek stories. They are often associated with women. The core of an apple cut in half is thought to resemble a vagina.

"But these apples were, at least in some of the victims, inserted near where their Adam's apple would be? Very interesting, don't you think? The Adam's apple is prominent in men, but not in women. I wonder..." His voice trailed off and he seemed to be examining a passing cloud.

"You say the weapon used in three of these murders is of Indian origin? Are you familiar with the Hindu concept of chakra?"

"Just vaguely."

"To give you an overview that hardly does justice to the spiritual depth of this great and ancient tradition: Basically, it is the belief that there are seven energy centers in the human body. These are areas that both receive and transmit a certain kind of force. The fifth Chakra is the throat and it is the communication center.

"I bring up the idea of Chakra because the weapon used in three of these episodes was Indian and directed to a particular part of the body. The killer seemingly attached a particular importance to the throat. Can you think of why?"

Delaney thought for a moment. "Not really, but if the throat is symbolic of the communication function, then perhaps the killer was punishing them for communicating something, or keeping them from doing so?"

"Good. That's what I think too. The question is both what and why?

"The other interesting factor here, the placement of the bodies. Your friend Puckett is right about the ancient Norse burial tradition, but the difficulty here is that lots of other ancient traditions did the same thing. Certain Hindu sects, for example, and they may be more relevant here. I wouldn't rule out that your killer was trying for some cultural symbolism here, but maybe not. It may be a referent to some tradition or nothing at all. It may have been done just to throw you off the track, so to speak.

"Now we need to ask, why did he, or she, administer the poison, which, for our purposes is what the muscle relaxant was? We know that this left the victims able to see and hear everything around them, but left them immobile. Why?"

Delaney answered immediately, "A sadist who wanted to inflict as much fear as possible on his victims."

"Sadistic? Perhaps. The infliction of fear? Probably. Did you know that poison is generally the preferred tool of women killers? And you say this tiger's claw is a weapon, not of warriors, but of sneak thieves and assassins? A weapon eschewed by warriors? Just like poison, no?"

"Do you think the killer could be a woman? You saw those pictures. It would take a man's strength to tear someone's neck apart like that, wouldn't it? And a beheading? I don't see a woman doing that."

"Certainly. But remember, those strong neck cords would be completely relaxed by the drug, making the job much easier. But in any event, it wasn't a woman who imitated your friend Mel's voice, was it?"

"Phil, it never occurred to me that it could be a woman. But with electronic voice technology, anything is possible."

"Then forgive me, please, but I have to ask, you're single, rich, seemingly intelligent and not overtly ugly. You're educated, have good taste and are capable of interesting conversation. Am I safe in assuming you've had a number of female friends? Perhaps even some one-night stands? Disappointed some women who may have been angered or hurt by your subsequent inattention? Is that a safe assumption?"

"No, quite the opposite, I think."

"The striking young woman who was with you on the day we met, do you still see her?"

Delaney hesitated. "No, we broke up some time ago."

"Was it an amiable parting?"

Camille, Delaney thought, Camille as a serial killer? Utter nonsense. "Yes," he finally said, "quite amiable and we're still good friends."

"Good for you. Of course, we should keep in mind that women killers of any kind are extremely rare. So, let me ask, are there any men who harbor deep-seated resentments against you? Any man who would want you on this case to prove that he could best you in this battle of wits and blood?"

"No one I can even remotely think of."

"Then, regardless of gender, might we safely assume he is simply seeking to add an element to enliven a contest of his own design? Someone who knows of the Maude Gruber case and mine? Someone who sees you as a challenge, not for your own sake, but for the sake of the game?"

"That was my thinking coming here and why I'm still open to the notion it might be someone in the police department. My work on those cases is not general knowledge. And I certainly never discussed them with any woman I may have been involved with." Delaney frowned. He had never talked with Camille about them, but she had heard about both cases from her uncle, Mel Thorogood.

Dr. Phil stood up and stretched. "Do you mind if we walk? Sitting for too long at a stretch isn't good for my chubby body. Walking's about the only exercise that interests me. Besides, at times like this I like to think of myself as behaving like the great teachers - the Buddha, Socrates, Jesus. You know they all walked while teaching their students? None of this classroom nonsense. Of course, our Minnesota winters might have challenged them, mightn't it?"

As they started their stroll Delaney said, "That sounds like a segue to your analysis of this killer."

"You anticipate me again. I must be so transparent. But yes, I have some ideas."

The morning was cool in the way of a southern Minnesota spring and the sky was now clear of anything resembling a cloud. The trees were just starting to sprout their leaves. It was easy to forget that this was an asylum that housed the state's most remorseless criminals.

"As you know, I am skeptical about this profiling business the FBI touts. I think they engage in unwarranted guesswork and vague, very vague, descriptions of potential perpetrators. Their methods take in too great a population and lead to too many innocent people getting unfairly targeted. Don't you agree?"

"Of course, and so do some very good agents within the Bureau itself, as well as lots of cops on the St. Paul force."

"Having said all that, let me venture a couple of theories about your killer. First, don't discount the idea of a woman. I think there's a fifty-fifty chance it is. It may not be someone you've bedded, but the methodology is not inconsistent with what a woman might adopt.

"By the same token, it could also be a man. The feral brutality of ripping out throats, slashing Detective Fortuno's face, that all seems pretty masculine to me. Wouldn't you agree?

"We talked about the tie to Hindu tradition – the throat chakra, tiger's claw and orientation of the bodies – but we don't know if that had anything to do with the killings. It could be that the killer just stumbled on the weapon somewhere and just wanted to rip out their throats, without any reference to Hindu tradition. But I think that, because of the apple and its placement, the idea of the throat chakra is entirely purposeful. If we take the apple in its Judeo-Christian mythological place, it's the forbidden fruit, the fruit of the tree of knowledge; knowledge that would make one become like a god."

"So, you think each of the victims knew some secret and were murdered to prevent them from revealing it?" Delaney asked.

"With one exception, that's exactly what I think, but we just don't know enough yet, so you'll have to stay open to other hypotheses. And, of course, it will be of paramount importance to discover if these victims are somehow connected or just random selections of a latter-day Jack the Ripper."

"What's the psychological profile, Phil?"

"In a moment, Conor. But first I think we have to assume that the person who murdered Ms. Martin is not the same as the one who killed the other three."

"That never occurred to me, but I think I see why you're going there."

Dr. Phil waved his hand, dismissively. "Look at the first three victims. There was a great deal of thought and planning that went into those murders and the subsequent placement of their bodies. They were killed with the same weapon. They were all laid out by the river with their bodies oriented due north. Rocuronium was used for each of them,

"All the evidence in Ms. Martin's case indicates a crude and extremely brutal method of killing. There is nothing of the, well, elegance, of the first three. The perpetrator knew of those and made a half-hearted attempt to make it appear as if his was done by the same person. But his effort displayed none of the elements that were clearly important to the Riverrun killer.

"We must conclude, however, that this killer has a connection to the first one."

"A connection? Do we have two multiple killers loose in the city?"

"Not exactly. I'll explain shortly, but for now let's return to our more interesting multi-victim murderer. Are you familiar with what psychologists call the Dark Triad? No? Well, it describes the most dangerous type of human being there is. It is made up of three psychological character traits - narcissism, psychopathy and Machiavellianism. Any one of these can be terribly problematic; in combination, they are absolutely deadly. This murderer of yours is certainly a psychopath, but in all probability a particular type known as a malignant narcissist."

They were at the end of the path and Phil turned around and started pacing back toward the main campus. Delaney's visiting hour was drawing to a close.

"The planning involved, the sadism, the neatness of it all. Plus, the killer is trying to communicate something, more than just killing his victims. He is sending some very broad hints, it seems to me. For instance, given the placement of the apples, I should not be surprised to discover that his name is Adam, or Adams. Whatever else he is hinting at, I leave you to discover, but to be sure, there will be other hints to uncover.

"A malignant narcissist believes himself to be a unique and wonderful creature, someone to be adored. He, or she, demands attention and to be taken very, very seriously. Anyone who crosses him is in for real trouble.

"In this case I think the muscle relaxant was used so he or she could do some kind of display for the victims. He wanted to show them his vengeance, power, or in his eyes, glory, before they died. He *needed* to show off for them.

"The manner of their deaths is completely consistent with what we know as narcissistic rage."

Delaney nodded. "So, a narcissist is not just someone overly taken with himself. But there is a particular kind of rage associated with narcissism? Of course, half the people we know think too highly of themselves."

"The people you know are nothing like this. This person suffers from delusions of grandeur that would put Napoleon to shame. I would be very, very careful here. Like all psychopaths, he is very intelligent, very observant and very determined."

"You also mentioned something about Machiavellianism. How do you reach that conclusion?"

"Ah, I can see your interest has been piqued. In addition to your empathic sympathy for the victims, you are now engaged at a kind of intellectual level; the kind that revels in a game. I would urge caution upon you, Mr. Delaney. This is not a person to be trifled with.

"Remember, we said that, in the killer's eyes, these murders were also about power? A Machiavellian brooks no opposition to the pursuit and preservation of his power. There is no sense of morality here. He simply loves power for its own sake. It is that will to power that drives him to win any contest he's involved in." Dr. Phil shook his head ruefully, and staring off into the distance, said, "He is so dangerous and so completely unpredictable. Given the way he has drawn you into his game, I feel some concern for your safety, Conor. Please be careful. Promise me that you will be cautious?"

Delaney laughed. "You do know caution is my middle name? Besides, I have the whole police department, my man Kyle and even Mackey's chief enforcer all looking after me. I don't think I have very much to worry about." He stopped. "But what about that second person? You had some ideas about him?"

"I have. You see, it would be unusual for a malignant narcissist not to have an accomplice – an Igor to this psychopath's Doctor Frankenstein. It would be someone psychologically dependent on him and completely under his control."

"That's rather spooky, isn't it?"

"Do not trivialize the potential of this person to break through all your defenses. Let's just hope he doesn't have you on his victim list. At this point, well . . ." He stopped then as if wrestling with another idea.

"What is it, Phil?"

"I do hope I am wrong about this, Conor, but your Riverrun fellow has drawn you into his plans and his next victim could well be someone close to you. I leave it to you to think of how to prevent that from happening." He paused and looked up at the clear blue sky.

"Finally, if these killings are not random, and I suspect they are not, then there are really only two things we can safely predict about him."

"And they are?"

"He's a show off and wants to demonstrate that he's much smarter and capable than his victims, the police and you, you in particular. He is likely to strew your path with red herrings and he'll try another stunt like that telephone trick or worse."

"What's the other thing?"

"He wants to be caught."

15

THE GOD OF PEACE

The first stop after the St. Peter trip was an unsought and unavoidable political foray.

As was his habit, Delaney stopped by the Indian on his way into City Hall. St. Paul is unique among American cities for its World War I memorial. The others, almost without exception, put up doughboys in tin pots, bronze cannons or granite slabs inscribed with names of the local boys slaughtered in the war to end all wars. They dot public squares and parks in every American city and town. St. Paul, flush with cash from a bond sale just prior to the market crash of 1928, commissioned a memorial to go into its new, art deco, City Hall/Court House. It did not hold a competition, nor did it commission just any run-of-the-mill sculptor. No, the fathers of the City of the O'Connor system went straight to the best. He was definitely the best in this country, and perhaps in the world; Swedish sculptor Carl Milles, who was given carte blanche to create whatever he saw fit.

Milles' creation was inspired by a vision of five Indians sitting in a semi-circle. Materializing from the smoke of their pipe, the splendidly serene Indian God of Peace rose majestically into the air. His right arm was crooked and held a pipe close to his body; the left hand was lifted as if in blessing or benediction. The sculpture was placed in the foyer of the new City Hall/Courthouse and, at a height of thirty-eight feet, was the largest onyx statue in the world. Its gleaming whiteness stood in stark contrast to the dun granite, brass and dark wood making up other elements of the vestibule. The calm dignity of the god's visage almost made

Delaney believe there was hope for his city and, by extension, for much, if not all, of humanity. But as he got on the elevator he was jolted back to reality.

He had not wanted to take this meeting, but Gene Swearingen had arranged it and Nate Muhammad thought he should go. So, he was about to step into the office of the most popular mayor in the whole odd history of this city on the river, to tell her that her signature program was not only destroying the neighborhood of one of her base constituencies, it was also founded on some terribly flawed economic assumptions that were going to seriously undermine property values, and with it the property tax base, throughout her city.

The reason for his coming here could be traced back to something his friend Swearingen taught him: that every professional person has an obligation to volunteer a certain percentage of his income and services to help poor persons and communities. Swearingen was religious in this conviction and devoted anywhere from ten to fifteen percent of his law firm's time to *pro bono* cases. He gave a similar amount of the firm's pre-tax profits to legal aid. Other lawyers thought he made them look bad.

Delaney's firm was one of the top corporate and financial investigations agencies in the country and that's why Nate Muhammad sought him out. They had met a couple of times before and Delaney liked him. The press condescendingly referred to Muhammad as a "community activist." He saw himself as a responsible citizen of his community. When he saw something threatening to his neighborhood, like kids selling dope on the street corner, absentee landlords turning apartment buildings into slums, or payday lenders ripping off sizable chunks of the neighborhood's wages, he took action. He was a gifted community organizer and his ability to mobilize residents in a good cause through his Neighborhood Action Coalition bothered the established powers, from the Chamber of Commerce to City Hall to the Trades and Labor Assembly to Eddie's Bistro & Tavern.

For Nate Muhammad, the idea of the Black Community was something to be cherished and preserved. He was not a racist. He was happy to have white residents living in his Summit neighborhood. But he didn't want them coming in as well-to-do "urban pioneers," forcing out poor Black families. That's what he had seen happening on a large scale, wanted to know why and had asked Delaney to find the answers. Delaney and his staff did, and Louisa Martinelli wasn't at all happy with what their research uncovered.

Mayor Martinelli was of a type, the liberal white American who had been in the forefront of the fight for equal rights for African-Americans. Delaney appreciated that people like her worked hard and put their money down to support efforts for integrated education, fair housing, equal employment opportunity and access to the same level of health care as white families. They fought the good fight and Delaney knew they deserved all the credit that future generations would heap upon them.

Still, he knew that Nate Muhammad rightly observed that too few of them got the idea of the Black Community. No one vexed Muhammad more on this score than Louisa Martinelli.

Delaney and Muhammad had met hurriedly the night before, after a newscast in which Martinelli held up a draft of the Delphi report and blasted it as inaccurate, unfair, biased and destructive of good public policy. She concluded with the one factual statement of her presentation, "These people didn't even have the courtesy of giving me a copy of this thing."

She was right about that. He'd given the first draft of the report to Nate and the NAC board of directors just three days before. But Nate was not entirely surprised to learn that a member of his board of directors gave a copy to the head of the city's planning department, a personal friend. But the planner was not about to miss this opportunity to curry favor with his boss and passed it on to Martinelli.

Smart politician that she was, Martinelli saw what was coming and jumped out front on the issue. Discredit the messenger and cast the argument in your terms; it's an old political strategy and an effective one. But neither Nate Muhammad nor Conor Delaney was going to play the straw man for her.

Muhammad normally would have gone to this meeting. It was, after all, his organization that commissioned the study, and he didn't need another white friend taking on a political battle that he could handle with greater skill. But he did think it a good idea for Delaney to go in and learn something about what Martinelli's strategy and moves were going to be in reaction to the investigation. In short, Delaney was to be his scout. Nate Muhammad understood he'd need all the information he could muster before taking on the powerhouse that was St. Paul's mayor.

When Louisa Martinelli first came into office it was by the thinnest of margins. She had the endorsement of the city's powerful Democratic-Labor party and Trades Union Assembly, as well as various women's organizations, good government groups and the African-American, Latino and Asian communities. Her opponent had the Chamber of Commerce, with its deep pockets' membership, and the reactionary Police and Fire Fighters Unions. In a tight election, minority voters provided the margin of victory.

That was three elections ago. Since then, Martinelli had consolidated power by winning over the Chamber and its supporters, vigorously defended the police and fire unions in lawsuits brought against them on affirmative action grounds, while giving them substantial raises in salary, and had hired more African-Americans, Latinos and Asians into city jobs than had ever been appointed in all the years prior to her mayoralty. In the last election she had only the opposition of a few unknowns who, together, tallied less than ten percent of the vote. In short, Louisa Martinelli was riding high. Delaney thought a concurrently high level of hubris might also be settling in.

Economic development is the name of the game for mayors and city councils. They are constantly on the lookout for ways to spur new development in their cities that will yield jobs, a broader tax base, economic growth, a sense of progress and political credit for themselves. Louisa Martinelli's genius in this game lay in her discovery of the latent potential of the City's Port Authority.

Before Martinelli the Port had been a minor agency that occasionally issued revenue bonds to finance the construction of small industrial parks along the river on the City's West Side. Shortly after starting her second term, she asked the question, "Is there anything that limits the Port Authority to just issuing bonds for riverfront development?" Her City Attorney assured her there were no such constraints and from that moment the Port Authority became Louisa Martinelli's vehicle for transforming the City of St. Paul.

Soon the Port Authority was issuing bonds to finance downtown shopping malls, office and condominium towers and hotels. It financed new manufacturing facilities and warehouses in the West Midway area, neighborhood mini-malls and parking ramps. And it financed the conversion of old and often decrepit apartment buildings into high-end condominiums in Summit, the poorest of St. Paul's neighborhoods.

Gene Swearingen was one of Martinelli's best friends and her earliest and strongest supporter. He had put a lot of money into her election and reelection campaigns. That meant when Swearingen called, she answered. She was also an attorney, and possessed every Minnesota attorney's sense of awe in his presence. He had obviously spent some time talking with her before this meeting, as he had with Delaney.

He opened by saying they should have met earlier and perhaps this whole unpleasantness might have been avoided. Delaney mentioned he was working on the Riverrun murders and might get a call that would require his leaving at a moment's notice.

Martinelli looked at Swearingen, then Delaney and said, "Gene told me you were working on that. I hope you can find the killer soon. Any progress yet?"

"Not really. We know more about how the victims were killed, a little more about the character of the killer and, well, more that can't go public."

"I'm certainly not going public with anything that's told to me in confidence. And I am the Mayor of this city. The chief's boss, if you will."

Delaney glanced at his friend Gene first and then replied, "After last night's performance I'm not feeling a real bond of trust here."

She leaned forward over her desk, "What did you say? Who the hell do you think you are?"

Swearingen held up his hand. "Time out. Louisa, I told you he would be blunt. And you," he peered down his nose at Delaney, "Let's try to get something done here. Recriminations won't get you where you want to go."

"OK," Delaney said, having achieved his first objective, "But I need to clear the air. She called the work of my firm into question. What do you think that will do for public trust when it comes out that I'm working on these killings, or any other future project?"

Martinelli interjected, "I'm prepared to walk that back."

Delaney acted stunned. "Did I hear that right?"

"It's either that or you're going to make me look like a damned fool, aren't you?"

Delaney smiled. "I'll do my best."

The great friend to both of them spoke again, "Your best may not be good enough. She handles the press in ways that would boggle your mind."

Delaney knew better but just nodded. He turned to her as she said, "Look, I just don't want this city to become another Detroit. We had to do something. This city's economy was stagnating and there was really nothing else to do."

"So, you had to destroy the Black community?" Delaney knew Swearingen thought he was unnecessarily goading her, but that wasn't entirely right. She deserved to have some taste of what Nate Muhammad would be laying down.

She ignored Delaney's dig and continued, "Here's what I'm prepared to do. That deserted area four blocks south of University? I've asked the Housing Authority to develop a one-hundred-unit low-income housing cooperative there. I'm also going to declare a moratorium on condo conversions in Summit. Finally, I'll get the Housing Authority to put up some front money and talk to some foundations and get them to fund Nate Muhammad's Neighborhood Action group. Is that enough for you?"

"You're going to say all this in a press conference?"

She gave Delaney a look that said he must be daft. "No. I'm not going to say any of it. It will just happen."

He nodded. "Of course. You'll fund the NAC?" That was Nate Muhammad's baby. He maintained the city didn't have to completely rehabilitate and convert old apartment buildings; they just had to enforce the building codes and provide the funds to rehab them to that level. That would make them habitable and keep the rents low. The economic models Delaney projected said this wasn't just the most economical way for the city to preserve low-income housing, it was the best possible way for the city to deal with problems posed by its growing number of absentee slumlords. The Neighborhood Action Coalition was the organization through which Nate Muhammad would identify derelict buildings and direct funds to the needed rehabilitation.

Since she talked in terms of actions already done or about to be taken, Delaney understood she had either done or planned all this before her press conference last night. That perturbed him, but he knew Nate would be elated with her moves and would want at least one other concession - that displaced Summit

residents be given first crack at getting into the new co-op apartments. Delaney decided to leave that for Nate Muhammad to negotiate.

Delaney looked over at Swearingen first, and after he nodded, said, "There are just a couple of other things I'd like to ask. I have a good team of professionals working for me. Good people who take pride in what they do. You shouldn't have smeared them last night. How are you going to make it up to them?"

She glared at him for several seconds before Swearingen spoke up. "Louisa, I know that look. Dial it back. He's right and you know it. That press conference was ill advised. You took a whack at destroying the reputation of the finest investigations firm in this state, and maybe the country, for all I know. Now the piper has to be paid. And that's me talking, not him."

Delaney's cell phone rang. Louisa Martinelli nodded to an adjacent room where he could talk in private. It was Shem. "Boss, you said to call if we found anything to tie the victims to each other?"

"What have you got?"

"Well, maybe nothing, but then again, maybe something. Shaun found it, but he called in sick today. He found out that Graham Byrd and Suzanne Porter both grew up in Kansas City."

"That's a pretty slim tie."

"But they grew up in the same neighborhood, went to the same schools and they were the same age. So, they had to know each other."

"Good. That's good Shem. It gives us something to go on."

"Boss?"

"Yes?"

"There's more. And this is where it gets really good. I found out that Fortuno met Porter in Milwaukee."

"Met her? How?"

"Through an escort service where she apparently worked as, well, an escort. Fortuno was in town at a cop convention. And there's an interesting coincidence here: Graham Byrd was in Milwaukee at the same time. For three days."

"Anything else?"

"There may be a tie between these three and the Port Authority."

"Really?" He couldn't resist smiling, "How so?"

"Well, Porter worked there, Byrd the realtor was involved in buying and selling properties for the Port and Fortuno called Porter at her office number several times. Nothing conclusive here, yet, but still pretty convincing to me."

"Shem, I'll be back in the office shortly. Keep digging, and would you transfer me to Marguerite, please?"

No, she said, there had been no strange occurrences at the office, no odd parcels, no skulking strangers. Not even so much as a marketing call. Shaun was out with the flu, but otherwise everything was absolutely normal. Was there anything else he'd like her to tend to? Delaney thanked the universe once again for the efficiency with which Marguerite looked after things.

He told Martinelli and Swearingen he had to go but had one other issue to raise before leaving. He knew his friend Gene would get the necessary public apology and it would be less galling for the city's mayor to give it as a favor to a staunch personal and political supporter.

Delaney sat on the edge of the chair to indicate he was in a hurry and said, "You're overbuilding condos in this city. The market isn't there, either for the new construction or the rehabbed older buildings. The market is going to tank and a lot of people are going to lose a lot of money, including investors in Port Authority bonds."

"That's your analysis," she said calmly.

"No, that's what the numbers say, exclusive of any analysis. Unless you have a wave of yuppie refugees from Miami, Chicago or San Francisco, you just don't have the population to support that much condominium development."

She sat back and took a deep breath. "You know, we had each proposed development reviewed by the planning board, bond counsel and the Port Authority staff and board. In addition, Pfeiffer & Ralston handled the bond sales.

An investment bank like that doesn't go around and market junk bonds to its customers. They'd lose the confidence of their investors if they did that, wouldn't they? And look at the grade the ratings agencies give to Port Authority bonds. They're AAA.

"But let's, for the sake of argument, concede your point. Now what do we have? Run-down buildings now made attractive and habitable, and new beautiful buildings that give a nice new look to our city. Which, without all of this, could end up looking like a minor league Detroit. We stopped that from happening, didn't we?

"You know, we have a great city. Beautiful architecture, parks, full employment, good schools, renowned health centers, and a housing stock that's affordable. We always finish at or near the top of every study of the country's most livable cities. I just want the city to keep all that and we can't do it if we stand still."

Delaney had neither the time nor inclination to argue further with her, but was struck once again by the naiveté of politicians. Pfeiffer & Ralston sold bonds and made money on every issue. They didn't care about their quality and they paid the ratings agencies, so of course the agencies were going to give them a high rating. They wanted more business too. As for the planning board and Port Authority, they had no capacity for economic analysis and floated merrily along on the tides of Chamber of Commerce induced boosterism. Anything tagged as economic development was good.

Delaney didn't go into any of that but just said, "I would advise both of you not to buy any of those condos until the market plunges, which should happen sometime between today and six months from now. Oh, and divest yourselves of any Port Authority bonds you might have. They're going to tank about the same time."

Martinelli sighed, but Swearingen nodded knowingly. As Delaney was leaving Martinelli asked, "Is this something that might break that case?"

He shrugged, "I think so, but I really don't know yet."

On his way out of city hall he glanced at the Indian again. The god still stood placid, serene and stately.

16

THE SONG OF ROLAND

Delaney joined Mel Thorogood behind the two-way mirror of an interrogation room shortly after Ann O'Leary and Natalie Puckett began questioning Roland Gadsen. Thorogood's deep frown told him all he needed to know about how the interview was going.

Gadsen said he understood why they were interrogating him and that he'd do the same if he were them. From his demeanor and speech, it was clear he was a pro. Delaney thought Gadsen probably could have scribbled down their questions before they were asked.

O'Leary thumped the table-top and pointed an accusing finger at Gadsen. "You say Fortuno called you the day after the second murder. Really? That soon?"

Thorogood turned to Delaney, "Guy came in this morning and confessed."

"Really? The actual, real killer?"

"Nope."

Of course. That would not have been at all consistent with Dr. Phil's profile. His suspect would never confess; would never feel the need to. Thorogood continued frowning at the three cops in the room.

"Well?" Delaney said.

"He's an immigrant."

"From India and he has a *bagh nakh*?"

"Tiger's claw, yes. It's being analyzed right now."

"And you're still grilling Gadsen, of course."

"Of course."

Of course. Both men knew they had a confessor; an innocent man who insisted it was he who committed the big crime. Several of them showed up for every high-profile murder case to put in their respective claims on the fifteen minutes of fame they were owed.

"Gettler is analyzing the tiger's claw right now," the Assistant Chief said. "I don't expect we'll find anything but the owner's prints on it."

Puckett asked why Gadsen thought Fortuno called him and why he couldn't just tell him what he knew during that call. Did Gadsen push Fortuno on this? Did he think Fortuno was credible? What did Gadsen think Fortuno had for him? Big Gad responded as evenly to her almost gentle style as he did to O'Leary's decidedly more aggressive approach.

O'Leary stopped Gadsen in the middle of a reply. "The word is, Fortuno was dirty."

Gadsen flushed. This was expected, but among cops, loyalty to one's partner trumps all other values. A partner is someone who guards your life, and you guard his. You protect, and are protected, from all enemies - criminal, civilian and departmental. The trust between partners has to be total and unwavering. There simply is no stronger bond for any cop. Anyone who tries to break it is a mortal threat, regardless of their position. Even partners a cop doesn't like, even a former partner one doesn't like, are still to be protected.

O'Leary's accusation clearly bothered Big Gad. His answer was steady, but defensive. "The word? C'mon, O'Leary, just whose word are we talkin' about here? You know that every cop has guys ready to bad-mouth him. More badgering, irrelevant questions like that, about a good guy like Danny Fortuno, and maybe I'll have to get my union rep in here."

Puckett gave that shy smile of hers, the one Delaney would come to know as the warning that something unexpected was about to land. "He's right outside, we thought you might want him. Should we call him in?"

"We have lots and lots more questions like this one," O'Leary said.

"OK, kids, might as well. Should I get my lawyer, too?"

It was O'Leary's turn to look uncomfortable. "You really want a lawyer here?"

"Nah, fuck the lawyer, bring in Milton. Then you two can go ahead and make a grievance for me against you. You didn't really expect me to turn on my own partner; are you two really cops? And you're not even internal affairs. It's kind of disgusting."

Delaney liked Keith Milton but knew that he was cut from the same cloth as other police union representatives throughout the country. Their job was to protect police officers from any and all insinuations, accusations or attacks, whether they were justified or not. The union rep was an advocate, period. Was an officer seen in the act of committing an axe murder by a crowd of fifty sharp-eyed witnesses? He had to be innocent: it was self-defense, an accident, the witnesses were blind or biased; the cop was a hero who put his life on the line every day.

Delaney's cell phone buzzed. He stepped away to answer. Henri Bouchard greeted him with: "I just sent you some photos you want to look at right away. Something odd is going on."

After glancing at them Delaney handed his cell phone to Thorogood.

The Assistant Chief' examined the shots before matter-of-factly-stating, "Russians."

Keith Milton immediately got to what he thought was the nubbin of the matter. "OK now, what the hell are you two up to? Roland Gadsen is a decorated, veteran officer. What are you trying to railroad him into?"

"Cool your jets, Miltie," O'Leary replied. "We're union too, remember? And we're not trying to railroad Gadsen. We just asked about his partner. The word is he was dirty."

"Oh?" Milton's eyebrows lifted slightly. He had heard the same word, but it didn't slow him down much. "Why are you asking Detective Gadsen about this? Why aren't you questioning the people who gave you that 'word'?"

O'Leary shifted in her chair, gazing first at Milton, then at Gadsen. "So, you guys don't care if there's a dirty cop in this department?"

Their reaction was immediate and heated. Both were objecting when Puckett raised her hand for silence. Strangely, it seemed to Delaney, they stopped and looked at her.

"I enjoy a good pissing match as much as the next guy," she grinned, "but maybe we can try to remember that we all want to see Danny Fortuno's killer brought to justice. Whether he was 'dirty', matters only if it helps us figure out who killed him. Are we agreed?"

Gadsen sighed, Milton nodded and O'Leary continued to stare at Gadsen.

Puckett went on, "Look, we know, and so do you, that Danny liked to gamble, snorted coke and was into rough sex with hookers. Not exemplary behavior, right? And any one of these bad habits could have gotten him killed. And the nickname no one ever said to his face, Dollar Danny? He didn't get that because he hated money, did he? Agreed?"

Milton and Gadsen both said "yeah" and nodded at the same time.

O'Leary, now speaking in a softer, more sympathetic tone, looked at Gadsen and said, "Detective, you were closer to Danny than anyone. You knew his habits, his vulnerabilities. We know you weren't crazy about having him as your partner. We also hear that his constant angling for a new financial bonanza got him into associates of Mackey for something north of two hundred thousand. Please help us out here, Detective. Do you know anything about that?"

It was a classic interrogation pattern. They had played good cop – bad cop and tried whipsawing him between friendship and enmity. Finally, they reeled him in with the appeal to common purpose, unwittingly abetted by his union rep. Delaney was surprised that they were playing a game Big Gad knew so well. He'd played it himself, several times with Danny Fortuno as his partner.

As he told it, Gadsen knew only a little about "that." Delaney knew Gadsen still wasn't telling them everything; and that what he wasn't telling could be key to the murder of former detective Danny Fortuno.

Delaney turned to Thorogood. "Mind if I join them?"

Thorogood, without looking up from the photos in Delaney's cell phone, nodded. "I was hoping you might."

Four sets of eyes widened as Delaney came into the room; Gadsen leaned back in his chair and his facial expression went blank.

"Mind if I join you, detectives? Detective," he said, looking into Gadsen's eyes, "who was the confidential informant Fortuno was dealing with?"

Gadsen nodded as the big question had finally been asked. Resigned, he said, "I don't know. He wouldn't tell me. Said it would be better and safer for me not to know."

"And so, he told you to wait another day? Did he indicate there was any danger in this for him? Or did he think he was somehow free of any threat?"

"That's about it."

"No one else in the Department was told about this contact, this lead, were they? It was going to be you and Fortuno, just like old times?"

"Danny said not to tell anyone else," Gadsen quickly interjected.

"Danny said that? I wonder what Thorogood or McArdle would have said? In any event, you waited too long for Fortuno to get back to you. The silence finally got to you and then it was too late."

"Yeah," he said, rocking back in his chair. "And you have to know, he told me nothing about this CI, nothing. Only that it was somebody important, somebody we couldn't fuck with."

"Mackey?" the two detectives said, almost in unison.

"No." He smiled wanly. "That would make everything so simple, wouldn't it? That was my first question and he said no, absolutely not. I believed him and we all know this ain't Mackey's style. Mackey's not going to kill even a former cop, is he?"

"Keep talking, Detective," Delaney said, "there's more."

"That's all I know."

"No, it isn't and it's time for you to stop playing the guy who's going to avenge his partner's murder, because that's what partners do, even for a guy who hasn't been his partner for two years. I've seen that movie a bunch of times and I love it. But it's not real life and you're not Sam Spade. You're doing a great post-mortem defense of Dollar Danny's reputation. But it doesn't wash and it doesn't matter. Now come straight or that guy behind the mirror is going to see that your life in this department becomes a living hell, regardless of what Milton here thinks. Are we on the same page now?"

"Okay, okay. But I've told you all I actually know. There were a couple of things he said though that might mean something."

"Keep talking, please."

"He said this person was not like anybody else in the city. He also said they were going to meet and the CI would bring the murder weapon to him. I guess he didn't lie about that, did he?

"Look, I didn't want to do this. I said let the guy mail it in or leave it someplace where he could pick it up. I said his CI could be dangerous. He just laughed and said the CI wasn't big enough to be able to do much to him. He said, 'where's your sense of adventure? You turning chicken shit in your old age?' That's what he said and now you know everything I know."

"No. There's more. Talk."

The Big Gad shifted uncomfortably. "The only other thing I can think of is Danny said the perp had a 'sexret.' I asked him what the hell that meant and he just laughed. Said, 'you figure it out, you're a detective.'"

"What do you think he meant?"

"I dunno, maybe that someone had a secret that involved sex. Like that's not ninety percent of the population. Now, honestly that's all I know."

Now Delaney knew what Big Gad knew, or maybe what he thought he should know.

Outside the room, a frowning Thorogood greeted him with, "What do you know about these Russian guys?"

17

THE SHOCK DOCTRINE

The Vory v Zakone are an elite leadership corps within the Russian mob and have an infamous criminal history and culture that extends back to the time of the Czars. The organization – its name translates as "Thieves in Law" - developed its unique code in Stalin's Gulags. The code, among other things, forbids a Vor from doing legitimate work of any kind. He is expected to live exclusively on the payoffs from his criminal activities.

An old Vory motto has it that "the natural home of the Vor is prison." As prosecuting attorneys around the world have learned, threatening Vory with extended time in confinement has no effect whatsoever. They view it as a homecoming opportunity.

Nor does a Vor feel threatened by torture or other bodily harm of any kind. He is too well aware that his comrades will do far worse to him were he to betray their trust. In his world, loyalty to the Vory brotherhood overrides all other values. His brothers guard his life, and he guards theirs. He is responsible for protecting all other Vory from all enemies - prison guards, rival gangsters, police and any other threat. The trust among Vory is total and unwavering. For a Vor this is the strongest bond possible. Anyone seeking to break it is a mortal threat and must be eliminated.

The easiest way to identify a Vor is by his tattoos. They amass tattoos like Boy Scouts collect badges and these are always inscribed in prison. A top level Vor carries an ocean of blue ink on his body that serves as a kind of biography and record of achievement. Even his fingers and toes may have something etched into them. Each tattoo has a special meaning and signals status, history and attitudes. For instance, stars indicate a high rank, a skull is the sign of a murderer and the letters OMYT on the fingers declare that this is a hard man to escape from. A crown is found only on the back of the hand of a criminal boss.

It was just such a tattoo that was causing Mel Thorogood's consternation.

The four photos Henri Bouchard sent to Delaney were all shot in the semi-mayhem outside the baggage claim level at International Airport. The first was of Marshall Pinckney, sporting a chauffer's cap and wheeling a large suitcase through the crowd. Right behind him was a big, completely bald man in a grey suit. Tattoos flared up from around his open shirt collar. The second shot showed Pinckney stowing the bag in the trunk of a black Lincoln Continental while the big man was climbing into the rear seat and looking over his shoulder into the crowd. A crown tattoo was clearly visible on the back of his right hand.

The next photo showed the group he was apparently looking at: two beefy men and a short, older woman, made to seem smaller by the big men flanking her. The final shot was of the three of them climbing into a black SUV.

Delaney and Thorogood both recognized Pinckney's passenger as Victor Boris Volkov, and Delaney identified the woman as Marta Voronova. " She has run financial fraud schemes and money laundering operations all over the world. She knows the dark side of money like no one this side of Lucifer himself.

"I've run into her twice before. Once on an inter-bank money transfer scam and later on a scheme to launder drug money through insurance companies' short-term investment funds. Delphi busted both of those games. Her presence here bothers me as much as Volkov's."

Chief Homer McArdle leaned back in his chair, his one eye shifting between Delaney, Mel Thorogood and Henri Bouchard, all seated on the other side of his desk. "I need a little more context here before I call Schmidt over at the FBI and have him loose his army of killer bureaucrats and knit-pickers on our City. So, this little old lady is part of the Russian mob? Who the hell is Volkov and what about the rest of that crowd? Just muscle? From what I know about Russian gangs, they plan and deploy pretty carefully. Do we have any idea of why they're here?"

After Delaney reviewed how Henri Bouchard had been employed to follow Marshall Pinckney and happened upon the Russians, Thorogood took over. "Our people are running facial recognition software to ID the other two guys. We suspect that they, like Volkov, are Vory. As for Volkov, he's a real force in the Russian mob. He's a top-level Vory leader and if he's here, there is something big going down. We are completely in the dark as to what that might be. I think we need to call in the FBI right now. They may have some notion of why these characters are visiting our city."

"I will be happy to call the FBI, and Homeland Security, too. But before I do, I want to know that I have all the information that's available. You ever hear that old adage, 'information is power?' Huh? Why do I need that power?" He waited a full two seconds before barking, "Well?"

His one eye glowered at them for a couple more seconds before he snorted, "It's simple. Our distinguished federal brethren may well fuck up at some point and I want to be in a position to make sure the whole operation in our City doesn't go south. The two of you know what I mean, don't you?" He looked at Delaney and Thorogood. Both men knew what he meant and winced at the thought of it.

"Now, Henri, these are lovely photos, but you saw more than they show by themselves. Tell me, how did you stumble across these beauties?"

Bouchard smiled. "It was simple enough. I was tracking Mackey's man, Pinckney, and he drove out to the airport. Only he wasn't in his own car. He was driving that big Continental. When he got to the last door on the baggage claim level he put on a chauffer's cap and walked into the terminal. He came out wheeling this muscle-head's suitcase through the crowd. While he was stuffing it in the trunk, the guy, Volkov, climbed into the back seat. He left his door open for Pinckney to close. I could see no sign that they ever talked to each other. I suspect Pinckney was playing some kind of undercover role as a driver, keeping his identity as one of Mackey's men a secret."

"Really? I hope you're right. Where did they go from the airport?"

Delaney interrupted, "I think Henri's right about Pinckney's undercover status. When I met him, he was outfitted in a slick three-piece suit and seemed to me to be a bit of a dandy. That chauffer's outfit he's wearing at the airport probably clashes with his normal fashion sensibilities."

McArdle's eye rolled toward the ceiling. "Where did they go, Henri?"

"I don't know."

The Chief frowned and huffed a frustrated sigh.

"No," Bouchard quickly said, "That's something you use on your cops, not a distinguished private detective. Now, if you were a good detective, instead of . . . "

McArdle chuckled. "What kept you from tailing them, Henri?"

"Now that's the question a good detective would ask, instead of huffing at his renowned guest. The answer is that, as the Pinckney car was pulling out of the jumble of traffic down there, I observed those three other passengers watching it. That little woman? She may be small, but she got a mean look.

"As soon as Pinckney's car left the area they all piled into that SUV. I never saw the driver because it had those tinted windows. I followed them to the Intercontinental Hotel in St. Paul. Right across the street from City Hall. My guess is that Volkov is also there."

"And then?"

"I sent those pictures and called Conor." Bouchard leaned forward. "What I don't get is why Pinckney played chauffer and why Volkov traveled alone, pretending to know nothing of the others following him. Looks to me like we've got one of those Russian dolls where you open it and there is another one inside: and another and another. Or something like that. But Pinckney is Mackey's man, so Mackey is involved somehow."

The other three swiveled their attention to Delaney. He nodded and said, "I'll talk to Mackey and see what he has to say, but I can't see him getting into the sack with the Russian mob."

"Get back to us as soon as you talk to him, OK?" McArdle said. "Is there anything else I need to know before calling the feds?"

After a few seconds of silence, Delaney started, "This is speculation on my part, but I think it's worth considering. Are you familiar with the shock doctrine?"

When only Thorogood nodded, Delaney continued, "It's the idea that the best time to force radical change on a government, or any kind of organization, is when it is distracted by a crisis."

Thorogood shifted uncomfortably. "You think they may be moving in here thinking this series of killings has us too distracted to notice them or respond to whatever they are up to?"

McArdle leaned back in his chair and looked at the ceiling. "Hmm... does anyone here suspect the Russians may be involved in our little string of murders?"

"If they are involved, it would only be tangentially," Delaney said quickly.

"What do you mean, 'tangentially?'"

"It looks like there are connections between our first three victims. They apparently weren't the random slaughter of a serial killer. I think if the Russians were involved they would try to create a serial killer narrative. And they may have taken a stab at doing precisely that."

McArdle shook his head. "Slow down, boy. What do you mean they took a stab at it?"

"The idea of a serial killer creates uncertainty, terror even. With our case we are down to looking for someone the first three victims have in common; someone with a motive for getting rid of them.

"Then we have the Karleen Martin situation. Dr. Phil is certain that she was killed by someone else. Elegance was the word he used for the first three killings. He thought the Karleen Martin killing to be too different from them. There was no use of the drug, no sign of the tiger claw, no use of the river or body being oriented in a northerly direction.

"By contrast, it was a simple, straightforward act of brutality. She was beaten to death and beheaded. In short, there was no cleverness involved here, no clues that might lead to, or away from, the identity of the killer.

"Phil thought this may have been done by what he referred to as an 'Igor' to our Riverrun killer's Dr. Frankenstein. I think it's possible it could have been done by the Russians to nudge along a serial killer theory for us, and the city, to react to. Whoever did it knew of the other killings and played on the Adam's apple theme."

McArdle suddenly stood. "OK, boys, I've heard enough speculation for one day. I'm going to call Schmidt right now and get his agents after the Russians. We locals will stay focused on the Riverrun cases, including the Martin woman.

"Henri, can you orient the Fibbies on where these guys are staying or where they're going in the city?" Seeing Bouchard's nod, he turned to his assistant Chief. "Mel, stay here for the call to Schmidt. And you," he nodded at Delaney, "can just leave and get back on the trail of whoever is assassinating our fine citizens. I'm not paying you extra to mess with the Russians. We have the FBI for that."

Delaney smiled. McArdle, he understood, had no intention of turning over the Russian intrusion into his city to the FBI.

18

THE ATTORNEY OF RECORD

Delaney logged on to find that the department had emailed the financial records for Byrd, Porter and Fortuno. They were all there, five years' worth of pay stubs and payments for mortgages, rent, telephones, internet, insurance, health care, cable television, furniture, clothing, restaurants, groceries, hardware, movies, contractors, credit cards and all the other detritus of the modern age. Of more interest to Delaney were their IRAs, pensions and investment portfolios.

He strolled down to Cy Kriegsman's office. "You got that squint goin' that says there's something odoriferous in the air. What smells like sour poop this afternoon?" It was a typical Kriegsman greeting.

Kriegsman was a recently retired IRS auditor who came into Delphi one day to announce, "You guys do interesting work." A week later he was on the payroll and within another day-and-a-half had established himself as the resident curmudgeon.

"Cy, you've looked over the Port Authority reports for Nate's project. What do you think of the Port's financial status?"

"We only looked at the stuff they have to report as a public agency."

"OK, but what's your suspicion?"

"Gamier than Lady Godiva's saddle."

"I want to know who's buying and selling their bonds. I don't think the market in their securities should be so hot. Wanna start digging?"

"Oh, yeah. Any limits?" That was code for could he get into personal financial files and other stuff that was supposed to be unlawful for anyone to pry into.

"Absolutely none. I think the Suzanne Porter murder may have something to do with her job at the Port. I don't want to miss anything." At this point Delaney thought it best not to mention any possible Russian gang involvement.

"You're the boss. Your command is my wish."

"Thanks, Cy. How soon?"

"Twenty-four hours, but maybe a hundred and twenty-four. How the hell should I know? I don't know what's there yet. When I do, I'll call you."

"OK, just move on it, will you? Of course, if you're too old to get this done . . ."

Kriegsman snickered. "Too old? I ought to sue you for creating a hostile work environment for the aged and infirm. Too old, my ass. The only thing slowing down this work is you, standing there and keeping me from my professional responsibilities." He grinned. "Get outta here, will ya?"

"One other thing, Cy. I've got our victims' financial records. I need to have your gimlet eye cast on them. I don't want to miss anything. You don't mind, do you?"

"Of course, I do. It's my nap time. You are one irritating bastard. Now scram so I can get some of your dishonest work done."

Delaney's next stop was Shem and Shaun's office. Outwardly the two of them appeared to have come from different planets. Shaun Neary was a perpetually disheveled, short, thin, pale and freckled redhead. No one could remember a time when his shirt was either pressed or completely tucked in.

Shandar Shivaji, on the other hand, was tall, dark, muscular and always immaculately dressed. Shem, like Delaney, wore tailored suits and silk ties. Unlike Delaney, he favored outrageously colorful suspenders that he lovingly displayed to the rest of the staff every morning after he hung up his coat. Buddy Holly glasses completed the hip persona.

But appearances were where the dissimilarities ended. In the cyber world, where they really lived, their instincts and actions mirrored each other. There they were twins who could effortlessly glide through endless rivers of ones and zeros, opening and closing gates at will. When working on a project their rapid-fire exchanges and language became impenetrable to the rest of the Delphi firm.

They shared a conference room-sized office, immaculately ordered with hard drives, screens, great big screens, routers, printers and miles of wire. Down the hall was a sealed room filled with high-powered servers and an emergency generator - the technical nirvana that drew them to St. Paul from Boston. They loved their space, their work and the pay. Delaney loved their competence, good natures and doggedness.

Shaun was out sick today, but Shem was excited, explaining that the first three future victims had all been in Milwaukee five years ago and there was enough in the phone records and subsequent emails to indicate the three of them had gathered together there. There were calls between Byrd and Porter before, during and after Byrd's trip to the city, and about a half-dozen calls between Porter and Fortuno during those three days. The first of Fortuno's calls to Porter came to Blue Light Escorts and was made late at night.

Delaney was puzzled. "Do we have any record of the three of them being in touch here? And when does Porter show up in St. Paul? And how does she move from being a hooker in Milwaukee to top administrative assistant at the Port Authority?"

Shem shook his head, "She may not have been a working girl then. It looks more like she was doing the admin work. Taking calls, bookkeeping, filing, making assignments. But still, it's funny. She moves here just a few months later with references from some of Milwaukee's top corporate executives. There is occasional contact with Byrd, but only a few calls from Fortuno over the years. She never calls him and his calls to her were always at her work number, at the Port Authority. At least that's what we've got so far. Of course, they could have used disposable cells and we'd never know."

"How about in the days leading up to her murder?"

"We thought you might ask, and we found that, between the deaths of Byrd and Porter, there are a flurry of calls, to her office and home. Strangely, or maybe not so strange, they are all from blocked numbers."

"How far along are you on some of that other stuff?"

"We've got what you wanted, I think."

"Good, give me the synopsis, starting with Fortuno."

"Apparently a highly talented cop. Grew up on the East Side and was one of several high school chums working in the department. A great-nephew of Chief McArdle. Married and divorced three times. He was overextended financially. He had lots of child support to pay and not just to his three ex-wives; there was lots of credit card debt and within the next year, unless something happened, he would have had to declare bankruptcy.

"But he was apparently quite a successful cop. His annual reviews were always laudatory, describing him as dedicated, courageous and creative. His case closure rate was among the highest in the department. On a scale of one to one hundred, he was always in the high eighties to low nineties on his personnel evaluations. He was the lead on several high-profile cases and got a fair amount of publicity for them. He was always prepared in court. As far as we can tell, he did not know Porter or Byrd before the meeting in Milwaukee."

"Check on how many of his closed cases, particularly of the high-profile variety, were dependent on the testimony of Gunnar Olafsson or the lab techs. What about Gadsen?"

"Oh, I get it. They could really make each other look good, couldn't they?"

"And they'd be conspiring to put innocent people away and letting the guilty skate. Now, what about Gadsen?"

"I don't think we need to go into detail here. Another East Side kid, but almost the polar opposite of Fortuno. His finances are always in order. He owns a house and lake cabin up by Brainerd. He was married, but his wife died, breast cancer, two years ago. No kids. Everything indicates he's a model citizen; responsible and no black marks anywhere. His departmental evaluations are not nearly up to Fortuno's standards, but still good in the mid to high eighties. Ready for O'Leary and Puckett?"

"Nothing unusual on Gadsen, really? Dig some more, will you? What about Puckett and O'Leary?"

"Clean through and through, although you may be interested to know that Puckett's maiden name was Bouchard and she is a first cousin to your friend Henri."

"She's married?"

"Divorced nearly three years now. One four-year-old child. A boy. Lives near Henri, whose wife does the day care for little Eli."

Delaney stared at Shem for a long second before asking, "Gettler?"

"Nothing here either. Looks like what you see is what you get."

"Doctor Thor Gunnar Olafsson?"

"The line on Olafsson: A North Dakota farm boy, undistinguished undergraduate student, finished in the lowest ten percent of his medical school graduating class, set up his medical examiner business with a bank loan, on very favorable terms. He currently owns a seventy-five percent stake in the business. The other 25 percent is owned by his brother. Two of his autopsies were successfully challenged in court."

Shem hesitated then said, "Boss, Gunnar made a call immediately after your meeting yesterday."

Delaney found himself hoping it would be something to implicate Olafsson in some kind of illegal, immoral or at least unethical scheme. Whenever he thought of Olafsson the old nursery rhyme came to mind:

> *I do not like thee, Dr. Fell,*
> *Precisely why, I cannot tell,*
> *But this I know and know full well,*
> *I do not like thee, Dr. Fell.*

But the news wasn't that good, at least not yet. "And the call was to?"

"His brother, you know, Jacob Berkeland?"

"That Jacob Berkeland, President of Pinnacle City Bank and Trust? That's Gunnar's brother?"

"Different dads, but they grew up together in North Dakota."

"He made the call right away?"

"He was still in the parking ramp." Shem typed a few keys on his laptop and the voice of Gunnar Olafsson said, "Jacob, I have just gotten out of a meeting and I have to see you at once. It is very urgent."

"What's it about?"

"I said it was urgent. I will be there in ten minutes."

Delaney frowned. He was saying, "Better add Jacob Berkeland to your list of deep backgrounds," when his cell showed O'Leary calling in.

"We have a hit," she said by way of greeting. "There were a couple of those muscle relaxer poisonings in Tulsa about twelve years ago."

"Just the drug? No strangulation, no knife wounds to the neck? Nothing but the drug?"

"That's it and it may not be related, but the prime suspect in the case disappeared and has yet to be located."

"You sound more excited about this than the facts warrant, detective."

"That's because of one other salient fact, consultant."

"Please share, detective."

"The suspect was a pharmacist. A young pharmacist with terrific grades from the University of Tulsa. He was a full-ride scholarship student with an undergraduate degree in chemistry."

"Sounds like a real whiz-bang young feller. I suppose you now have a life history and know where his trail went cold?"

"You want it all now or should I spend some more time on this and give a better picture of the guy at the debrief?"

"I'll see you then."

"Oh, before I forget," she hesitated, "Puckett thinks Porter's employment at the Port Authority has something to do with her murder. What do you think?"

"I think Officer Puckett is catching on to this detective business pretty quickly, don't you?"

Cy Kriegsman stepped into the room, a broad grin creasing his face. "Angels, Mr. Delaney, angels bearing glad tidings of off-shore gifts, Cayman Islands gifts."

"Thank you, Cy. Can you take another look and see what law firm is representing those off-shore angels?"

"I already got that, Delaney. It's a local outfit – Aguilera Perkins Nathan and Bennett – and the attorney of record is one Camille Bennett."

19

A NARCISSIST, A PSYCHOPATH AND EVEN A MACHIAVELLIAN

Dreams From My Brother: Tuesday, May 6

Upon receiving this latest message from Cody, I was put in mind of lines from Blake:

> Did he who made the lamb make thee?
> Tyger! Tyger! Burning bright
> In the forests of the night ..

I think the message here is about how, in childhood, we create whom it is that we become as adults. Our hopes, fears, dreams, experiences and imaginings all tossed into a roiling mulligatawny stew of memory and emotion, out of which emerges our sense of identity, our self.

That self always has a dark side, a Tyger if you will. Most of us are able to keep it imprisoned deep enough within our psyche that we pose no real threat to our fellow human beings. For the psychopath we are hunting here in St. Paul, it's simpler. He has become the Tyger.

Then there are those, like the narrator of this dream, for whom it's more complicated. He is engaged in a perpetual struggle with his own dark side. and because he has come to know it so well, he intuitively understands the character and sensibilities of the psychopath.

That makes him an invaluable partner in our Tyger hunt:

Oh dear, I am going to sound so grandiose and pathetic and I know what you are going to think. As a practicing psychologist it might have been my first professional reaction, too. Except, you must understand, this was a real phenomenon that I experienced. It was as genuine and tangible as reality gets. Please don't dismiss it out of hand as a self-induced delusion.

The first time it happened I was a chubby little eight-year-old, who understood he was already a disappointment to his parents. A child with no brothers, sisters or friends. A child already alone and adrift in the world. Such a boy would be likely to create his own imaginary world, wouldn't he? One with himself as the centerpiece of a great drama, engaged in ever more heroic adventures?

The problem with that theory is that I had, and still have, a terrible paucity of imagination. I never had those narcissistic phantasies about myself. Nor did I ever have any religious inclinations up to that point. It wasn't until afterwards that I knew my vocation lay with the priesthood.

Oh my, I am about to reveal something to you that I have never shared with another soul and I am feeling quite trepidatious at the prospect of finally doing it.

So, very well, here is my story, the one that will tell you who I really am. As I said, I was just eight years old the first time it happened. I was alone in the apartment on that Saturday afternoon, absorbed in a book about western outlaws. Normal fare for a boy of that age, wouldn't you say? I felt a faint chill creep into the room and thought that was rather strange. Mother kept the place stiflingly hot. But it kept getting colder and as it did, the lights began to dim, and the darkness of the cloud-covered day started soaking up all the fading light in the room. I was prepared, at that point, to get a flashlight and blanket so I could continue reading. But then, as blackness enveloped the room, I heard a low rumbling growl, deeply resonant and insistent. I feared a tiger or wolf, or some other beast had made its way in.

As the rumble grew progressively louder it became something more akin to a howl. I felt myself quaking and unable to move. I was panic stricken and just wished that I might fall into some kind of unconscious state. But I couldn't. I was being held captive by dread as the howl and the darkness together filled the whole room.

Then, just as I thought my heart must burst, the universe fractured. My hair stood on end and my body was pulled in every direction. The world around me was spinning and things were falling apart. There was no center. The howl continued to grow, as if it must be orchestrating the chaos. Any sense of time was lost, and space was obliterated by the material destruction spiraling wildly around me.

Oh, my goodness. You must find this so . . . No, you want me to just continue? Well thank you, I will.

As I said, time had seemingly ceased to exist, but at some point the howl stopped and the universe reversed itself. Now I found myself encased, not in terror, but in an irresistible, overpowering sense of perfect love. It gave me such comfort and warmth. Now I was swaddled in a blanket of divine care and protection.

I was now possessed of an entity who would, in this moment, admit nothing into my psyche but itself. Indeed, I believed immediately that the power binding me was the same as that which created universes in a momentary thought. This experience of total immersion gave me, you see, a fleeting glimpse of a terrible, timeless, Creator and Destroyer.

As I felt myself being gradually released, I wondered what I should call the deity that had so blessed me and I heard, not in words mind you, but with a clarity that words can never achieve: I AM who I AM. With that phrase echoing in my brain, I slid back into this so-called reality, but with such an overwhelming feeling of relief and joy. I was at peace and nothing anyone could say or do could change it.

Tell me, do you think Moses might have been an alienated fat kid? I mean, I didn't know it at the time, but when he asked the burning bush who He was, God replied, "I AM who I AM." Basically telling Moses, and me, that it was impudent to even think such a question. He is who He is, and He does what He will do. Period.

Oh, good heavens, you must think me completely addle-brained. Comparing myself to Moses and describing an encounter with the Divine? Thank you for not laughing out loud.

It is, however, all true and it is why I became God crazed. Who wouldn't? After that encounter I saw God in everything – things as disparate as darkness and light, love and greed, fear and power. There was nothing anywhere that wasn't God. And so, naturally, I joined the Society of Jesus and entered seminary. How I gloried in the exercises of St. Ignatius. I was far more proud of the SJ after my name than the Ph.D.

But even as I prayed, meditated and studied, the reality of the world intruded, imposed itself. First came the awful realization that we live in a predatory world. Don't you find it strange that the fundamental nature of our loving God's creation requires that there be more death than life? It is a hard paradox to resolve, isn't it? I was able to do it by remembering that I AM who I AM means we lack the wisdom, the standing, if you please, to even question or understand such things.

Having practiced the exercises of St. Ignatius, however, I could not help but shudder at the fate of all those poor animals that, over all the millennia of this earth's existence, were victims of the predators that endlessly stalked them. All those innocents, all those weak, preyed-upon creatures. The fear, the terror, the sheer horror of being ripped to pieces by some monstrous tiger or wolf, to say nothing of human predators, with their meatpacking plants and the cruelty of cages and feed lots. Who made the tiger, indeed? Who created the ravenous hunger of the wolf? And worse, who made such indifferent human beings who could slaughter lambs without so much as a flinch of conscience? Now you know why I am a vegetarian.

You have probably already guessed that that's when the revelation came to me: Almighty God was exceedingly cruel and sadistic - A narcissist, a psychopath and even a Machiavellian, if you will. And so, I focused my studies in psychology on socio-psycho pathologies, the idea being that if I could understand these conditions, I could some- how draw close and once again be possessed by the Power and Holiness.

The Church, other than my poor bewildered confessor, was unaware of my unorthodox sense of the Divine, so it allowed me to work among the psychopaths at Leavenworth prison. My order, ever mindful of these things, felt that learning in this area could yield important scholarship and lead to new ministries.

I was actually quite happy among the crazed murderers of the federal penal system. The pure viciousness and utter lack of human empathy in these psychopaths had a certain admirable clarity about it. They were untroubled by doubt, stress, regret or conscience. They were all, without exception, unapologetic predators. I wondered if they, in their utter certainty about themselves, were also touched by the Holy Spirit.

Those happy days ended when Rome (Rome!) intervened and insisted I head up that deplorable "rehabilitation" program for sexually abusive priests. Oh, my. Me! How absurd. I, who had never had a sexual feeling in my life. I, who knew that no one got to pick his sexual orientation. I, who knew that these priests would not, and could not, be changed through the offices of The Church. But belief, faith, superstition - call it what you will – was immune to the pleadings of science.

Then there were those priests. Some of them were so penitent. Feeling intensely miserable about their "perversion," they had joined the priesthood believing it would remove them from temptation, give them a retreat and solace from a hostile world. But soon they learned the unhappy truth: they were living in the most fertile fields of enticement imaginable – surrounded by compliant young boys and girls. And in those days, who, really, would believe priests capable of succumbing to that kind of temptation? They were, after all, men of God, were they not? But their unholy desires overcame them. For many, their repentance was real. They mortified their flesh, wept, fasted, prayed and begged God's forgiveness. And wondered, always wondered, why had He created in them this horrible and insatiable urge – why had He cursed them so, weren't they created in His image, too?

You can see their dilemma, can't you? Think of how it would be if you lived in a world where your attraction to women was considered a "perversion." But then there were those other priests, the ones who felt no remorse for their predations, no pity for their victims; men who felt their remorseless hunger was a gift from God. Really, they were ravenous beasts, wolves who preyed upon defenseless lambs. Their confessions were pro forma and repentance was not in them. I hated them and hated that they would leave our "rehabilitation" program and return to tend to new, unsuspecting and vulnerable flocks, despite my desperate pleas that they be sent to a monastery.

That's when I finally left the order to live a more Christ-like life. I joined a traveling carnival. Living among the barkers, the thrill ride operators, food vendors, animal trainers, drivers and drudges gave me a new lease on life. It was quite wonderful; I found my place in the world.

I have always been interested in "trigger events;" the singular incident that pushes someone over the edge and is the precursor to their committing otherwise unthinkable acts. For me that occurred on the afternoon that one of those wolfish priests came through the carnival with a group of children in tow. I could see him for what he was, but I knew no one else could, except for one young lad in his entourage - a poor child with a vacant stare to his brown eyes, uninterested in any of the lights and noise around him. His victim, I thought, just as the priest saw me. His black eyes widened with fear as he saw the angry glare that I could not help directing at him. His evident fear inspired the idea. I would kill him, and if I were not apprehended, I would kill more and more of his monstrous brethren.

I was at the doorstep of his small rural rectory just a few weeks later, a pistol in my hand and my heart racing wildly. I was giddy with anticipation. When we got to his living room my breath started coming in great gulps. Have you ever felt like that? I had never before had this feeling of power and joy. Believe me, when you, and you alone, have the authority to declare life or death, you feel like a god.

That priest, did he want last rites? I was prepared to administer them, if he liked. No, his death was not negotiable. A snap, a snarl, a challenge: who the hell did I think I was? What gave me the right? He became grotesque with indignation, but got on his knees when I waved the gun and told him to get down. How my heart was pounding! My breathing came in shallow and quick bursts and I was crazy with power and the knowledge of what was coming in just a few short seconds. The hard, cold metal in my hand, the sweat coursing off his face, the dread spreading in his eyes. He was becoming more wild-eyed and more desperate with each passing second. I could see it and feel it in the air – his terror. It froze him in place and had the odor of feces and urine. I smiled, almost laughed.

Then, the shot. As the howl of it drowned out everything around me, I felt the all-powerful, all-absorbing Presence enfolding me once again. It was a rapturous reunion. My whole being trembled and collapsed with ecstasy, just as it had decades ago. After all those barren years, I was once again cloaked in the ineffable purity of the wondrous I AM. I felt again its marvelous intensity as it spoke, but not with words, "Well done thou good and faithful servant." And with that I knew perfect peace once again.

I also knew that I had been given a mission and purpose for this life. I was now the chosen instrument to avenge the preyed-upon and to prey upon the predators. It was now my vocation, my calling, to bring soul-freezing fear and horror down upon these predators. I lived that commitment fully, just as the Spirit directed. Of course, being possessed by the I AM every time I destroyed another one of those evildoers filled me with joy that was beyond bliss and fulfillment that was total,

But it was not long before I knew that one day I would have to be incarcerated. You see, even though I felt such profound purpose and serenity in my new vocation, guilt, in the form of a still, small voice, would not let me go on. This voice was a quiet one, but insistent. I knew it would never stop and it has been with me every day, every minute, of my life, for so long as I pursued my beloved vocation.

Now, you see, those moments of joy and power are gone, and I know full well that I will never again, in this life, feel the thrill that only the embrace of Holiness can give. Once He said, "Well done, thou good and faithful servant." Today and for every day to come, I will hear or feel nothing of the great I AM. Every day I will be reduced to feeling as lonesome and adrift as I was as an eight-year-old child.

You are able to understand what a sacrifice I made, aren't you? You can see, can't you, that I gave up absolute happiness? Sometimes I wonder, will I ever be given the opportunity to feel it again? I know there will be times, in the long hours of the night, when it will become an obsession and I will pray with great fervor that I might once again be imprisoned by the wonderful horror of the great I AM.

And that still, small voice? Even now it is as insistent as ever, but offers no comfort or joy.

WEDNESDAY

. . . .we are living in one of a vast number of universes.

—*Alan Lightman*

Whatever you dream be aware that it is just a dream.
Yet, since there are infinite parallel universes, whatever you
dream must be real somewhere in the multiverse. And if it is
real, no matter where, then it is not a dream anymore.

—*Franco Santoro*

I urge you all, fervently I urge you, to state unto the universe,
unto the multiverse: I AM, I AM, I AM! I am life. I am God.

—*St. Germain*

I am"... I cried/ I am"... said I
And I am lost, and I can't/ Even say why

—*Neil Diamond*

20

THE WAY OF THE WORLD

Injustice is the way of the world. Delaney believed that and accepted it, but not with total resignation. He was grateful for those occasions when he could engage in a struggle to balance the scales. The Riverrun case was starting to smell like of one of those rare opportunities.

It was 7 a.m. and Mel Thorogood was moving to the whiteboard to review all that his team and the rest of the St. Paul PD had brought in over the last thirty-six hours. The mood of this meeting was decidedly more comfortable. The actors now knew each other. They were all feeling a little more comfortable in Delaney's offices. Gunnar Olafsson was not in attendance.

"I can tell you," Thorogood began, "That the FBI reports 234 murders involving mutilation of the throat over the past ten years. They're spread all over the map, with one having occurred in Minnesota, one in Iowa, two in the Dakotas, and five in Wisconsin. California led the nation, but none of these cases rose to the level of creativity we have with our first three victims. Beheadings are still rare. Ours is apparently the first one done in over five years. No previous cases anywhere in the country involve an apple or business card.

"There are no instances of homicides with the neck mutilations we've encountered, and none had any kind of an apple motif. Finally, there were two unsolved murders featuring an unusual poison substance, both in Tulsa, Oklahoma. Dalton, give us an update on the poison?"

Gettler, uncomfortable with any kind of public presentation, began with, "It appears that a proximate, if not determinative, cause of death for our first three victims may have been some kind of a rocuronium substance."

Thorogood raised his eyebrows. "English, please, Dalton."

"Yes, I was getting to that. Rocuronium is a muscle relaxant, not a poison. Of course, when we use a term like poison, we have to be a little bit careful. Nicotine is a terribly potent poison, but we usually don't think of it that way. You see, when we say poison, we usually . . . "

"Dalton, to the point. please."

"Uh, OK, yes. You see, rocuronium is a pharmaceutical agent, one that doesn't affect the nervous system and has been used extensively to relax patients undergoing surgery. Also, uhm, it has often been used as part of the cocktail for lethal injections. For executions. In death penalty cases, that is."

Already knowing the answer, Delaney asked anyway, "So it is an anesthetic?"

"No. No, not quite. You see, while it relaxes one's muscles, one is still fully aware of one's surroundings and can still feel pain. Anesthetics must still be used to deaden the pain."

It was O'Leary this time. "So, you mean to tell me they were alive and knew what was happening to them when they were killed?"

"Well, it is almost certain that the first two of them would have been able to see and hear the killer as he moved in and began to, uhm, kill them. Detective Fortuno, despite the nature of his wounds, may have died the same way. I would think it might have been quite terrifying and painful, although the victims would, to all outward appearances, appear blissfully calm, even serene. Of course, I guess that is how they looked, isn't it?"

"We've got a deep-down, unholy sadist running loose in this city," Thorogood muttered.

Gettler continued, "Ms. Martin, on the other hand, may present another kind of problem. You see, well, " he glanced nervously around the room, "it appears she may have died some time ago. Her head shows signs of having been refrigerated. For how long, I can't say yet. That and her bruises and wounds from a severe beating indicate the circumstances of her death were quite different from our first three. What we do know for certain is that she had no rocuronium in her system at the time of her death."

"That," Thorogood interjected, "and a profile we had done convinced me that Martin's death was at the hands of a second perpetrator. So, we will continue to focus our attention on our original three victims. The Martin case has been assigned to other detectives."

Delaney, hoping to quickly get the discussion off Karleen Martin, turned to Gettler. "You said it was a form of rocuronium. What do you know about the specific drug?"

Gettler hesitated, choosing his words carefully. "I have started to match it against the agents most commonly used in surgical procedures, but so far it, well, it appears to be somewhat different in its molecular structure."

"Dalton, just get on with it, please." Thorogood was impatient.

"Normally, this agent acts quickly, but this altered substance would have an almost immediate effect. It appears the killer may have used a singular rocuronium pharmaceutical agent. I mean one that is not in any pharmaceutical formulary."

Delaney jumped in before Thorogood could react. "You mean it's unique, there's nothing else like it in the world. It's a substance that, up till now, has not been seen?"

"Yes, yes, I believe so. It is really quite a feat of chemical engineering. I think whoever designed this drug must be quite brilliant. Or lucky."

It was Puckett's turn. "What do you mean, lucky?"

"Well, what makes this drug different, is that it appears capable of completely relaxing someone in less than thirty seconds, unlike other muscle relaxant drugs, and would take up to five or six hours before eventually, uh, suffocating them. It could be that the chemist just stumbled upon this while trying to do something else, but that's just speculation on my part. We don't yet know how it was administered, whether by inhalation, ingestion or injection, but we should be able to determine that in the next day or so.

"If the chemist was trying to design a drug to act in just this manner, well, he would be, as I said, quite brilliant."

"Great." The Assistant Chief drew the word out as if it had two syllables. "Anything else, Dalton?"

"Not yet, but I am doing a national survey to see if other crime labs have seen this substance."

"Detective O'Leary, why don't you take it from here? Do you two have any good news?"

"Yes, Assistant Chief, indeed we do," said O'Leary. "We have finished our examination of the St. Paul Police Department files and are able to report to you that none of these personnel are brilliant chemists. Although within the force there certainly are some sadists. We finished reviewing those files and neither of us saw anything out of the ordinary. If anyone in the Department was involved, there's nothing in their files to lead us to them."

"There is one other thing you should be aware of, if no one's told you yet," Puckett joined in. "The three bodies were all oriented on a north-south axis, so we're developing a theory that these may have been ritual killings. What Dalton just said about this poison seems to lend credence to this idea. It may have something to do with old Norse Viking ceremonies."

O'Leary continued, "The chief suspect in the Tulsa cases was a young and apparently brilliant pharmacist who disappeared shortly after the second killing. He just vanished and they have no lead on where he may have gone. Then there's a case in Kansas City. The victim had ingested some kind of muscle relaxant, a rather weak strain as it turns out, and he doesn't show up in the statistics because he didn't die. He snorted the stuff mixed with coke. He said he didn't know the coke was diluted and wouldn't say who he got it from. We're asking our friends in the KC department to talk with him again. We also believe that cocaine use in this country would fall dramatically if this particular mixture were more widely distributed."

"Thank you for that strategic insight, Detective. Anything else?"

Puckett languidly raised her hand. "At the risk of stating the too obvious, would this case indicate our victims may have snorted their designer drug, as well?" She looked at Gettler.

Gettler nodded slowly and noted that, "Given the absence of needle marks or evidence of oral ingestion, that's a fair assumption. Please note I said no *evidence* of oral ingestion. They could have taken it that way and it was just digested by the time we looked at their gut."

"Thank you, Dalton." It was Puckett again. She gave him an outrageously flirtatious smile and said, "Could they have thought they were snorting coke? We know that Fortuno liked the stuff, what about the other two?"

"Well, what about them, Detective?" the Assistant Chief demanded.

She looked sheepish. "We'll have to get back to you on that, Chief."

"Just one other thing, Chief," O'Leary said. "We think the chances are good the Kansas City perp has moved here and he's our guy."

"I would agree with that," Gettler interjected. "The technicians in Kansas City said the strain of rocuronium found in their victim, while it has a slightly different molecular structure from what we have, is also something they've never seen before or since. I've put out a bulletin to labs around the country to see if anyone else has found anything like this, but so far nothing."

"I wouldn't call it nothing, Dalton," Thorogood said. "If we can narrow the suspects down to someone in KC, as well as Tulsa, we'll be in pretty good shape. By the way, O'Leary, do we have a photo of the Tulsa pharmacist?"

"Yes, but the picture itself is not real helpful. It's from his high school yearbook and it's his freshman year. However, there is something that goes with the picture that kind of confirms that this kid is our Riverrun freak." O'Leary sat back and smiled broadly.

At Thorogood's scowl, she quickly continued, "You know how in high school yearbooks the kids often have some kind of motto or favorite saying? Adam Bierce's favorite was, 'Tyger, Tyger, burning bright, in the forests of the night.' That's a line from a poem."

"William Blake," Puckett added.

"Given our guy's preference for a tiger's claw as his murder weapon," O'Leary concluded, "We think this is a pretty strong clue that he's our man."

Thorogood paused for a few seconds before responding. "It doesn't confirm that he's the Riverrun killer, but it is an indicator, isn't it? Nice work, you two. Now, what about that photo?"

"Chief, we ran it through our facial recognition program but there's nothing on the guy in the system. Here's copies for all of you of his high school photo. I've got the sketch artist down the hall. She's done a couple of computerized updates, but they're not going to be real reliable."

The high school photo showed a thin, smiling kid with a light mop of hair falling over his forehead and ears. He had a kind of intense and confident look rare in kids that age. The caption said Adam Bierce and the unspoken question was in the air: how did he become their sadistic killer? Delaney wondered what stories the kid had since invented about himself in order to hide his real self.

Just then Marguerite opened the door and let in the sketch artist. She dropped a sheaf of papers on the table. "Good morning, everyone." she said, addressing the group. "For those of you I have not met, I'm Georgia Kane and I'm the department's sketch artist. And here are some sketches. I ran that photo through the computer programs, and I did some sketches too. You know, this is a hit or miss proposition. If this guy is in hiding, he's probably dyed his hair, could be bald by now, maybe has whiskers, maybe even had plastic surgery. And he'll have put on weight and, well, who knows what all. What O'Leary has are three different sketches that I hope give you some bare notion of how he could look now. Any questions?"

Thorogood frowned. "Sit. Sit until we've had a chance to look at these." The sketches were all of a middle-aged man without the kid's smile. The differences in the three drawings all had to do with how much heavier he might be, where his hairline could be and, in one, how he might look with whiskers. On each page there was a frontal and side perspective.

Delaney had to ask, "In all these you seem to make the assumption that he would be aging and filling out like your average American male. But to me, this kid looks a bit feminine and I'm wondering if you could do another sketch to emphasize that quality?"

"Oh, good idea. You mean, he stays thin and is, uhm, no offense here, but gay like?"

"Let's just think of him as a single guy concerned with his appearance, and a bit effeminate."

"I can do that, but can I ask why?"

"You may not, sorry. Information on this case has to remain closely held. How soon before you can get this for us?"

"Ten minutes be OK?"

As she walked out, Thorogood turned to Delaney. "I can ask why."

"Two things. First, look at him. He's small, slight and that grin is positively girlish. Second, we think he knew Graham Byrd and, while Mr. Byrd undoubtedly had lots of straight acquaintances, there's always the possibility that his killer was gay and that he knew him. The place and times of the murders may also indicate the killer is either gay or homophobic."

"I'm not liking this at all," O'Leary interjected, "but I have to admit it does have some plausibility."

"It's just another avenue to explore that might narrow our list of suspects. Mel, do any of these sketches look like anyone in the department?"

"A couple, maybe . . . but no, the resemblances are too distant." Thorogood asked what O'Leary and Puckett thought. Both found any possible resemblances far-fetched.

The sketch artist came back with fresh copies and asked if this was what Delaney was looking for. Now the face was slightly elongated, but otherwise kept the same features, with large eyes, a full head of hair and a dimpled smile. Delaney was not the only one who found that last touch a bit exaggerated from the high school photo, but no one commented on it.

Thorogood looked around the room. "Can we excuse Georgia O'Keefe for now, or do we need her to do up the guy as a cowboy, construction worker and fireman, too?"

It was too much for O'Leary. "Chief, we had no idea you were a fan."

He gave her a two-second stare before turning to Delaney. "You have some things to report?"

With one eye still on the sketch, Delaney said, "Officer Puckett, you remember yesterday you said Porter's job at the Port Authority might have something to do with her murder? What led you to that conclusion?"

"Not so much a conclusion as a speculation. The Port Authority has gotten so big in the last five years. It's controversial and has pissed off a lot of community groups. It's really tearing up some old neighborhoods and displacing a lot of people out of their homes. The stuff Nate Muhammad's group is coming up with is probably just the tip of the iceberg. I just think that, given her position there, it's worth looking into."

"You have great instincts, officer. In fact, the economic models we've developed in this office indicate that the Port Authority is headed for financial disaster. The only reason it hasn't fallen yet is that there is an angel, or flock of angels, buying its bonds at strategic times. Of particular interest to us is the bank through which those purchases are made. It's Pinnacle City Bank and Trust of St. Paul, whose president is Jacob Berkeland, the half-brother of our own Dr. Thor Gunnar Olafsson."

"No shit?" Thorogood looked as puzzled as everyone else. "But what, if anything, does this have to do with our murders? And are you somehow implicating Gunnar?"

"Not yet, but we do know that, after our first meeting, he made a beeline to his brother's bank." Delaney couldn't tell them about the urgent phone call Olafsson made. It would have raised too many uncomfortable questions, uncomfortable for Delaney.

"But let's set Gunnar aside for now. The more suspicious matter is the source of the money used to purchase the bonds. Some of it came from offshore accounts in the Cayman Islands and Bermuda. But many of the purchases were made with cash."

"I'm in over my head here," Thorogood was still frowning, "and I'm glad we've got your financial expertise to help on this, but is there a problem with cash?" Then he paused, the idea bulb flashing behind his eyes. "Somebody's laundering money, aren't they? And Porter knew about it, maybe was part of it, or was going to blow the whistle on it? Drug dollars, maybe counterfeit?"

"Given that Port Authority bonds are denominated, at their lowest levels, at $50,000, I'd say you've made a pretty good guess."

Puckett was exuberant. "This is so great! Do you guys get to do this stuff all the time? Pulling down the power! What could be better?"

Even Thorogood was smiling as O'Leary put a restraining hand on Puckett's forearm. "No, dear, we never get to pull down the power and remember, our job is to catch a killer, not bring down the Port Authority."

Delaney used that as his segue. "I think the two may be linked. And my guys think they may be able to track down the sources of the funds. We should have that sometime in the next couple of days. I can't guarantee this will lead to our killer, but I have a feeling it will.

"Keep in mind that before coming to the Port Authority, Suzanne Porter was working for an escort agency in Milwaukee. There is something mightily suspicious about her suddenly moving into her St. Paul position. She was put there either by an inordinately successful social worker or some darker figure working an angle."

"Wait a minute." O'Leary was stunned. "How do you know that and why weren't we told?"

"Sorry, O'Leary. I'm getting ahead of myself. I only just found out about it." Delaney gave them the run-down on what Shem had uncovered about the first three victims, their rendezvous in Milwaukee and subsequent contacts in St. Paul.

"So, we really are dealing with a killer who targeted these individuals and not a serial killer who's picking random victims," Thorogood said. "If that's the case I have to admit to feeling a sense of relief.

"As for our three victims being linked and targeted by the killer, well, that's what it looks like," Delaney answered. "And we have definite connections to the Port Authority with Byrd and Porter, but none so far with Fortuno. What we have found out is that Fortuno was in up to his eyeballs with three loan sharks. I met with them last night and found out he was desperate to get a nut for a hot 'investment.' Somehow, I have to believe this has something to do with a Port Authority development project or bond issue. But that's just a hunch on my part. My people are looking into it."

Thorogood chuckled. "You met with them?"

"At Mackey's."

Thorogood laughed, but O'Leary and Puckett's puzzled expressions were tinged with a hint of anger. O'Leary spat out, "What's this about meeting with Mackey and loan sharks? Aren't they the people we usually try to put away?" She shook her head, "Mackey . . ."

Thorogood looked at his two detectives and said, "Look, one of the reasons Delaney is on this case is that he has access to some unsavory people who can maybe help us. You know how that goes, don't you, Detectives? O'Leary, how many street-level drug-dealing confidential informants do you have? Delaney's contacts just happen to be at a higher level. Any problem with that?" When neither detective raised an objection, he turned again to Gettler. "Dalton, anything else?"

When he shook his head, Thorogood spoke in a quieter voice, "O'Leary and Puckett, keep on the Adam Bierce trail; Dalton, continue pursuing the drug angle and see if any cases turn up where there are neck mutilations as well. Conor," he looked at Delaney, "you want to start?"

Delaney, joined by Thorogood, reviewed their earlier meeting and subsequent call from McArdle to Eric Schmidt, Special Agent in Charge of the local office of the FBI. Thorogood was cautious. "We don't think the Russians have anything to do with our case, except for one thing. Conor?"

"How many of you have heard of the Shock Doctrine?"

The door flew open and Marguerite called in, "Conor, now! Something horrible has happened."

21

TYGER, TYGER, BURNING BRIGHT

Missy Skarda liked nerds. Geeky and brainy, that's how she liked her men, and no one fit the mold better than Shaun Neary. She spotted him on her first day as Delphi's new receptionist, just a month ago. Two weeks ago, they began carrying on a light flirtation. A glance, a wink, an occasional laugh over coffee or lunch. Oh, he liked her all right, she thought. No one missed that.

Missy knew that it would proceed beyond its current stage, it was just a matter of time. She had his attention and in little ways let him know of her interest. She had lots of questions about her computer's programs that he, and only he, would be allowed to answer. She plied him with questions, questions about the Large Hadron Collider, artificial intelligence and string theory. At every opportunity she briefly touched his arm, hand or shoulder. And he, in his own awkward way, signaled his interest. Taking too much time to answer a question about a non-existent problem with her computer, trying to carry on a conversation without falling into geek-speak, laughing too energetically at her lame jokes.

The real glitch in their budding romance was one of those qualities that Missy so admired in a nerdy man; Shaun was shy and doubly so with a woman to whom he found himself attracted.

It was Wednesday morning when Missy, just turning up another floor in the building's parking ramp, saw the door of the black SUV swing open. A body was hurriedly pushed out and the SUV squealed away. Missy quickly drove up and jumped out of her car. She was horrified to see that it was Shaun sprawled on the concrete. But she didn't scream until she saw his throat.

By the time Kyle Lilly carried him up to the office, a small crowd was gathered, joined almost immediately by Delaney, Thorogood and the others. Thorogood called for the paramedics from Phelan Hospital as soon as he glimpsed Shaun's limp body.

A verse was typed out on a page pinned to Shaun's shirt. It read,

> Tyger, Tyger has a hungry maw,
> And needs to exercise his claw.
> What immortal god of symmetry,
> Brought this throbbing neck to me?

After tearing it off, Delaney had everyone move back to their offices except Missy, Shem, Kyle and Marguerite.

"Marguerite, Kyle, you have us in lockdown?" Lockdown meant no one could get onto the floor unless someone in the office turned off the electronic locks in the elevators and the three doors that led to exit stairs. When they nodded, he turned and, after a glance at Thorogood, said, "Missy, would you wait for me in my office, please? I need to get as much detail from you as I can."

The paramedics were hurried through lockdown and the first one through the door gasped, "Whoa, what's this?"

Thorogood was quick, "Be sure to have them check for the poison immediately."

As they were loading Shaun onto the gurney, the paramedic replied, "They've got the test ready and have antidotes."

As they wheeled him out, Delaney looked at Shaun's neck again and marveled at the artistry of the thing. Shaun's new tattoo was a colorful rendering of an open and torn throat, complete with green apple.

"Nice to have a poison center so close, isn't it?" Thorogood said quietly.

Delaney nodded. Phelan Hospital was as famous for its poison control center as it was for its burn unit. He stepped away from Thorogood and the others, motioning Kyle Lilly to join him. "How soon can you get the plane ready?"

"Hour, hour and a half."

"Do it. Plan for an overnight. Get flight plans ready for Tulsa and from there to Kansas City and home. Call right away if there are any delays. Otherwise, I'll see you at the airport shortly."

Turning back to Thorogood, Delaney smiled. "The tattoo, the use of that drug again; I think we just received confirmation that Adam Bierce is our man and that someone else killed Karleen Martin.

Looking to Marguerite he continued, "Would you please get the parking ramp tapes ready for the detectives? Then I'd like you to go to the hospital and stay with Shaun." She nodded at O'Leary and Puckett, "It'll only take a minute. Right this way. It's easy to operate."

To Shem Delaney said, "I know you want to go to the hospital, but we need you here to help find out who did this."

Delaney went to his office and shut the door. "Missy, have you ever been hypnotized?"

She shook her head. "No, but if it will help..."

"Good. There's nothing to worry about. It will simply help you to remember details you might otherwise have forgotten that may be locked away in your subconscious. Give me your hand?" Delaney took her right hand in his and covered it with his left as his voice fell into a low and easy cadence. Missy found herself relaxing and later apologized to Delaney for having fallen asleep and wishing she could have been of more help. He told her she was welcome to spend the rest of the day with Marguerite at the hospital.

Within the hour the word came in that Shaun was safe, the poison control center had the right antidote for rocuronium. She wondered aloud, though, who would want to do such a thing to someone like Shaun, a mere slip of a boy who posed no danger to anyone? Delaney would tell her, and the rest of the staff later that Shaun wasn't the real target and that each of them would now be given a twenty-four-hour security detail.

Missy wondered if that meant there would be two security details at Shaun's room because that's where she planned to stay until he was released.

22

HOMELAND SECURITY

"We're the ones who decide what's a matter of national security and what's not."

"And, as you may know, we're the ones who are responsible for the safety of the citizens of the City of St. Paul," Homer McArdle rejoined with a grin only barely suppressed. The meeting may have been a serious one, but that wasn't going to spoil his fun.

"*Special* Agent Dee-Wayne Hanson of the Federal Bureau of Investigation, let me introduce *Special* Assistant Chief Melvin Thorogood of the St. Paul Police Department and *Special* Consulting Investigator Conor Delaney. I do believe he is known to your boss, having pulled his ass fat from the fire a time or two?"

Hanson extended his hand. "Mr. Delaney, good to see you again. Chief Thorogood, I've heard good things about you."

The Prankster McArdle shifted in his chair and with his one eye looked askance at Hanson. "Do they teach you that kissy-ass stuff at Quantico or is it just your natural inclination? You've heard good things about Thorogood? Sure you have. And gentlemen, this other fellow here is Mr. Arnold Rakovitch, straight from the Federal Department of Homeland Security."

The man introduced by the still smirking chief sighed. "Arne Ratkovic, gentlemen, and I'm pleased to meet you. You're wondering why we're here?"

"You came to tell us we won an award for being the finest force in the land? Which we are, you know." The Chief of Police was having a good time.

Duane Hanson said brusquely, "Can we stay on business please?" He sat in a slouch, hooded eyes glaring at McArdle. Delaney and Thorogood were unhappy with being ordered to McArdle's office less than an hour after the assault on Shaun Neary and with the growing suspicion that the FBI might now make their case a Homeland Security matter.

"Would you like to explain to these gentlemen what Your Specialness is doing here and will you please sit up a little straighter? You look like you're either gonna fall asleep or strike." The last comment was a not-at-all-veiled allusion to Hanson's nickname within the Bureau: Snake Eyes.

Delaney wondered if the nickname came from the way the man's upper eyelids drooped or from Hanson's barely disguised hostility toward the rest of humanity. Delaney had met him briefly once in the Bureau offices. Just long enough to have been introduced and exchange a handshake. The man's hand was as cold then as it was today.

Hanson snapped, "We have reason to believe that this series of killings is tied to grave and extensive matters of national security. I would therefore direct you to immediately turn all your files over to the FBI and to share with me any information you have relevant to these murders."

"Whoa," Thorogood barked, "what 'grave and extensive matters of national security' are we talking about here?"

"You know I can't reveal that, Mr. Thorogood. It's classified and on a need-to-know basis only."

"What he means," McArdle's voice now had an edge to it, "is that less than twenty-four hours after us local Keystone Kops notified the FBI of the presence of some high-level Russian gangsters in our fair city – Russians they should have already had under surveillance – less than twenty-four hours later they are using said Russians as an excuse to take over a strictly local, but high-profile case, that has absolutely nothing to do with the Russian tourists.

"He means to tell us, gentlemen, that we have a national security emergency going on, right here in River City, but us first responder Mayberry cops are not sophisticated enough to even be told about it, much less assist in helping deal with it. That about right, Arnold?"

"That's hardly fair, Chief. You know that where national security is involved, information is on a need-to-know basis and the fewer the people in the loop, the better the chances of critical secrets staying secret."

"Horse pucky," McArdle snapped back. "You think you're going to be able to finally nail Mackey and you want to keep us out of the loop because you think there are elements in this fine, nationally recognized police department, that have been compromised and support Mackey in his evil-doing ways. National security." His one eye glared at Hanson and Ratkovic. "You guys are just obsessed with putting a small-time operator out of business when you should be concentrating on these Russian invaders. They're the real national security threat."

When McArdle's broadside was met by silence from the two feds, Delaney squinted and licked his lips before addressing Hanson. "You're a Utah guy, aren't you?"

Hanson flushed. "My state of origin has nothing to do with this. Or my religion either."

Delaney smiled. "But your bureau chief isn't from Utah, is he? And who said anything about religion?"

"There are people," Hanson said as he looked at each of them, "who have an anti-Mormon bias. Not that I'm accusing any of you of that, Mr. Delaney. But no, the chief is not from Utah."

"Then my question is a simple one. If this is such a big deal, why did he assign such an inexperienced and low-ranking agent to handle this case? No offense, but you haven't exactly made your rep as a crime fighter yet, have you?"

It was Ratkovic who intervened: "I specifically requested that Agent Hanson be assigned to this case."

McArdle: "Oh, I get it. You thought he could just charm the pants off us and we'd hand over our files. You went for charm over experience or competence."

"It so happens," Ratkovic continued, "that agent Hanson has some special training and expertise that we feel are essential in handling this matter. We believe he brings a blend of expertise and competence to this arena."

McArdle's eyebrows shot up. "Oooh, I see. *Expertise* and, what did you say? *Competence?*"

"Mr. Hanson has a Ph.D. in accounting from Purdue University." It was Delaney offering the agent's bona fides.

"Accounting?" McArdle blurted.

"What does financial expertise have to do with the Riverrun cases?" Delaney asked, watching their reactions. He expected them to cite the presence of Marta Voronova as their reason for needing Hanson's fiscal and monetary know-how, but was disappointed when Ratkovic replied.

"I'm afraid we can't tell you that. It's classified."

"That's it, gents." The rictus smile was now gone from McArdle's face. "When you play the classified card, the game changes. We're the fucking first responders, remember? Does your boss even know you're here, Hanson? You guys come back with a federal warrant and we can talk business. Before that, stay the fuck outta here. Hanson, next time I see you here, I'm calling Schmidt. I don't think he wants to hear from me, do you?"

Snake Eyes was silent, but the Rat wasn't. "I can't tell you how disappointed I am that you feel this way, Chief. You can expect to hear from us again very soon," he said as he stood up to leave.

Delaney waited until both men were at the door before asking, "Aren't you going to tell us what the connection is between our string of murders and the Russian mob?"

"As I said before . . ."

McArdle cut Ratkovic off, "Yeah, we know, it's classified."

As soon as the door closed McArdle turned on Delaney: "Why did you ask them about a tie between our cases and the Russians? They're not supposed to know we are even thinking about some sort of connection."

"They already knew it, Chief. Neither of them so much as raised an eyebrow when I said it. You've got a leak in this department. They already knew it and so did Mackey. Speaking of whom, I think you're right, they see these cases as the avenue that will finally get them to him. Hard to figure out why else they'd be interested in cases that so clearly don't involve national security."

McArdle stepped over to the office door, opened it, shouted, "Megan," and returned to his seat.

If anything, thought Delaney as Megan Hartley walked into the Chief's office, she seemed even more aloof and frosty than in their previous meeting. McArdle started as soon as she came into the room, "Megan, me darlin', did you see those fellows that just left? You did? Wonderful. You know they are feds, don't you?"

When she gave him a cursory nod, he continued, "I want to see something done on the great cooperation we have between the St. Paul Police Department and the local office of the Federal Bureau of Investigations. You know your counterpart over at the Fibbies office pretty well, don't you? Can you give him a call and see if the two of you can't put together a nice sort of press package for our local news media? They'll love it, won't they?"

Hartley was visibly startled by the notoriously uncooperative Chief's request. She hesitated a moment and said, "Yes, as you know, I do know Walt Moran 'pretty well.' I will be glad to work with him on a press package for the local media. Anything else?"

Now McArdle's voice took on a more aggressive tone, "That's quite enough, isn't it Megan? Get that done and I will be happy as a clam."

"It explains a lot, doesn't it?" McArdle spat when she left the room. "She's their mole in the department. Knows Walt Moran *pretty well*. She should know him fuckin' well, she's been shacked up with him for the last three months."

Delaney thought McArdle was too quick in tabbing Hartley as the mole. She could not have picked up any information from their earlier gathering at Delphi and passed it on to the FBI that quickly. It had to be someone who was in the meeting.

When McArdle paused, Thorogood broke in, "But she is not spying for Mackey."

"Of course not, and when I find the bastard who is he'll wish he'd never been born." Delaney and Thorogood both understood this to be an empty threat. Mackey clearly had more than one informant in the Department and McArdle himself talked with Mackey on a semi-regular basis.

"Maybe he's the same guy who took your phone," McArdle said softly to Thorogood. To Delaney he said, "Copies of all the files are in your office computers? Good.

"Mel, I'd like a confidential memo outlining everything we've found out, and any suspicions you have, so far. Can you do that?"

"Sure, Chief, but is that a good idea? I mean, if we're turning over the case..."

McArdle stopped him. "Look, they just pissed me off and I had to yank their chain. I'm going to call Schmidt in a couple of minutes and have him tell those boys to forget about getting their little writ from a judge. I'll turn over all the stuff they want and you two should cooperate with their investigation. It won't hurt to have their help, especially if those Russian bastards are involved.

"And, by the bye, boyos," the chief paused for a split second, "what's the accounting angle on this?"

23

RU = < >

They were both finishing brief phone conversations. Delaney was talking with Kyle Lilly who was at Holman Field, St. Paul's airport for jets and other private aircraft. Thorogood was on the line to his counterpart in Kansas City.

As he put his phone away Thorogood said, "He remembers the case, also wants to help. Apparently it has stuck in their craw. He can pull the victim in and have him waiting for you whenever you arrive. The guy is a street dealer and a long-time CI."

Delaney said that Kyle and the plane would soon be ready to leave Holman Field. He thought he could interview the right people in Tulsa and Kansas City and be back in time for the morning debriefing session on Friday. "If I'm lucky we'll know more about Adam Bierce forty-eight hours from now."

Thorogood smiled at that. On the surface it looked like luck, or something very like it, was part of Delaney's genetic make-up. He first noticed it when they were in college. Whenever Delaney played poker with other students, he always won; well, no, that wasn't quite right. He did lose once in a while and at other times it looked to Thorogood as if he strategically lost so as to not be too obvious in his winnings. Luck, as Thorogood observed, may have had something to do with it, but there was more. When the two of them were grad students in DC and took a trip to Atlantic City he became convinced of it. Thorogood watched as Delaney played cards and won moderately; moderately at six different casinos.

His take for those two nights was well over $100,000. That's where Thorogood caught on to Delaney's penchant for reading other people.

At the Atlantic City casinos Thorogood studied Delaney as his grey owl eyes flowed over each opponent, performing a subtle examination of each of them without ever catching their eye or by any outward gesture seeming to give them any kind of extraordinary attention. It was at their third casino that Thorogood saw that, after just a few hands, Delaney seemed to know most of the other players' tells. When he asked Delaney about it later that evening, his friend was evasive, claiming that he was just lucky that night.

"That," Thorogood said, "is bullshit. What's really going on?"

Delaney grinned. "Kinesics. You can look it up. You know that old saw about 'You can only play the hand you're dealt?' I play the hands the other players have. With another five years of practice, I should make what I'm doing on this trip look trivial."

Thorogood knew Delaney now flew off to Monaco and Macao every year to win big and bolster his firm's bottom line.

Every cop on the St. Paul force was trained in the practice of reading body language. But Delaney went far beyond that. In an interview or interrogation, he seemed able to draw meaning out of every movement, every statement, a person might make. And in that setting, he could also, at one point, be deeply empathic and at another, utterly alienating.

Thorogood thought the man's intense focus on reading people was almost mystical. When he asked Delaney about it last year, his friend laughed and said that he did nothing that any other man or woman couldn't do after ten or fifteen years of concentrated study and practice. He laughed again when Thorogood accused him of being a closeted Buddhist monk.

So it was that Thorogood was convinced that Delaney's flight to Oklahoma and Kansas City would be worth the expenditure of time and resources. "Just a little curiosity question, though," he said. "What *exactly* do you expect to achieve from this quick little hopscotch around the country?"

Delaney glanced out his office window at the clouds beginning to crowd out the noon-day sun. "We need to learn more about Adam Bierce and I don't think we can do that without talking with people who actually knew him, who dealt with him face to face. Right now, we know only that he's a smart psychopath, has a morbid sense of humor, may have a connection to the Port Authority, may have one or more plants in this department and is likely to kill again. We know he started in Tulsa and Kansas City. Were those random acts of cruelty or did they, seemingly like our murders, have a purpose? Let me talk to his mother, people who knew him, the local police and the victim in KC, and, with a little bit of luck, I'll come back with something tangible. Worst case scenario, we'll know more than we do now."

He stopped for a moment, staring out the window again. "I'm only pausing because of what Phil said about the possibility of this guy strewing the landscape with red herrings. We are building our whole case on the premise. . ."

The interruption came from Shem entering the office. "Don't know if it's important but, that tattoo? At a three-point magnification you can see this on the apple." He handed them a scrawled note with the inscription, *RU* = < >.

Thorogood squinted at the note. "It looks like the formula for the classical Greek notion of *agon*, 'Are you equal to, lesser than, or greater than, me?' It's the inherent challenge between any two bodies when they meet. This came from the tattoo on Shaun's neck?" Delaney watched his friend's eyes narrow. "Is that message for you, Conor, or for all of us?"

"I don't know, but I better get going. It's all set in Tulsa?"

Thorogood, still troubled, nodded. "Yeah, and the Tulsa PD will have somebody waiting for you at the airport. If there are any hang-ups with KC I'll let you know. Hope you find something. Coming back with nothing will not be good for morale or McArdle's disposition."

"He'll just be happy that I'm paying for it."

"One other thing, Boss," Shem said, "I don't know if it's important, but I talked with Shaun just a few minutes ago. He's still pretty bleary but he said he saw a moustache. He couldn't remember anything else about it. I mean he couldn't' recall the face attached to it, wasn't even sure he saw it. 'It kinda floated' was how he described it and thought maybe it was from a dream and not real. But I thought I should mention it."

Delaney looked quizzically at Thorogood, who shook his head.

"This may be nothing. You know Shaun has always wanted to grow a beard, a moustache, anything. But so far he just can't grow whiskers thick enough to do it."

Delaney smiled. "If he just saw it 'floating,' it is probably just a power symbol for him and he is associating power with the person holding him."

Thorogood nodded in agreement. "Makes sense, especially since he didn't see it attached to a face."

Forty-five minutes later, in the speeding Gulfstream, Delaney received another message from Shem: "Jacob Berkeland just called Mackey."

24

POWER AND ITS DISCONTENTS

This isn't the first time Cody has used a McArdle replica as his messenger. In this instance I think the message is confirming that the Riverrun murders are not about one sick person's psychopathic pleasures. The flamboyant methods displayed in these cases are a diversion, as is the perpetrator's insistence that I be involved in the investigation. Dr. Phil did say the killer was likely to strew our path with lots of distractions.

Somewhere in this City there is a Machiavellian zealot whose goal is to wrest power from McArdle and Mackey. He has begun the process of driving a wedge between them. As the essay from Cody's universe makes clear, McArdle's own Machiavellian mind-set is ill prepared to meet the complex challenges posed by this character. Mackey? I think he may be, by instinct and experience, better able to flush out and destroy this threat.

It's power. It's always about power.

Here's a Final Jeopardy question for you: who's the most powerful guy in any city in the land? If you said Chief of Police, collect $200, pass go and get out of jail free. If you're the Chief you're holding a royal flush in the eternal game of power poker.

But enough of games and mixed-up metaphors, here's the facts: One, when you're the Chief, you're the one and only Commander-in-Chief of an army. That's what the force is, despite what some of these lefty reformers say. We're military and damn proud of it.

Two, nobody, and I do mean nobody, tells you what to do. The Mayor? City Council? Give me a break. They are no threat whatsoever. Their staff handlers move them around like puppets and they are forever sucking up to their donors; you know, those good corporate citizens that finance their pathetic fear- and ego-driven political ambitions.

Then there is the public, the voters; those homespun folks who love and support their local police. The politicos need to be adored, or at least paid attention to by them. And that's the simple-minded end goal of every godless politician. That means they operate from a gut full of fear and loathing. They pose zero threat to any Chief who halfway knows what he's doing.

Three, Chief of Police is the last unfettered position of power in this country. President, Senator, Congressman? They're all checking and jamming each other and that's mostly the only kind of power they have. Sheriff? Glorified process server with a shitty case closure rate. Governor? Generals? See politicians, above. Really, the only people who wield my kind of power are the heads of the CIA and NSA and their operations are too big for them to wield their authority effectively. In short, if you're really interested in power, at least in this universe, you'll aim for my job, period.

There are some simpletons out there who would disagree with me, and there are so-called reformers who want things like body cameras and Civilian Review Boards. They think they'll cockcrow into existence some kind of new day in law enforcement. But that's really old stuff that I can fend off with a wave of my pinky. In truth, there really is nothing new under the sun and these times are no stranger than years or eons past. Oh, I know, the political nincompoops of today have the power to fry our asses into nuclear nothingness, but that's really a change in degree, not substance.

The public struggle between the so-called forces of light and darkness goes on and on. In reality there is very little that fits into one category or the other. It's mostly an unending series of skirmishes along the edges, between shades of gray that, truth be told, are almost indistinguishable from each other. Trouble is those battles can create a lot of chaos for your community. Unless you're a Chief who's smart enough to forge a compromise, an agreement.

Here's another thing that's unchanging and it's something every Police Chief, King, Emperor or Hottentot Pooh-bah knows deep in his guts - it's lonely up here at the top. There's no escaping that. Maybe it's different in some other universe, but here in this one it's the way it is.

Mackey knows. That sneaky cripple of a peckerwood, he knows the feeling. He's had it ever since he weaseled his way onto Pigs Eye's rickety throne.

Mackey. He came to see me just before Eddie James went in for that final shave and haircut. He offered his version of a new agreement. That was the first time I met him, and I was impressed. Eddie was making retirement plans and Mackey was not his designated heir. Truth be told, Mackey was far more impressive than Eddie James ever was. James was a pure, assholic thug, period. He dealt in intimidation and fear, exclusively. Mackey was an asshole, too, but clearly miles ahead of his boss in the charm and brains department. From the beginning he had a more nuanced understanding of power and how to wield it.

Mackey had it all figured out, what businesses he'd do and what he wouldn't, where he'd operate, where he wouldn't. He had a whole business plan and even a fuckin' organization chart. Here were the loan sharks, here the gamblers, the pimps over here, the dope peddlers in this corner and here, off to the side, the enforcers. He even had a plan for moving into legitimate business and getting out of town, but with a succession plan in place. He was smart enough to not offer any bribes and promised to stay away from the unions and politicians. Mackey, the city's biggest asshole, is also the linchpin for regulating crime in this city.

From that time to this, we have been like a pair of Spartan kings, Mackey and me. We depend on each other and neither of us thrives without the other. We make this City what it is. Our grand, secret agreement means there is no war among the criminal element and leaves my cops with little to fret about except traffic and domestics. The Agreement also keeps this city from degenerating into just another Detroit.

In truth, all any of us have flapping around between our ears are our thoughts and memories. Every Chief needs to come into office with a memory bank full of the right kind of experiences. He needs to know you can't just erase history. History and culture, time and place – you don't just decide one day to abolish them. They're too strong and they will eat you alive if you don't respect them.

When you're the Chief, there are no friendships; you are alone, perfectly alone, and you'd better damn well accept it. It's all or nothing when you're the Chief. You try to make too many people happy, you are finished. Same thing if you alienate too many of them. You become a tightrope walker – alone in a dangerous balancing act.

Every big operator has to learn and internalize a few basic facts of power: Never tell anyone the real reason you're doing something. There's no percentage in it. Besides, a Chief should never believe he has to justify his decisions. When you do give reasons, tell them what they, in their willful ignorance, want to hear. That way they think you're on their side and, ergo, they owe you.

An undeniable proposition: Human beings are, by their very nature, devious liars. They are all, deep in their bowels, looking out for number one. Ninety-nine percent of them have this vicious streak under that patina of goodness and kindness. Even the guys on the force – well, especially them. They don't trust anyone when he first ascends to my position. A new Chief, he needs to know that he absolutely cannot trust them. Immediately, some gutless wonder and his cabal will be trying to make him look bad so they can take over. The new Chief better know who those bastards are so he can snip their balls before they get his.

You have got to be political, know who to suck up to until you're in a position to make them eat shit. The Mayor, a couple councilmen, the union, the chamber, one or two reporters; pretend you think they have good ideas, toss a little flattery their way and you've got them locked down. Now the media weasels are reporting that you're popular across a "broad spectrum" and you are suddenly more powerful than any one of them. Now you are The Man. Truth is, you have to pretend to know what you're doing, do what you think you have to do, and take it all on yourself, without apology.

You rely on your own experience, your own counsel. And you remember, always, it's about power. Power: the aphrodisiac, the demon, the tiger that crushes the bones of its enemies.

Power, the succubus who consoles you in the loneliness of your dark nights.

THURSDAY

...using hypnosis, scientists have temporarily created hallucinations, compulsions, certain types of memory loss, false memories, and delusions in the laboratory so that these phenomena can be studied in a controlled environment.

—*Scientific American: July 2001*

Is hypnosis dangerous? It can be. Under certain circumstances, it is dangerous in the extreme. It has even been known to lead to murder. Given the right combination of hypnotist and subject, hypnosis can be a lethal weapon.

—*George Estabrooks*

The covert hypnosis techniques I developed needed to work quickly at the unconscious level. And they did. I easily gained control, commanded attention and compelled compliance from anyone.

—*Igor Ledochowski*

25

COLLECTIVE AMNESIA

Gene Swearingen grew up in Oklahoma and said he never regretted leaving it. It is, he claimed, a great state for cattle, oil, football, rodeo, pickup trucks and Baptists, but not much else. He called it home to a corrupt, nasty brand of politics, equal to Louisiana's, but lacking the charm of Cajun food and music.

Swearingen compared Oklahoma to his new home state: education, life expectancy, employment, health care, income or any other measure of quality of life. Minnesota was at or near the top in every category; Oklahoma at or near the bottom. And, a real bonus for Swearingen, Minnesota was far more hospitable to class action plaintiff's attorneys. But, he had to admit, Minnesotans were not all that hospitable on a personal level. What they called politeness, he saw as culturally approved passive-aggressiveness. Where his Oklahoma relatives and friends were quick to warm up to new acquaintances and open their homes to them, Minnesotans all seemed to have an aloof reserve that made new friendships almost impossible to establish. He thought it was a function of the State's Scandinavian heritage.

Once upon a time Oklahoma was Indian Territory, home to Trail of Tears survivors. Now there were five civilized tribes in the east, plains Indians to the west.

Oklahoma Sooners: They were cheating pioneers who snuck early into the newly opening territory to lay claim to the best land. Were there Indians already there? Fuck 'em.

Only now tribes have money; oil money, casino money. The times now called for Sooner descendants to pucker up and plant one on a big red ass and convince anyone who'd listen that grandma was a Cherokee princess. Or Chickasaw. Or Osage. These days, for a great many Sooner descendants, the only good Indian is a rich relative.

In this matter, Minnesota and Oklahoma were similar: Both had treated their Native American populations shamefully. Minnesota, in fact, perpetrated the largest mass execution in the country's history when, on the day after Christmas, it hung 38 Dakota Sioux men in the aftermath of the tribe's uprising in 1862.

Tim Fredrickson claimed to be part Chickasaw, although his family came from Amish stock and he was only a second-generation Oklahoman. He became a patrolman in the Tulsa PD two years ago in the aftermath of yet another wide-ranging departmental scandal. Cops were found to have fabricated evidence, consorted with hookers, dealt drugs, robbed immigrants, brutalized suspects and lied in court, among other things. It was of a piece with the department's history.

In the 1921 Tulsa race riot, the single worst racial attack against African-Americans in the country's history, Tulsa cops deputized members of a lynch mob and urged them to "get a gun and get 'em, boys." Tulsa's prosperous Black community was razed and somewhere between 100 and 300 people, all Black, were killed. No government official bothered to keep count. No one was arrested, no one tried, no one convicted. Nothing was said, nothing was done, and a collective amnesia and silence settled over Tulsa and the rest of the country. Not until 92 years later did a Tulsa police chief apologize for the conduct of the force.

Good ol' boys with a habit of winking at the antics of other good ol' boys - that was the culture. But the conduct of the force finally got to be too much of an embarrassment and in the housecleaning that followed, experienced cops like Fredrickson, from other, rural, jurisdictions, got hired.

Delaney was now on the Turner Turnpike heading south for Bristow. As he finished rereading the case file on the two Tulsa murders, Tim Fredrickson said, "I wasn't on the Tulsa PD when they had those investigations. Not sure it wouldda helped if I had been. That investigation was real thorough. As I told you, it's too bad, but the guys who did it are off the force now. Retired. I tried to find 'em to get their help, but no luck."

Delaney already knew that one of them had been forced into retirement; the other was doing hard time at McAlester State Prison. Delaney said, "It says here that Enid Bixby was found lying on her back with an apple placed over her heart. Did anyone think that meant anything?"

"Not that I know of and you can probably tell from the file that that Adam Bierce kid was real smart. Very intelligent, as I recall. I had this case once that involved his mother and a sister of his. It was my rookie year and I don't really recall his mother too well, so I don't know if she'll be much help. But her daughter, that poor kid. Her and her mother and aunt got worked over by this guy. Of course, they was trying to squat in his house, so he had reason enough. But that poor little child, all bloody and crying. I was glad to help out on that one, let me tell you.

"I left a message at the nursing home that we were coming. I have no idea if Adam Bierce is in contact with her, or anyone else, or not. Until you guys located her, I didn't even know she was there."

"Do you know anything about the people who run this place?"

"Hell, yeah. I know everybody in the county."

"What are they like?"

"Money grubbing sons-a-bitches, like all nursing home operators. They keep the old folks doped up and mostly immobile. No problems that way. Please Lord, let me be kicked in the head by a bully mule before I'm booked into one of them places."

"When we get there, I'd like to talk with the old woman alone for a while. Could you do a scan of their records then?"

"Hell, yeah. But you better not take too long if we're goin' to get back to Tulsa afterwards.

"Them ones you're seein' back in Tulsa? Professors, huh?" Delaney nodded. "Them bastards like to talk. We could get stuck there all afternoon, we ain't careful."

As they pulled into the parking lot Fredrickson grinned. "Good luck with that old woman, hope she's got some good information for ya."

Three hours later Delaney was back in Tulsa meeting with two retired professors who remembered Adam Bierce as a student. Both wondered why he had settled for being a pharmacist when he might have aimed higher as a first-rate chemist.

"Of course, I never knew him very well, just by reputation," Professor Claude Lawton started off, "and, well, I did have him in a couple of classes, I guess. I just don't remember much about him, except he had these strange eyes. We've been retired for a few years now. Memory slips as you get older, you know. I'm afraid I don't recall anything else about him, just those blank eyes. So many of those students, they all blend together, and I've forgotten so many of them, even the nasty ones. Not too many of those were there, Wally?"

"Not really, Claude."

"Dr. Bixby knew him best, being his advisor and all. Perhaps you should talk to her?"

"Professor Bixby is one of the people the police think Adam Bierce murdered," Delaney replied.

"Enid Bixby, murdered? By her advisee? I didn't know that, did you Wally?" Professor Lawton looked distressed

"I knew about it, yes. Everyone did. She was drugged and strangled."

Delaney shifted to look directly at Walter Duncan, "She was drugged and strangled, that much is in the public record. What else do you know about her death?"

Duncan shifted uncomfortably, "Strangled, yes. But the killer wore gloves or something, so no fingerprints. Really, I only know what I read in the newspapers."

"Was it in the newspapers? I don't remember reading about it. Did I read about it, Wally? Did I know?"

"It was a while ago, Claude, easy to forget. Lots of people have forgotten about it."

"Why this collective amnesia, Professor Duncan? One of your colleagues, the head of the department, is murdered by one of her star pupils and people just act as though nothing happened?"

"It wasn't quite like that. It's just that, what were we to do? We told the police everything we knew, but nothing seemed to happen. What could we do? Dr. Bixby was buried and life went on. Isn't that the way it's supposed to be?"

"Dr. Duncan, what aren't you telling me?"

"I suppose it's OK to talk about it now. Enid was a bit, uhm . . . unusual. She practiced an esoteric kind of eastern religion – a mixture of Buddhism, Hinduism, something exotic like that. And then there was that other thing. Times are different now, but back then some people would have thought Enid to be a pervert and a danger to young minds."

"Please explain, Professor."

"You see, she swore me to secrecy before she agreed to come here. I was the head of the department and hired her. When I interviewed her, she told me she had published several major research papers, but I would never find them under her name. I would have to look under the name of Edwin Ardmore. You see, she was a transgender and in Oklahoma at that time, well, she could never have been hired into any position."

"But you hired her, why?"

"It was a decision I never regretted. She was just fabulous. Smart, a brilliant teacher and scientist and the students all loved her. She was the sweetest person you could ever want to meet."

"But you were the Department Head and she displaced you. Sounds like she knew how to wield a knife in the internal academic wars."

"No, it wasn't like that at all. I asked her to take over. Among her many virtues was a talent for organization. She revamped the department and somehow managed to keep everyone happy with their class assignments and even their office placements. Everyone just loved and respected her. I always thought it a great injustice that she had to hide in plain sight."

"Wally, I didn't know that about her. Are you sure?"

"After the autopsy revealed her 'secret,' the rumor mill ran full force, of course. One said a jealous boyfriend did it, another that it was a girl she had an affair with. There were several permutations on these theories, including that drugs were involved. I think Adam Bierce became a suspect because he seemed to be close to Dr. Bixby. Some thought too close and that they had pervert parties. Such a boatload of crap. She didn't even like Mr. Bierce."

"She didn't like him? Why was that?"

"About a month before her death she came to me, as the one person that knew who she really was, and told me that Bierce had somehow found out about her. He claimed to also have gender identity issues and was pressing her about her history and how she had handled everything."

"So, Bierce was also a trans?"

"That's the hitch. Enid said he wasn't, really, but that he seemed to want to know all about it so he could just change his identity if he ever wanted or needed to. She thought him to be a narcissistic, asexual creature who was irresponsibly dabbling in some very serious matters. She disliked his cavalier approach to matters that were so fundamental and dangerous for her. She said he was not truly a trans-gender person, but was probably harmless."

"So, you don't think Adam Bierce was the killer?"

"No, I think he probably was. Given what she said about him, I don't really think there's any other logical suspect. She said he was *probably* harmless, but I don't think she meant it. Plus, the use and dosage of rocuronium indicates the killer was likely someone from the chemistry department, doesn't it? It's not something commonly found in one's medicine cabinet. No one else in the department would have dreamt of hurting Enid and he disappeared right after her death."

Professor Lawton looked distressed. "Rocuronium? Oh my, I didn't know that."

26

THEY'VE GOT SOME
CRAZY LITTLE WOMEN THERE

Beau "Dealy" Bulgave earned his nickname in two worlds. With the junkies on the street, he was Dealy because that's how he made his living. With the cops he got it by his reliability as a confidential informant and jailhouse snitch. He was dependable and always ready to make a deal. In a half-dozen cases he sealed the fate of men who almost trusted him. Not that they always knew. Dealy lived in mortal fear that one or two of them might find out and his fate would be sealed. But the Kansas City cops took care of Dealy. He was a dealer and they let him deal. Life as a stoner was uncomplicated and sort of good.

But what was this about? Sergeant Billy Sherwood, his own personal handler-man picked him up and told him he had to meet some guy from up north. Dealy did not like the odor of this. North meant cold. He was never there, knew nobody there and wanted nothing to do with faraway cold places. And this room, a fucking interrogation room. Sherwood coulda done better than this; an office maybe, with big comfortable leather chairs. Maybe the room wouldn't be so bad, but after half a night in a cell he was getting a little twitchy, he would need a fix pretty soon.

The guy came in and called him Mr. Bulgave. A well-dressed dude, real dignified; he shook Dealy's hand, one of those two-handed handshakes, real friendly like. He seemed okay, kind-like, and had a soothing voice. Dealy relaxed.

Did he remember, years ago, when he snorted some bad stuff, real bad stuff, the stuff that put him in the hospital? Put him near death? Yeah, Dealy could remember and every time he did it gave him the shakes all over again. The guy wanted to know, did he remember who gave it to him?

Yeah, Dealy remembered, but who wanted to know? Was this guy a fed? He wanted information, Dealy had it, what was the guy ready to deal for it?

"It has come to our attention - " fuck yes, a fed. Only feds talked like that - "come to our attention" - Oh, fuck. It came to their attention that Dealy had a relationship with certain members of the Kansas City Police Department and that relationship was not only about to be terminated, but the agreements from past cases? "We have reviewed those and determined that they are illegal and therefore non-binding and unenforceable. You understand what that means Mr. Bulgave?"

Dealy looked around. Where was Sherwood? They couldn't fuckin' do this. "Where's Sherwood? I wanna talk to Sherwood." Not possible.

"You're dealing with me now, I have the cards. By the way, did you know we have Marshall Pinckney in St. Paul now?"

Pinky? In St. fuckin' Paul? When did he get out of Leavenworth? So what? Pinky was in on the deal. She said so. Uh, oh. Christ, where is Sherwood? I'm getting stressed now, gotta get outta here.

Dealy was starting to get the serious twitches and wondered what Pinky said, or thought, or if that woman was in this thing, too. "It's easy enough, Mr. Bulgave. Just tell me who gave you that stuff and we can let everything go back to the way it was," the guy said in a soft voice that was no longer soothing, "and you can leave. We don't want to keep you here. We will only do that if you force us to. Here's the deal, we think the guy who gave you that stuff is killing other people with it. Terrible way to die, isn't it? We need his name and then we're done."

Dealy wrung his hands to steady them. "I don't know, man. All I know is this blonde come and bought some stuff from me. It wasn't a guy, but this bitch, see? Real high class, ya know? Paid premium price, too, then wanted to get high with me." The walls were getting closer and the mirror was flashing distorted images. "Man, I need something for my nerves, ya know?"

"Would you like some coffee, Mr. Bulgave?"

"C'mon, man, I need something stronger than that. I need my stuff."

"I know, Mr. Bulgave, but the Kansas City Police Department doesn't stock your 'stuff.' They do have coffee. But quickly, Mr. Bulgave, we're running out of time, aren't we?"

Dealy's forearms began to itch and he started scratching them. A sound somewhere between a sob and a moan issued from his mouth. "That bitch, that bitch, she said, you're gonna die, Dealy, The Man can't leave a loose end like you dangling around here. Guess I fooled 'em, huh?"

"So why don't you just tell me who it was?"

Dealy groaned again. "Gimme my dope, goddam it! I'm tellin' you nothing 'til I get my dope."

The guy talked slowly, softly, "But we're almost done, aren't we? Such a little ways to go before you can be free. You should know by now, I hold the keys to this room; you want out, you give me what I want. By the way, you're not afraid of spiders, are you? That looks like a nasty one on your wrist."

Dealy jumped, swatting at himself, but the spider didn't budge, didn't seem to even be affected by his blows. It just kept changing colors and staring at his eyes. Dealy sobbed and slammed his wrist against the metal table. "Oh Christ, get this thing off me! Help, goddam it!"

The guy took Dealy's hand and snapped his finger over the spider. It disappeared. "You should see a doctor about your wrist, you may have broken it. Now let's talk about that bitch that hurt you, Mr. Bulgave. We don't want her coming back to hurt you again, do we?"

Dealy, eyes tearing up, nodded and said, "She come to me in the hospital and said Mr. Civella rethought through it, ya know, and he, Christ this hurts, and he's gonna be watching me. Maybe he got a use for a man of my talents. But, I open my mouth about the deal sending Pinky away, or this bad dope, and I'm dead, bad dead. The Civellas don't mess around, ya know. Aw, Jesus mister, you ain't tellin' 'em are you? Please?"

"The woman, Mr. Bulgave, what was her name?"

"You gonna tell, mister?"

"I'm not after the Civellas, Mr. Bulgave, your secret is safe with me. But I do want to know about that woman. Her name?"

"She never told me, man, and I didn't ask. I just thought I was getting pussy, what did I need her name for?" Dealy was getting worn out, tired, felt like he was going to fall asleep.

"You wouldn't be lying about that, would you?"

"I ain't shittin' you, man, honest. Christ, I'm tired."

"Just one more thing, Mr. Bulgave. Would you look at this drawing, please? Do you recognize . . ."

"Yeah, yeah, that's her. Now leave me alone dammit. Please, mister?"

The guy stood and looked down at Dealy and said, "That's OK, you've been a real help, a really big help. Now go to sleep and when you awake you'll have forgotten all about this, you will remember nothing, nothing at all."

27

ALL ABOUT EVIE

Dreams From My Brother, Thursday

There was a welcome consistency in the characters described by Professor Duncan and Dealy Bulgave. In both cases, one could trace the outlines of a psychopathic predator. I could make nothing, however, of the indecipherable utterances of Bierce's mother. The only word or syllables I could make out were, "E-V." She repeated it almost like a mantra throughout an impenetrable monologue. It meant nothing until Cody sent the following:

That Adam.

I coulda told you about him once, Mister, even if you was a cop, which you say you ain't. So why you coming out to this here shithole of a nursing home in the middle of Nowhere, Oklahoma? You ain't come to see me outa kindness, I know that. Something else I know, whoever sent you never told you about me; that I'm just a li'l old lady, sitting alone and talking to nobody but herself. Ain't nobody else I can talk to. But it don't make no never mind to me. I really got nothing to say to nobody about that Adam or anything else.

You see, it was them doctors named my li'l Evie, Adam. I told 'em, she's my li'l girl and I don't care what she got atween her legs. But they think they know everything those dirty bastards.

Only I knowed from her stirring in the womb I had a li'l girl in me and when she come out I could tell a way she cried she was the darling girl I yearned for. But them peckers at the hospital, they said, "Ma'am, you got the drugs in you and you got some confusion. You ain't got a Eve here, you got a Adam," and that's what they put on the birth certificate. But it weren't no drugs talking, it was me and my mind as clear that day as it is now. Now what you thinka that? Like they think a mother don't know her own child?

But we get outta that hospital and I treat her like the baby girl she is and she always appreciate it. I call her Evie and that's what she call herself. And smart? I tell you, she was smart as a gospel preacher, that one. She start telling me what to do and bossing everyone around when she's only three.

I lets her hair grow long in them curly blonde locks of hers and dress her purty in dresses and li'l skirts and her with them cute li'l dimples. She was a real princess, I tell you. Beautiful li'l girl like you ain't never seen. And them li'l boys? They come sniffing around her afore they knowed what they was sniffing for. But she knowed. She wrapped them li'l peckerwoods around her finger and made them do whatever she wanted. That Evie, one thing about her, she was always the boss.

Of course, that's what got us in trouble. She was eight years old, no, nine? Something like that. Me, my sister Becky and her, we was moving from place to place in them days. We was going around Creek County, outside Tulsa. You know, there's a lotta them truck stops out there. Cause we didn't have no money then, we'd get into one of them deserted ranch houses or a barn an' stay 'til we had to move on. Me an' Becky, we turned tricks in them trucks at the truck stops to earn enough to keep our-selves and Evie fed and maybe a li'l extra for some stuff to smoke. OK, Mister, we was getting high in them days, smoking weed and meth and anything else we could find. Don't go judging me for that. I got right with the Lord and he forgive me them sins. Besides, I took good care of my Evie. Always done that.

But one day she says, "Ladies, we's gonna stay in a better class of place." What she did, was she read them obituaries and seen where a old man died and she said, "We can move in there, cause he sure don't need it no more."

So, we went ta this ranch outside Sapulpa and I tell you it were a fine house. Evie says that old man he lived upstairs and now he's dead and ain't nobody livin' downstairs so we went in and went up them stairs. We was almost ta the top, with

Evie leading the way, when a man yells, "Hey, what y'all doing going up there?" and Evie yells back, "It's OK, we's kin to that dead man," and we keeps going 'til we get into this real nice room up there.

But that man, he comes right up after us, his wife pussyfootin' behind him. "My ass," he says. "You ain't no kin to my old man. I knows all our kin an' you ain't nothing but squatters, so git." Then he says to his wife to call the sheriff.

But Evie, she gives him this look of hers and says right back, "Mister, I don't know who you are, but we is staying the night in our kin's house an' maybe tomorrow night too. We's kin and gotta right."

That man, he looks at Becky and asks, "You her ma?" and Becky shakes her head an' points at me and that man he slaps me right across the face. "That's cause yer smart-ass kid is too li'l for me to slap, now git her an' git out."

Well, I tell you, my eyes was all teared up from that swat. I seen Becky already heading down them stairs, but Evie pipes up and says, "Mister, you can beat us all up, and I'm sure the cops will be real proud of you beating on a bunch of women and children."

Ooooo, that Evie, she had some real grit to her and she weren't afraid of that guy for a second. But I was and I wanted outta that place right now. But Becky, my poor dumb sister, she come back in right behind that li'l wife and shoves her outta the way and she's got that man's shotgun and she's pointing it right at him. Only it didn't frazzle him one bit, he jus' yanked it outta her hands, then he slams the butt of that shotgun right into her forehead, real hard. Becky, she went down like a sack of groceries and lay there bleeding and moaning and I start to wail, too. But not Evie.

That man, he looks at Becky, then me, then Evie. He yells at his wife to go downstairs and call the sheriff right now. Then he walks over to where Evie's sitting in this window well and takes hold of her chin. Looking her straight in the eye he reaches back and without even looking, snaps a backhand right across my face. Oh, it stung real bad, but even teared up I can see Evie is just giving him the stink eye. "Well, well," that man says. "I do believe we have us a li'l so-sho-path here. The cops, my li'l shithead, is too good for you," he says, "We's gonna turn you over to the social workers and psychiatrists. They's gonna have a ball with a li'l girl like you."

I'm worried real bad then. Worried they's gonna take my li'l girl from me and I let out a real loud wail, but ain't nobody much payin' me no mind. That man, he just give me a glare and I shut my face right then. I don't want no more of his slapping me around.

Evie, she's still cool and says, "Mister, you is a first rate fuck-up and so's your li'l wife. You just wait."

Then we hear that sheriff's car coming up to the house and as the car door is slamming Evie doubles up her fist and smacks herself right in the face and then does it again, right on her nose. I tell you, blood just gushed outta there and Evie starts screaming and runs over and hugs me real tight, with that blood gittin' all over my sweatshirt and jeans. I think that's the only time she ever hug me.

Then that deputy comes in and looks us all over and says, "Jesus Christ, Bob, what the hell . . . ?" That's when Evie runs over to that deputy, crying an' hugging him around the waist. "Don't let that bad man hurt us no more, please?"

That Bob, you can see he's getting worried now. He says, "Now wait a minute, Freddy. It ain't what it look like." But that cop, he don't buy it, what with Evie screaming an ableeding all over him.

The good thing is, they took that Bob away in handcuffs. But then some social worker takes Evie when they finds out we ain't got no place ta live. I hollered at them for that and Evie, she like to have a conniption. But when they put her in the car she stopped hollering and carrying on, just like that. I tell you, that's the last I saw of my li'l girl.

After that I got right with the Lord and got clean. Me and Becky went to working in fast food joints, on account of we can't read. Can't write neither. Poor Becky, she weren't never quite right in the head after gettin' thumped by that shotgun. But justice was delivered onto that Bob and his wife. They was murdered one night, blasted to hell by somebody shooting them with that very same shotgun. Vengeance is mine saith the Lord.

They brung Evie back to me a year later, only she don't look like Evie no more. They done made her into Adam. I hardly reconize her, lookin' like a boy in boy's clothes and shoes and short hair and all. She was a handsome boy, but I knowed in my heart it was still my Evie inside. When we's back together, she tells me, "Ma, I'm still Eve, but we gotta play along with these bastards, so call me Adam an' pretend I'm a boy. That way they won't take me away again."

We did that and that Evie, so smart, finished high school two years ahead of time and got her a scholarship to TU. I tell you, she was a genius that one.

She come to see me once after she been away at TU for a couple of years. She come back for Becky's funeral and after she start saying that we gotta be real careful nobody know that she's really Eve, not Adam. She says, "We gotta take precautions, right ma?" And I say, "You betcha, Sweetie." Then she says we gonna take care of that right now and she takes out a needle and says it's medicine that's gonna help me and her keep our secret. I didn't understand what she meant, but that medicine sure felt good when she shot me up.

Now I'm feeling real good, real dreamy and drifting on a sea of calm. I'm thinking, that Evie, she just gimme a jolt of the balm of Gilead, only then I see that Adam is taking out a knife. It ain't no ordinary knife neither. It's a fish fileting knife, real sharp and he's putting on some rubber gloves. Then, that Adam, he went and reached into my mouth and I'm too doped up to stop him. He pulled out my tongue and he took that knife an' sliced it right outten my mouth.

I tell you, Mister, or I would if I could, but that goddamn Adam he seen to it I can't tell nobody nothing, not ever again.

FRIDAY

Psychopaths... people who know the differences between right and wrong, but don't give a shit.

—*Elmore Leonard*

Most psychopaths are subtle. They are more like poison than a knife, and they are more like slow-working poison than cyanide.

—*Sam Vaknin*

The eyes of a psychopath will deceive you; they will destroy you. They will take from you, your innocence, your pride and eventually your soul. These eyes do not see what you and I can see. Behind these eyes, one finds only blackness, the absence of light. These are of a psychopath."

—*Dr. Samuel Loomis*

28

ANOTHER AGREEMENT

Chicago, when they were still young. Delaney, one week into his insurance company job; Mackey in town for what he could not discuss. That's when The Deal was made. There was no written contract, not even a handshake. They clinked their glasses, each filled with a double shot of John Jameson's Twelve-Year-Old, and downed them in one gulp. Delaney gagged, sputtered, coughed, teared up and laughed. Mackey roared until he, too, had tears coursing down his jowls.

As they started on their divergent professional lives they knew the chances were better than fifty-fifty that one day they would find themselves up against each other. It was, they agreed, to be avoided at almost all costs. The one who first discovered the inevitable conflict was to contact the other immediately. Then they would palaver and decide which one of them would back out, if he could, or whether they would have to fight it out, and may the best man win. It was unspoken, but understood, Delaney would recuse himself from the first of any potential conflicts. He owed Mackey that much.

Both dreaded the day it would happen, but the Jacob Berkeland call sent a clear cock's crow signal to Delaney. He called Mackey on the flight from Kansas City and set up the meeting for a back room at Holman field. Mackey would meet him when his plane landed. It was not a meeting Delaney could tell Thorogood about, nor could he tell Mackey he knew about the Jacob Berkeland call.

This day was of the kind that often hits Minnesota in the early spring – rainy, windy and cold. It was turbulence all the way down. Kyle Lilly thought of it as something that made a flight interesting. It left Delaney feeling vulnerable and mildly pissed at the universe. He was convinced that turbulence, like mosquitoes, served no real purpose other than to annoy the rest of creation.

Delaney shook the rain from his coat as he walked into the room. His annoyance level rose by a couple of degrees when Mackey said, "No wire?"

"No recording devices of any kind, absolutely none, shithead. And thanks for coming out here to meet."

Mackey grinned. "It was convenient. I'm flying to Cleveland in an hour. By the way," he hesitated for two beats, "you haven't forgotten about Evelyn's dinner invitation, have you?"

His face, his posture, the faint stutter in his speech, nothing fit with what he was saying. Delaney thought it probable that Mackey wasn't going to Cleveland. He was unsure about Mackey's reference to Evelyn and said, "How could I forget any kind of invitation from Evelyn? Especially if we get to talk about John Rawls?"

"Oh, fuck John Rawls. Who gives a shit about philosophers?" Mackey laughed nervously as Delaney sat. "Now tell me, where's our problem? I thought you were just working that Riverrun case. You got something new?"

"It's about that case and the Port Authority has something to do with it. And, my friend, you are conducting business with the Port Authority, lots of business."

"Yeah? So what? Port development projects and bonds are legitimate business and I like moving my money into legit enterprises. You think I should expand some of my other concerns? I thought you'd approve of this."

"Do you know why Suzanne Porter was killed?"

"No, and don't you think if I did I would have told you?" Disappointment dripped from his voice.

"I'm sorry, Mack. Let me explain, as much as I can. Suzanne Porter was secretary to the Port president and privy to lots of inside information. There's a lot about the Port that's suspicious, including the regular infusions of cash and transfers from offshore accounts, all run through Pinnacle City Bank and Trust. This, in addition to those projects where the properties were sold cheap just before the public announcement that they would be part of a new redevelopment, sending their prices up and away. Yesterday I was in a meeting with guys from Homeland Security and the FBI. They now have the Riverrun case and the FBI is going to use it to try to get to you. You know they've been after you for a long time and now they think they have the hook to reel you in."

He paused as the roar of a corporate jet taking off filled the air. "Face it, Mack, there isn't anyone else in this town who has the juice to juggle the money, the bank and the Port Authority like this. I know that's the theory the FBI has to be working from.

"It would be naïve to think Porter and her friend Graham Byrd were not killed because of their Port Authority connections. The FBI won't know where else to look, except in your direction. Can you help me out here?"

Mackey was startled and looked at his friend for a moment before saying, "Here, look. The bank, yeah, I own part of it, not the controlling interest either. I'd like to own it outright, but I don't. Jacob Berkeland has a lot of juice in his own right.

"You can't run a business like mine if you don't have a partnership with a bank. You know the old saying – 'all major business is an inside job' – so I have a large interest in the bank. It's good for hiding a lot of deals that can't be public. Same with the Port Authority. I can park big chunks of cash there and it's like hiding it in plain sight - legitimate plain sight, know what I mean? It cleans the money and helps the City of St. Paul. If I lose a little on it, that's OK, it's just the price of doing business.

"Suzanne Porter tipped us off on redevelopment plans, so we bought properties and cleaned up when we sold them. But I also do business with Goldman Sachs, Chase, and lot of others. You gotta diversify your income and expenditure streams or you get to be too obvious.

"But the murder of those people? You know better. Sure, you're fishing here, hoping I do know who did it, but I don't. Which leads me to believe this theory the Fibbies have cooked up about the Port Authority connection being what got them killed is bullshit.

"You and your cop friends have got to look at something else if you want to catch this freak. What happened to that notion it was one of these guys listening to voices in his head?"

"I haven't ruled that out yet."

"And what about these neighborhood crazies that are so pissed off at the Port Authority? That Nate Muhammad and that crowd - wanna bet that some of them have mental problems? Did you check to see how many of them did time at St. Peter? You ever think of that?"

"There's something else, Mack. I think it's related. You know about the Russians that flew in yesterday."

"Volkov. I'm watching him. Do you know why he's here?"

"No, don't you?"

"Not yet. But you said 'Russians.' I only know about him. There's more?"

Delaney hesitated before deciding it didn't matter if his friend was being truthful or not. "Yeah, at least three others."

"Do you know what they're doing here?"

"That would only be guesswork at this point. Marta Voronova is one of the others. Heard of her?"

"No. You think she's important?"

"She's like no one else on the planet when it comes to money. She's the best at stealing, laundering, printing and selling, investing, manipulating, hiding and any other illicit thing you can do with money."

Although Mackey just nodded, Delaney saw his face flash something between surprise and anger. He continued, "So here's what I do know. Volkov is near the top of the Russian mob pyramid, and he's been the point man on several expansions into new territory. But the Russian mob never just moves into a new place and takes it over. They're too cautious, too smart for that. They plan carefully, always find some local partners first and split the action with them. They might jettison them later, but they never, ever, expand into a new territory without local allies."

"The feds think the Russians want to come in here and I'm their contact, don't they? I hope you know better."

"Yeah, they're looking at you. But I think the real kicker is Marta Voronova. She's the top Russian money person. She operates on a global scale and I don't get why she's in St. Paul."

"You got a tail on her?"

"No, but the FBI does."

"McArdle?"

"I'm sure he does too."

"Volkov?"

"The same." He didn't mention that he also had Henri Bouchard tailing Marshall Pinckney.

Mackey snorted. "Volkov may be the most watched man in America." It was Delaney's turn to be surprised. Mackey already knew about Bouchard.

Delaney was about to speak, but Mackey stopped him with a wave of his hand. "Here's another *theory* about what's going on in this city. There's some guy – maybe an organization - that wants to displace me, so they contact the Russians and leave a trail of crumbs that brings you and your friends in law enforcement to the idea that I'm involved in this Riverrun shit. I'm thinkin' there's all kinds of stuff you guys ain't thought of yet. I'm right, ain't I?"

Delaney smiled. He actually hadn't thought of Mackey's last proposition. It was preposterous on the face of it. Mackey was too big, too well protected by his insider status to be challenged by another local mobster, even one with the backing of the Russian crime syndicate. That, thought Delaney, was precisely why this theory had legs.

With this idea beginning to take on the shape of plausibility, he asked, "Mack, my good friend, have you ever heard of the Shock Doctrine? And, by the way, what can you tell me about Marshall Pinckney?"

29

A LEISURELY BREAKFAST IN THE SUBURBS

"I thought you should know, Pinckney is having a leisurely breakfast up here in Anoka County." Henri Bouchard called just as Delaney turned the Prius out of the Holman Field parking lot.

"Yes?"

"He dropped Volkov at a local motel about an hour ago. It's one of those suites motels, but I thought the Intercontinental was more Volkov's style."

"Yes?"

"Pinckney drove away in his own car, a Lexus. He left the Continental in the motel parking lot, along with that little cap and sunglasses."

"Maybe Volkov wanted to drive himself from there."

"Maybe."

"I hear doubt in your voice."

"You haven't heard anything from the cops or FBI tailing Volkov, have you?"

"They don't report to me, Henri."

"If they did, they would have reported they lost him somewhere around the I–35W construction mess going on in Shoreview, Arden Hills and New Brighton."

"They lost him, but you didn't."

"No."

"And?"

"I called and let them know where he was."

"Good."

"Maybe not."

"Why?"

"They lost him again."

"Fill in the blanks, Henri. If I have to keep goosing you it will be next week before we finish this conversation."

"The feds and cops got to the motel quickly enough, but there's no Volkov there. The Continental is there, but no Volkov."

"Don't stop there."

"Could be he had a different car waiting for him, or someone else picked him up. There's a lot of possibilities. Your guess could be better than mine."

"It could be a Higgs operation." Delaney paused. "Except that I just saw Mackey at Holman field. He says he's flying to Cleveland, but it's not like him to take off during an operation that would be this big."

"Pinckney still hasn't moved. He must be having a very big breakfast."

A realization hit Delaney suddenly and hard. "What's the name of the restaurant?"

"This one? Matthews Family Restaurant, why?"

"I should have guessed."

"What? Your turn to fill in some blanks, if you don't mind."

"Pinckney is no longer there and certainly didn't have time for breakfast. Matthews is run by Matteo's Aunt Amelia. She named the place after Matteo, her favorite nephew. Matteo and Mackey are friends and occasional business partners. He let Mackey use your restaurant as the rendezvous place where Higgs, or whoever else was involved in capturing or killing Volkov, could meet. They left by a back entrance and they're halfway back to St. Paul by now."

"Did Mackey know I was tailing Pinckney?"

"I don't think so. He was just being cautious in case the cops or FBI might have still been on Pinckney's tail. You know, when Mackey told me that he was going to Cleveland I was pretty sure he was lying."

"He would lie to you?"

"Only if it served his purpose."

"What does that mean?"

"It means I expect to get a call from him later today."

"Why?"

"Because he will either have Volkov in his custody or Volkov is dead."

"And Pinckney is a big part of this operation?"

"Mackey told me earlier that Pinckney was a loyal guy who could be trusted."

"I can't help but think how cool it is if Mackey actually does have Volkov. There'd be lots of crimson faces in this town, including McArdle's."

Delaney resisted the urge to comment on the inability of people in high places to feel embarrassment about anything. As Henri hung up Delaney eased the car into his parking spot at Delphi.

A feeling of weariness washed over him as he got out of the car and stepped into the elevator. He was about to inwardly curse the universe for this but couldn't. The universe, he admitted, had actually been pretty good to him over the last few days.

30

NO EXIT

Arne Ratkovic and Duane Hanson came reluctantly to the morning debrief session. They wanted the St. Paul Police off the case and worried their attendance would be seen as encouraging the department. But curiosity overcame their qualms.

Dr. Phil was also in attendance, smiling benignly down at them from a large screen set across from the floor-to-ceiling windows that gave a full view of the hard rain lashing across the city and the dark river. It had taken a call from Homer McArdle to get him, but the St. Peter Hospital administrators finally allowed Dr. Phil to participate with the group assembled in Delaney's conference room.

Following McArdle's lead, Thorogood had agreed beforehand that everything the department had uncovered would be shared with Ratkovic and Hanson, as well as Dr. Phil. Thorogood had Delaney start by going over his findings from Oklahoma and Kansas City. Dr. Phil's smile broadened when Delaney touched on the sexual ambiguity of their prime suspect. "This is marvelous, just marvelous," he said. "It helps to explain so much."

"We're going to ask you to expand on that in a few minutes, Phil. But first, we've found a couple of other things you might also find just 'marvelous.'"

"It's about former police detective Danny Fortuno. We know he was acquainted with Suzanne Porter and possibly Graham Byrd. What we also know is that in his time with the St Paul PD, he was involved with six fatal shootings. The bodies were all autopsied personally by Dr. Gunnar Olafsson."

"Why is that important?" Ratkovic wanted to know.

Thorogood turned to Hanson. "Special Agent Hanson, would you like to answer that?"

"I would, if I understood why this is such a big deal."

"Would it interest you to know that Olafsson is the half-brother of Jacob Berkeland?"

Hanson's face turned deep crimson and Ratkovic sullenly crossed his arms and said, "Sorry for the interruption, please continue."

"Within the department we're re-reviewing those shootings in light of what we now know about Fortuno and his subsequent demise. We will, of course, keep the two of you apprised of any new information we develop."

The door opened and Marguerite peeked in. "Chief? There's a call for you, they said it was urgent."

In less than a minute Thorogood was back in the conference room and barked, "Jacob Berkeland is dead. He was found at his desk just a few minutes ago. Dalton, O'Leary and Puckett get over to his bank and secure the scene right now. You know where it is."

It was O'Leary who voiced everyone's question, "He was killed in broad daylight?"

"It *looks* like suicide. Get going. And Dalton, see that someone, anyone other than Olafsson, does the autopsy right away. I'll send someone to go see him to break the news."

Hanson jumped up. "I'm going to the bank, too."

Thorogood exploded, "No, you sit your ass down, goddamn you. You squeezed him, didn't you? Gave him the full treatment; told him the only way out for him was to give up Mackey. That's what you did, isn't it?"

Hanson glared sullenly from beneath his hooded eyes. "And you didn't get anything out of him, did you? Did you think, really, for one fucking instant that he would be more afraid of you than Mackey? Or that deranged killer? Do you know what you did, you insufferable buffoon?"

Standing, Hanson sneered, "I don't have to take this crap, not from you or any other St. Paul cop. Now I'm going over to that crime scene, or whatever it is."

"Before you go, Agent Hanson," Delaney sharply broke in, "consider this. You left the man no exit. In his mind there was little difference between you and whoever it was he was afraid of. Remember that the next time you decide to scare somebody into cooperating with you."

"I offered him witness protection."

"And any decent hacker can find anyone you have stashed away in witness protection. Your system, the marshals' system – they're playthings for a skilled computer jock. I suspect Berkeland knew that."

Hanson, still red-faced, stormed out and Ratkovic muttered, "I suppose I should stay for the rest of this séance, shouldn't I?"

"Yeah, and you just might learn something," Thorogood snapped and slumped in his chair.

Delaney turned to the screen. "Still with us, Phil?"

"Oh, yes. Quite the melodrama you have going on there."

"We have some more questions for you," Delaney said, turning to the screen. "A few minutes ago, you said our suspect's sexual identity explained 'so much.' Care to expand on that?"

"Happily, Conor, quite happily. Your suspect's name is what? – Adam, and he's whimsically placing Adam's Apples in his victims' throats. But Adam – first man – is what? Hiding, masquerading, assuming a new identity as a woman? I think none of those is quite right. He's too full of himself and I think he may be wearing his feminine identity quite proudly. He thinks of himself as Adam *and* Eve. This would be entirely consistent with what you learned in Oklahoma."

Delaney's owl eyes widened imperceptibly. Now he knew Adam Bierce's other identity.

Ratkovic asked Dr. Phil, "You mean he has a split personality?"

"No, quite precisely, no. What we commonly think of as a split personality is a dissociative identity disorder where the two identities take turns at controlling a person's personality and behavior. They may not even know of each other. That is decidedly what we do not have here.

"This person – a psychopathic, malignant narcissist - has integrated both identities into his/her personality. The two may even have conversations with each other or may just be identities he assumes when he, or she, wishes."

Marguerite opened the door again. "Conor, Chief Thorogood, it's Detective O'Leary."

Delaney switched on the speaker phone and O'Leary said, "Have you ever heard of a suicide shooting himself right straight in the eye? I never have. It's always the temple, in the mouth, under the chin or something like that, know what I mean? But Gettler says the gunpowder residue on his hand and face indicates the shot came from the gun being held by Berkeland right up against his eye. Makes you wonder if he was hoping to see the bullet coming at him. For the time being we're going with the obvious, it's suicide."

"Where did you find him?" Delaney asked. "On the floor with a north-facing orientation?"

"No, he's sitting in his chair, behind his desk."

"Is there an apple within his reach, or would it have been if he hadn't met such an unfortunate end?" Dr. Phil wanted to know.

"Yeah, it's right there on his desk, and a bite has been taken out of it. But it would have been out of reach unless he stood up. I can send a live feed of our scene, if you want."

"Please do," Delaney responded and swiveled to turn on the room's other large screen so Dr. Phil and Ratkovic could watch. It lit up with the scene: Jacob Berkeland in a dark suit with red tie, slumped and listing to his left, arm hanging over the side of the chair. His right eye socket was a black hole and his fingers dangled just inches from the revolver lying on the carpet. On his desk, just to the left of a small stack of file folders, was a small green apple.

"Detective," Delaney asked, "is that pistol a .22?"

"Sure is, and we'll be checking it for prints. Something tells me we'll find Berkeland's prints on it and no one else's. Hey, how did you know it was a .22?"

"It's what a woman would use. A man would go with a .38 or 9 millimeter. Officer Puckett, any observations?"

"Do you think it wasn't a suicide? That a woman killed him?"

"Not necessarily, but I'd hold off on making that suicide judgement."

"They found him when they opened up this morning, but the staff here, they don't seem as surprised or shocked as they should be. We need to do some serious interviews with them."

"Would you concur with that, O'Leary?"

"I would have said we need to interview them regardless of their reaction, but yeah, this gives us the angle for talking with them. Uniforms are getting their IDs and statements now. We'll be here for a while questioning them."

Puckett interjected, "Mr. Delaney, why do I have this feeling that this is going to lead us back to your friend Mackey?"

"Because you have good instincts, Officer Puckett - very, very good instincts."

Duane Hanson stepped before the camera. "It's because we all know that Mackey's responsible for this, including you. Why are you protecting him, Delaney?"

"Mr. Hanson, when you have *evidence* of Mackey's culpability, and *evidence* of my protecting him, or any other suspect, we can talk. Until then, please confine yourself to fact gathering, as opposed to guesswork and speculation. One of the facts you may want to gather is whether or not it was common for Mr. Berkeland to have an apple on his desk, or if it might have been put there by someone else."

Thorogood said, "Dalton, you'll get that apple into an evidence bag, won't you? We should check it for prints and see if there's some DNA in that bite mark."

"If I were to hazard a guess," Delaney said, "I'd say it was placed there sometime before he got to the office and it was a clear threat of what was in store for him if he talked with you, Agent Hanson."

"Detectives, bring those files on his desk, or copies of them, back here with you. Good luck and good-bye," Thorogood said.

Delaney turned once again to the large screen. "Well, Phil, what do you think?"

"Fascinating, truly. The ubiquitous apple, and an eye rather than the throat. Shooting him through the eye, was his executioner trying to tell us something?"

"What if it was nothing?" Ratkovic interjected. "I mean – why didn't he just write his name if he wanted to tell us something?"

Delaney replied, "Good questions and we'll know more in a little while, when O'Leary and Puckett return. Could be the function of the apple here was to make a threat clear. It may be that he didn't even know who it came from. Phil, what else do you have for us?"

"We are dealing with purposeful Judeo-Christian symbolism. Remember, the fruit of the tree of the knowledge of good and evil was strictly forbidden to Adam and Eve. After they did eat what is commonly believed to be an apple, the gods - the gods plural, by the way - make the astounding statement that, 'The man has now become like one of us, knowing good and evil. He must not be allowed to reach out his hand and take also from the tree of life and eat and live forever.'

"Something else. Remember my thinking this egomaniac had to show off for his victims? I now think he took his clothes off to display unusual physical characteristics - feminine and masculine gender traits, together in one body. With great pride, I should think."

"That explains what Shaun told us, that he was doped up and his vision was blurry, but he thought a naked man and a naked woman both danced after tattooing his neck."

Dr. Phil nodded and continued, "The last of our original three killings is different, though. Mr. Fortuno looks more like a crime of passion. The killer didn't take a lot of time with him."

"What about Karleen Martin?" Ratkovic wanted to know.

"I believe she met her fate at the hands of someone else, someone who may have wanted her death to seem as if it came at the hands of Adam Bierce."

"The Russians?"

"Oh, Mr. Ratkovic, you are now treading outside my area of expertise. I would only venture that if it were Russian gangsters, they may have purposely made a sloppy job of it as a warning to Adam Bierce or others. But really, that's just a layman's poorly informed guess."

"Jacob Berkeland," Delaney broke in, "His bank was being audited by the FBI?" Ratkovic nodded when Delaney glanced his way. "And he was terribly afraid of someone who didn't want him talking with the FBI. The apple announced or reinforced the threat."

"Does this lead you anywhere? Do you have any other suspects in mind, yet? Or can we expect this fiend to disappear, like Ambrose Bierce, into the Mexican desert?" Dr. Phil paused for a full five seconds. "Conor, just an idea, but maybe worth following up. Your killer's name is apparently Adam Bierce. It would be entirely consistent with what we know about his trickster tendencies that his adopted feminine name incorporates both Eve and Ambrose. Do you see what I'm getting at? Does that seem right to you?"

Delaney's brows were furrowed and when he hesitated Dr. Phil, his smile broadening, said, "Oh, Conor, you have that look again. The one you had when you apprehended me in the carnival. You know who it is, don't you?"

Purposely not looking at Thorogood or Ratkovic, Delaney replied, "I wish I were as good as you think I am, Phil, but I'm as lost as I ever was," and he winked at the screen.

A few minutes later Ratkovic left the room and Thorogood looked at Delaney. "Eve Ambrose?"

"Try Evelyn."

As the realization grew, Thorogood laughed. "He's been hiding in plain sight."

Looking down from his perch on the screen, Dr. Phil patted his belly and smiled.

31

THE DEATH OF LOVE

Cody is never very direct. The communication tools at our disposal work against that. Although this occasion looks like the exception, I assume it isn't. I suspected Ida had something to do with our break-up. She and I are great friends, have been ever since Thoro introduced us years ago. So, I take it that she really is looking out for Camille's best interests. But it stings to know that someone so close to both of us, caused our separation. The universe sometimes plays dirty tricks.

But Cody is conveying more than that. He is, I think, indicating that Camille is somehow entangled with the Riverrun cases. She and her firm represent the Port Authority, but Cody wouldn't have sent this if that was the whole story. I think her phone call must be more important than I thought.

No.

Uh-uh.

It's not happening

No way.

You want to know why? Well first off there's that age thing. He's Melvin's age, my age. Twelve, fifteen years older than you. I'm your godmother and I was your baby sitter. You want to marry somebody the same age as your aunt and uncle? Same age as your godparents? He's more like us than you. And face it, girl, he's not really like us, is he?

No, don't you go getting in my face about this race stuff. You know I won't object to you marrying some nice white man. Oh, I know you're not talking about getting married, but you know, one thing leads to another and pretty soon you haven't got control over events. You know how it goes; you smile, then a kiss, then you're in bed and then it's either a wedding or heartbreak. And I know you, little woman, so don't go telling me marriage isn't somewhere in the thinking here.

And look at the way he looks. You, you're beautiful; absolutely the most beautiful young woman in any room you walk into. Him? He's not exactly what you would call handsome, is he? Why, with those oversized eyes and that odd nose of his he could practically qualify for federal disaster aid. Now wait, I'm just saying, you're beautiful, he isn't and you will always look mismatched. People are going to be saying you hooked up with him for his money. Yeah, I know it wouldn't be true, don't I know you well enough to know that? And you a big shot lawyer now, making plenty of your own money. But still, that's what people are going to say when they see the two of you together, she married him for his money and he married her because . . . well, you know what they'll say, don't you?

Wait now, don't go blaming me. I'm only telling you what you already know. You want to live with that? Besides, doesn't he strike you as a bit peculiar? Even Melvin says that.

Another thing here, what's with him and all this Port Authority stuff? That is just stirring up a lot of trouble. Yes, sometimes you have to do that, and maybe this gentrification business requires more attention than it's gotten. But why is he into it so deeply? He is supporting a lot of first-class troublemakers. You know his company is doing a study and helping that Neighborhood Action Coalition against the Port Authority?

Of course, they're right, but a simple meeting or two with the mayor and a few councilmen could have fixed it. Without all this public confrontation, too. You can always get more with honey than vinegar, and that's double-true in this town.

What do you mean that wouldn't make for any long-term institutional change? Hmmphf. Look at what Melvin's done with the police. Notice how few Black men have been shot by cops since he moved up? There's your institutional change. And don't give me that look.

But look, there's another thing and it's really the big one. You know he don't want children? You didn't know that? It's what he told Melvin a long time ago. Melvin thinks it's because he ain't got no family of his own. And don't you think that's a mite mysterious? Don't got no connection with any of his foster families. So, you got this man, no family and not wanting one. And I know you want babies; the women in this family know how to make babies, beautiful babies and lots of them.

You don't want the kind of life you'd have with him. That life would just be too lonesome after a while. You know how it is, we got big families. We have a good time with all the aunts and uncles and cousins and grandmas and grandpas. We practically have a party going on all the time. And you are my big sister's baby girl and I don't want you making a big mistake about your life.

You know, we have met some of his other girlfriends. He hasn't had many, but the one's we've met, they are all, older, white and usually looked to be, ahem, on the experienced side, know what I mean? None of which you are. You are still young and can attract a more, shall we say, appropriate kind of man.

No, I haven't talked with your uncle Mel about this. You know he thinks that man walks on water. But he doesn't think like a woman, does he? But you have to.

32

WE NEED TO TALK

"Delaney? We need to talk. Meet me at the warehouse this afternoon. Two o'clock."

"Chief McArdle, I was just getting my bill ready for you."

"I'll see that a check is expedited and delivered promptly by wagon train. Now cut the comedy and listen. Your buddy Mackey had a panic attack and kidnapped that Russian bastard, Volkov, and has him marinating at the warehouse."

"A panic attack. Mackey? Not likely, Chief."

"Listen, him and me agreed that I'd keep Volkov under surveillance and we'd arrest him as soon as he stepped out of bounds. But then, this morning, without provocation, Mackey packs him up and personally delivers his carcass to the warehouse."

"And your guys botched their surveillance assignment, didn't they?"

"Enough. As long as Mackey has him, I think we should find out why the Russians are taking an interest in our fair city."

"Yes?"

"In order to do that I will need to use some of your unusual talents. Know what I mean?"

"Not yet. Two o'clock you said?"

"Yeah, and Delaney, I don't want to hear any of your liberal sermons about treating felonious assholes like family. The Russian mob is mean and vicious and I don't want them fucking up our town. Got it?"

* * *

"We need to talk, Delaney. Right now."

"You're not in Cleveland."

"The right people think I am."

"Do you know who these right people are?"

"The Russian friends of this bastard Volkov and the fuckers in my organization that're working with them.

"Yeah, do you know who those *fuckers* are?"

"Yeah, of course. Not all of them. But I don't have that many ambitious or smart people in my crew, do I? How long have you known?"

"Less than an hour. But McArdle says you've got Volkov stashed at the warehouse."

"Yeah, and I know he wants you here in a couple of hours."

"Yeah."

"But there are a few things I need to go over with you that McArdle doesn't need to know about."

"Be careful, Mackey. You don't want to screw around with McArdle."

"I just said it's something he doesn't need to know about. It's not anything against him."

"But he won't like it, will he?"

"Let's stop talking in these, waddya callems?"

"hypotheticals?"

"Yeah. Now listen. Maybe I don't want you to do anything. Maybe I just want you to probe a little bit."

"I'm hearing lots of maybes."

"Here's my thinking, and by the way, it doesn't involve any real risk. You ain't gonna be in any real danger."

* * *

"Conor? We need to talk."

"Always happy to talk with you, Evelyn, even by phone. Talk away."

"It should be face-to-face. You will be here this evening, won't you?"

"Is there something wrong?"

"No. Not yet."

"Not yet? Sounds dire. Does Mackey share your concern?"

"Mackey is in Cleveland tonight. I wanted to talk with you while he's away."

"Hmm, well, sure, I can make it. What time?"

"About eight? I'll have dinner brought up from downstairs."

"You're not doing this just so we can talk about John Rawls?"

"This actually involves other important matters."

"You'll have to make room for another person."

"What? Why?"

"Since our last encounter with that mass murderer, McArdle has decreed that everyone at Delphi must have a police escort at all times. And the escort is to keep a detailed calendar of where we are going and when. I don't like it, but what are you going to do?"

"No."

"I'm afraid so."

"I'll have one of the girls show him around the back-room downstairs while we talk. He'll find that interesting, won't he? I'm telling you, Conor, we need to talk."

"Eight o'clock you said?"

"Yes. I will see you then."

33

THE VOICE OF

The warehouse. It was the department's secret holding pen; an old, out-of-the-way, red brick building where it could temporarily stash a suspect without drawing the attention of the press or public. Its existence in the industrial midway district was known only to a select few within the department and no one outside of it, except for Conor Delaney, Mackey Stately and their closest associates. Within its walls, unusual interrogation techniques were the rule, not the exception.

On this day a sedated Viktor Volkov was seated there on a heavy oak chair, his forearms duct-taped to the armrests. When Butchie lifted the hood from his head, he found himself still in complete darkness. He was left like that for an hour, an hour that felt more like six hours to Viktor Volkov.

An overhead spotlight flashed on without warning. When he tried to look beyond the cone of harsh light surrounding him, he found only blackness.

Another much dimmer spotlight came on. Within its faint island of light Volkov could make out the indistinct head of a man. With a deep scowl it barked, "Viktor Volkov, do you know who I am?"

"Yeah, you McArdle. This bullshit don't scare me, McArdle. Why we don't just talk, you know, like normal people?"

"You are not normal people, Viktor Volkov. You are low-life scum. Why are you infesting our fair city?"

"You don't want visitors to your city? I'm tourist come to see your most livable city."

"Cut the bullshit, Viktor. "

"I tell truth, no BS."

The beam illuminating McArdle went out. Ten seconds later Viktor Boris Volkov felt a needle plunge into the base of his neck. He became sleepy, but did not fall asleep. Five minutes later a voice spoke out of the darkness.

"Mr. Volkov, do you know who I am?"

"Show me your face."

"Why are you here, Mr. Volkov?

"Fuck you."

He heard the murmurs off to his left and then felt someone's fingers on his wrist, taking his pulse.

The voice spoke to him again, this time slowly and rhythmically, urging him to relax; relax every fiber of his being. He tried to fight the effect of the serum but, as the fog of sleep began drifting over him the voice became more and more distant, until he was forced, first, to imagine what it was saying and then to make up words to fit with the airstream and sound waves falling so softly on his ears. The voice was so calm, so reassuring. Viktor felt comforted in ways he had longed for his whole life. He wondered if it could be the voice of God. The voice was kind, protective and curious. Whatever questions it had, Viktor was joyously eager to answer. He felt a brief pang of regret when the voice later told him that he would forget all that had happened to him that day, but he wanted to please the voice, so he did.

When he awoke he was seated on a Delta Airlines passenger jet bound for St. Petersburg. He could not remember when he was called back to Russia and checked his pockets for any clue there might be. As the sleep continued to wear off he became aware of just how uncomfortable it was to be wearing pants, so he took them off, along with his too small briefs. The woman seated next to him reached frantically for the call button, but was too short to reach it. Volkov smiled and asked if she would like him to push the button for her.

The St. Petersburg police were waiting for him as he strode into the terminal, the tattoos covering his legs and buttocks exposed for everyone to see. They delivered him to one of the Vory offices where a syndicate council was awaiting his report on the potentially lucrative St. Paul project. Now in its beta phase, the St Paul venture, led by Volkov and Voronova, was key to the Vory gaining clandestine access to the fiscal resources of several Midwestern state banks.

It was rumored that his fevered insistence on going pantless led to Viktor Boris Volkov's disappearance just a few weeks later. Other sources claimed that in St. Paul he had talked too freely about syndicate plans to the wrong people.

He never returned to St. Paul.

34

FIRST DATE

Mel Thorogood could see no harm in it; at least it was an idea. He knew they were thin on the kind of evidence that persuades a judge or jury. Evelyn Rose might be responsible for the deaths of at least three citizens of the City of St. Paul, but unless prosecutors could meet the normal evidentiary standards of the Minnesota Criminal Courts she was going to skate. Nor did the narrative about her names leading to her real identity meet any known legal standard. Thorogood cursed equally the lack of DNA from Adam Bierce and the skill of plastic surgeons.

He also thought Delaney's strategy for dinner this evening was entirely too simplistic: Delaney would have a small recording device sewn into his suit jacket. His cell phone would also be on record for the entirety of their meeting. Delaney would try to steer the conversation in such a way that Evelyn would somehow either confirm her identity as Adam Bierce or as the Riverrun killer. Thorogood admired Delaney's talents, but thought his expectations were a real stretch.

Delaney, for his part, neglected to mention that Mackey needed information, too; the kind of intelligence that would lead him to Evelyn's collaborators. He knew Jacob Berkeland was one and had suspicions about a couple of others. But that's all he had; he hoped Delaney could tease out some other names before he was forced to move on Evelyn.

At police headquarters, Delaney and Thorogood both objected to posting Natalie Puckett as Delaney's bodyguard. McArdle however, simply shrugged and said the two of them didn't really know Puckett, and she was more than capable of taking care of herself and Delaney.

That evening, as the two of them approached the entrance to Eddie's, Natalie Puckett smiled and said, "I've been on some weird first dates, but this one is easily the weirdest. How about you, Delaney?"

Puckett was a continuing revelation. At just five-foot-six in her steel toe pumps, she showed no signs of tension or fear at the prospect of entering the den of a sadistic, psychopathic killer. "I don't really do dates," he replied.

"So, you've already decided it's a one-night stand?" She laughed as she stepped through the doorway.

Butchie was waiting for them.

Delaney took Butchie aside and Puckett thought she heard him say something like, "Butchie, muffin Butchie." She was sure she misheard it, especially since she could not make out any of the other few words Delaney directed at the big man. But she had heard Delaney's hypnotic trigger right. Butchie was now dedicated to their safety and well-being for the night.

As he led them upstairs, she cast a raised eyebrow at Delaney, who whispered, "He's a good fellow."

She rolled her eyes. "Yeah, he looks like it."

After opening the door to the clubroom, Butchie left them.

Seated on a couch next to Evelyn was a short, thin, older woman. Her dark pageboy framed a wrinkled, puckish face with lively brown eyes made large by thick, black-framed glasses and a barely suppressed grin.

Glancing at Puckett, Evelyn Rose said, "Conor, I'd like you to meet my mothe…"

"Ms. Voronova, I presume?"

"Very good, Mr. Delaney." Marta Voronova laughed. "You know, I've been waiting a long time to meet you."

"Perhaps," Evelyn interjected, "you could introduce your friend, Conor."

"I think introductions are hardly necessary at this gathering." Voronova beamed and Evelyn frowned slightly as Delaney went on. "You've never met her, but you do know about Natalie, don't you?"

Looking off in the distance, Evelyn said, "In Mackey's business we have to know a few things about our police department, don't we? Natalie Puckett, formerly of the Domestic Violence Unit, now playing detective and helping you find that deranged serial killer. She is divorced and the mother of a delightful little four-year-old boy. Have you got her in over her head?"

As Delaney was about to speak, Puckett touched his arm. "Do you two mind? I'm right here. And I'm definitely not in over my head." Voronova smiled at Puckett and quietly clapped twice.

Delaney scowled. "What's this about, Evelyn?"

He noted that Marta Voronova was relaxed and comfortable; unusual for someone in a foreign land, dealing with strangers. He had a fleeting notion of asking about her drug of choice. Evelyn, as always, had an edge to almost everything she said. Sometimes it was so slight as to be unnoticeable. But Delaney always noticed.

"It's about cooperation, Conor. Compromise and cooperation."

"And, we sincerely hope," Voronova added, "collaboration."

"I believe this is the point," Evelyn said, staring at a sculpture across the room, "where your 'date' should be entertained elsewhere for a short while."

"Oh, I can't be shuttled off. I'm to stay with Mr. Delaney at all times. That's the express order of Chief McArdle, so I know you understand."

Voronova laughed quietly. "Oh, I like her. My dear, you are welcome to stay. More than welcome. What do you say, Evelyn? I think she is OK."

"Conor?" Evelyn shifted her gaze to a Turkish rug near Delaney.

"A moment, please." Taking a few steps back, he spoke quietly to Puckett. She finally nodded and Delaney turned back to Evelyn and Voronova. "We think it will be OK for her to leave, as long as she's still in the building."

Evelyn picked up a small handbell from the side table. The petite blonde entering the room in response to the bell registered surprise when she saw Puckett.

Evelyn did not look at the woman as she spoke. "Martine, would you please give Ms. Puckett here a tour of our facilities? Butchie will let you know when to return."

To Delaney's relief, that meant Butchie was stationed just outside the room.

"Before we start," Evelyn said as the two women left the room, "drinks?" And as she brought Delaney his usual shot of Irish whiskey, Marta Voronova talked about how much she was enjoying St. Paul.

"I just don't understand how Nabokov could conclude that this is a boring city. It has such exhilarating possibilities. Don't you agree?"

"I can't wait to hear about what kind of potential the City holds for a woman of your talents." Delaney's sarcastic tone was met with a wink and half smile from Voronova. "Evelyn, what's up? What are we doing here?"

Her gaze was now focused laser-like on the Mille sculpture. "First of all, Conor, I have some terrible news for you. Mackey won't be coming back from Cleveland."

Delaney remained as still as the sculpture.

"It's unfortunate, but he alienated the wrong people there – something about impeding their market growth and expansions."

"He was getting too big for their comfort?"

"I really don't know the particulars. It's something I've been afraid of for a long time."

"You sold him out." Delaney remained still, but his now intense owl eyes bored into Evelyn's. She shifted her stare onto the Klimt painting.

"Mister Delaney . . ." Voronova paused. "Your voice is ripe with unjustified accusation."

"Unjustified?"

"No one here is responsible for what has happened to Mr. Stately. I am much aggrieved if you think I would have anything to do with his demise."

Delaney caught her use of the singular first person and let it slide for now. Did it denote some kind of a split between them? To Evelyn he said, "His demise? You have confirmation of his death?"

"Only the word of a highly placed source in the Cleveland operation. They called at two o'clock. I still haven't told Butchie or the other men."

Cleveland. Did someone there encourage Evelyn in some way, only to be overruled later? Or was Cleveland in on Mackey's scheme from the beginning? Once again he marveled at how betrayal seemed imprinted into the very fabric of organized crime. No Godfather ever slept easily.

Even as Mackey had jokingly called it "Another Theory" several hours ago, he was plotting how to suppress the reality of an internal threat. The Cleveland source had confirmed Evelyn's treachery. Volkov, under the influence of the sodium pentothal and Delaney's gentle coaxing, sealed her fate. All that was left was to find and eliminate her supporters and allies.

"You didn't bring me here just to tell me about my friend's death. What do you want?"

"Of course, Mr. Delaney." Voronova leaned forward, ready to ditch the social blather for the more pious tones required of business transactions. "We'd like to offer you a deal."

35

HE WAS A SHAMAN

"We'd like to offer you a deal."

Those were the same words Viktor Volkov used with Mackey a year ago. Mackey turned him down cold and then called McArdle. And that, McArdle would later tell Thorogood, was precisely why he kept a man like Mackey in power. Mackey was a hedge against stronger, more troublesome crime syndicates. McArdle was convinced that Russian gangsters, the Mafia, Yakuza and other highly organized crime syndicates posed immediate threats not only to the power structures of cities where they operated, but to their national governments as well. His exhibit #1: the Russian Federation.

Mackey's call further solidified their alliance and from that day forward, had them united in their commitment to keep the Russian mob out of St. Paul.

Delaney, confronting the Russians in the person of Marta Voronova, wondered about what kind of deal she and Evelyn were empowered to make, while still casting about for ways to unmask Evelyn.

"Are you interested, Mr. Delaney?" Voronova pushed him for an answer.

"Probably not, but I am curious. What did you have in mind?"

"So predictable, Marta. He wants to know all about what he knows he's going to turn down."

Delaney smiled.

Voronova nodded and Evelyn rang her dinner bell once more. Just seconds later the two men flanking Voronova in Henry Bouchard's photo walked in. After one of them frisked Delaney, his partner waved a flat wand over him from head to foot and finally took Delaney's cell phone and suit jacket. The two big men left as quickly and silently as they had appeared.

Evelyn smiled. It was not a pretty smile. She pressed a button on a remote-control device and Delaney heard a recording of his Monday conversation with her, *"I'm curious about your thoughts regarding government entering into partnership with a criminal enterprise. Ostensibly this partnership is for the benefit of the public. What do you think?"*

"That's what your friend Thorogood is listening to now." She pressed the remote again. "So predictable, Conor. Trying to bug our time together this evening. For what? It would never be admissible in court, you know."

Delaney glanced at Voronova. "Is there any chance Boris and Natasha will bring my coat back?"

"Yes, of course, just as soon as they remove the offending technology."

"And are they going to administer some kind of punishment for my bringing the 'offending technology' in here?"

Voronova was emphatic. "Mr. Delaney, I have no intention of harming you. You have become precious to me. I have too much respect for you and that Delphi organization. You may have cost me a little money in those insurance and banking deals you scotched…" She paused as if reflecting back on those incidents. "And Evelyn? She speaks so highly of you that I fully expected your entrance to be heralded by a flock of trumpet-tooting angels. But still, I am shocked that you would think we would stoop so low as to physically harm you. Or Ms. Puckett, of course."

"You are free to leave at any time, Conor, although I hope you won't." Evelyn was no longer smiling as she gazed at the Mille statue again.

"Shocked? Strange you should use that word, Ms. Voronova. *Shock* is what the two of you have been deliberately fostering in this city, isn't it?"

"Conor, whatever are you going on about? We haven't done anything to shock, terrorize or stupefy anyone in this city." Evelyn was getting exasperated.

Delaney was mildly surprised at the tone of authenticity in her voice. He had never been able to read Evelyn. Now he knew why. She was a psychopath and psychopaths have no emotional canvas to read, their slates are blank.

As she turned to Voronova and said, "Can we get on to business?" Boris & Natasha returned with Delaney's coat and cell phone. One of them held the jacket for him as he slipped into it. Evelyn's glance briefly went across the room to her desk. "By the way, Conor, I appended a message at the end of my recording assuring Thorogood that you and Miss Puckett were just fine and he could call you if he wanted confirmation.

"Conor, we really want you and Delphi to join us in creating a new city. A city like no one has ever seen before," she said and nodded to Voronova.

"You see, Mr. Delaney, Evelyn and I have a great deal of respect for your ability to - how should I put it - connect with people. Everyone seems to like you, to respect you, and, most importantly, to trust you."

"Why do I get the feeling that a deal with you would involve betraying that trust?"

Voronova shook her head slowly. "No, absolutely not. That would not in any way suit our purposes."

"And what are those by the way, your purposes?" Looking at Evelyn, he said, "See? I'm interested."

"Down in Bolivia," Voronova began, "there is a mid-size city that has grown fourfold over the last ten years. It is booming with construction of all kinds of buildings, new businesses opening almost daily, with a living standard that has raised family income to the highest level on the continent. It is nearly crime free and the people who live there wouldn't think of moving to any other part of their country. And do you know how all this good fortune fell upon this heretofore obscure rural town?" She paused for two heartbeats. "Cocaine, Mr. Delaney, Cocaine.

"Our Latin brothers learned some time ago that they had to do something with their profits from the cocaine trade. They simply had amassed too much money; literally, it was more than they knew what to do with. So, they cast about for ways to invest it for the long term; ways that would make their families financially secure for generations to come. They arrived at the bold idea of corralling and centralizing all of their investments in one place and chose that unremarkable township.

"I'll be happy to share with you just what they did and how we propose to make St. Paul achieve a level of success that far surpasses the Bolivian economic miracle. But only after you agree to participate in our venture. As a full partner, I might add."

"You understand, don't you," Evelyn joined in, "we are talking about resources far, far in excess of what the cocaine cartel brought to rural Bolivia. Just think of how that could help the city and your bank account."

"So, you want me to help you gain control of a few, or several, or maybe all, of St. Paul's independent banks? You will also want control of the Port Authority, Housing and Redevelopment Authority and partner financial institutions, law firms and related agencies?"

"You're a fixer, Mr. Delaney. You can deal with the people who can make this happen. Think of what this could do for your city and for you. You would be a key leader in the creation of a real City on the Hill." Voronova's fervor impressed Delaney; he had always envisaged her as cooler, less emotional.

With his eyes still on Voronova, he said, "Evelyn?"

Watching out a window, Evelyn replied, "Yes, Conor, your guesses at the broad outline of our program are close. We will need to direct the resources of a number of financial institutions in order to reach our goals. And yes, you are every bit as critical to our success as Marta has said. But you should also know that we will proceed whether you are with us or against us. You do understand, don't you?

"Here's what you need to understand." She looked directly at him for the first time that night. "You are being given the opportunity to participate in the most revolutionary social experiment of all time. One that is going to bring more money here than you can even dream of. We can wipe out poverty in this city. Doesn't that appeal to your liberal instincts?"

Delaney, sipping on his whiskey, laughed out loud and gagged. Between coughing and laughing, he blurted, "You two want to stamp out poverty? Evelyn, you have never given the slightest thought to alleviating the poverty of anyone and, no offense, Ms. Voronova, but I'd bet every dollar in this universe that you and yours have never directed one ruble of your mob's filthy lucre to anyone outside of your syndicate."

Still choking and laughing, he lifted his glass and sang:

"Hurrah for the Revolution and more cannon shot!
A beggar upon horseback lashes a beggar on foot.
Hurrah for the Revolution and cannon come again!
The beggars have changed places, but the lash goes on.

"Old Willie Yeats knew all about your revolution. How'd it work out at home, Marta? Now, if you don't mind, I'd like to collect Detective Puckett and get away from the two of you."

Voronova sighed and, after asking Evelyn to have Puckett rejoin them, said, "I would hope we might not get entangled in the traps that language sets for us. How about if we call it social change, instead of revolution? In that context, Mr. Delaney, I wonder if I could prevail upon you to step into another room just to very quickly look over one of our plans."

Seeing his hesitation, she quickly said, "Oh, don't worry. We have it all pasted up on a wall in the Blue Room. You don't have to look at anything too detailed, just a few visuals that will, we think, allay your fears about our enterprise."

Delaney resisted the urge to simply walk out on the two of them and followed Evelyn down a short hallway, lined with small landscape paintings, to the Blue Room. It was directly across from where he met with the loan sharks. But this was nothing like that cramped meeting space.

This room was as spacious as the Club Room and the walls, ceiling, doors, and carpet were all different shades of blue. But what drew Delaney's eye immediately was the collection of art noveau and art deco paintings on every wall and sculptures scattered throughout the room. Facing each wall were benches of various sizes, each inviting a visitor to sit and gaze upon works by Klimt, Toulouse-Lautrec, Aubrey Beardsley and others of those eras. In among them were displayed sculptures by Brancusi, Moreau and several others by artists unknown to Delaney. There was another Edwardian desk with a single chair and computer tucked into a corner on the far wall from the door. There were maps, organizational charts and other visuals hanging from the walls near the desk. Boris and Natasha were already in the room and Voronova gave them instructions to wait by the door for Butchie and Natalie Puckett.

The two women led Delaney over to the far wall where there were four poster boards with graphics showing how funds would be shuffled from the Russian Mob's criminal activities - identified only as enterprise 1, 2, etcetera - into a stream of charitable foundations, non-profit organizations and other community groups involved in improving health, education, housing and employment opportunities for St. Paul residents. Delaney marveled at the complex simplicity of it all. He looked at Voronova with a renewed appreciation for her unusual abilities.

The sheer amount of dollars being projected for this "Community Funding Initiative" was staggering for a city of just 230,000: $2 billion over three years. The economist in him noted that this amount, if simply divided among them, would give every low-income family in the city much more than a comfortable upper-middle class life. Poverty in St. Paul would become nothing but a memory.

"In addition to these contributions – impressive, aren't they? - we are prepared to strictly abide by the terms of The Agreement."

When Delaney's eyebrows arched, Evelyn quickly added, "You don't think St Paul got picked out of a hat, do you? The infrastructure's already here and we can build on it."

Delaney smirked. "I suppose we should forget about the means by which you came into all this cash – child porn and prostitution, dealing dope, loan sharking, counterfeiting, financial fraud and theft – we should look away from that and instead focus on this fine example of Christian charity?"

"If we didn't do those things someone else would," Voronova chided. "You know that. Isn't it part of the core beliefs on which this, your city, was founded? You know all about the Agreement and how this city is run so don't get pious with me, Mr. Delaney."

"Leaving aside, then, the means by which you came into all this cash, what percent of annual pre-tax profit is represented by this fund?"

With her smile still firmly in place, Voronova replied, "Why, five percent, of course."

Delaney smiled back, but it wasn't a pretty smile. "Ms. Voronova, do you think me a fool? I said, 'annual,' not monthly. Oh, and I forgot, you don't pay taxes and it's all profit."

Evelyn stopped him. "Listen, you're no fool. You have to know that pumping something like an additional $55 million just for charity, and millions more into business enterprises, financial instruments and other opportunities into the local economy each and every month will make this city the richest in the world. What's wrong with that?"

"You know full well what's wrong with it. Just ask San Francisco or Seattle. First, housing prices will explode, then everything else from cabbages to caviar will follow suit. Then It will become a city of American oligarchs ready to peel off rolls of big bills to buy an army of office holders to safeguard what they will come to believe is their right to wealth without limits."

On the other side of the room Butchie was escorting Puckett into the room. Evelyn saw Puckett trying to get around one of the Russians and set out across the room. Despite Delaney's bitter reaction to her "plan," Voronova insisted that, "We can take steps to ward off those kinds of unintended consequences."

With her eyes on the carpet, Voronova continued in a quiet voice, "I'm curious, how much do you know about me, Mr. Delaney? More importantly, what do you know about my father?"

Using the same quiet tone, he replied, "I know you were born in the Siberian taiga and you were very young when Stalin threw your father into a gulag. I assume that's where the connection to the Vory was made."

"Anything else about my father?"

"No."

"He was a shaman."

36

SHARK EYES

Martine felt a rush of hope mingled with apprehension when she saw Natalie Puckett. Five years earlier Puckett had answered a 911 call from a neighbor who heard Martine's screams. By the time Puckett and her partner arrived Martine was beyond screaming and her pimp was nearing exhaustion from beating her.

From her half-closed eyes the semi-conscious Martine watched as her tormentor turned his rage on Puckett, who floored him with a kick to his kneecap. Martine faded into unconsciousness and didn't see Puckett stand back as her partner jerked the pimp's arms behind his back and put on the cuffs.

Puckett came to take her statement two days later. Tears welled up in Martine's blackened eyes as she said she would not be cooperating with any criminal investigation into this "incident." Even as a rookie Puckett knew why. The pimp had associates who would visit her. Best she be a good girl and accept her beating as a cost of doing business. Permanent disability or death were her other options.

Life was better now. Three years ago, Mackey, Mackey the Merciless, put out the word that he would no longer tolerate pimps beating up their whores. It ruined the product; if they were selling cars, would they smash their windshields or dent the hoods? Shortly thereafter Mackey cashiered a couple of misbehaving pimps to make his point.

As they made their way through the card games, craps shooters, diners and drinkers in the Back Room, Puckett saw Martine's mood undergo a decided uptick. When they reached the bar, she saw why. The bartender came over to them right away, his eyes fixed on Martine.

Martine smiled. "Tommy, this is Natalie Puckett. She's a cop, but a good one."

"We don't get many cops in here, except the guy over by the emergency exit." He nodded to his right. When she glanced that way, she saw Roland Gadsen playing cards with three other men.

"I heard you was with Delaney, I'm Tommy Swenson."

"Word gets around fast. Pleased to meet you Mr. Swenson."

"If you're a friend of Delaney's, the drink's on me."

"You know Delaney?"

"We all know him here. Him and the boss are buds and he's a good guy. You drinking that expensive Jameson's, like him?"

Puckett laughed. "Tonight, it will be a Shirley Temple. Tell me, when you say he's a good guy, what do you mean? What makes him such a "good guy?""

"I'll give you an example. He's here with the boss one night and Mackie suggests that the two of them should sit in on a card game for a couple of hands. They go over to Lucy's table and ask if they can sit in for three hands, no more. Of course, it's okay. Who's going to tell Mackie no?

"The first hand, Delaney takes, but it's a small pot. The second hand, well that's entirely different. The pot just keeps growing and it's down to Delaney and Marty Sheets, who's a regular and a pretty good card player. They go back and forth raising each other, musta been a dozen times. Finally, Marty calls and Delaney lays down a full house with three aces and two queens. Marty sees it and tosses in his cards."

"So, did he take the third hand too?"

"This is where it gets interesting. The pot grew pretty large again, but not nearly the size of the other one, when Delaney calls. The other two players left in the game hold a flush, jack high and a straight, king high. Delaney folds and him and Mackey get up and go about their business."

"So, what's the big deal about that?"

"The big deal is that Lucy takes a sneaky look at Delaney's hand before tucking it away. Delaney had a straight flush and he walked away from a $500 pot, which is exactly half of what he won in the other hand."

"Why would he do that?"

Swenson laughed, "Hey, you're the detective, you tell me."

As he stepped away to get their drinks, Puckett asked, "How about other people, are they as frightened of Evelyn as you are?"

Martine, startled by the suddenness and directness of the question, replied with a quiet, "Yes."

"Why is that? What makes her such a scary character?"

"You know how she doesn't look at you when you're talking?"

"I noticed. Yeah."

"That's bad manners, sure, but it's better than when she does look at you. She's got shark eyes. To her eyes you could just be a piece of meat. There's nothing human there, it's like she sees you, but to her, you're about as interesting as a cockroach."

"You know what some people call Delaney behind his back? Owl eyes. The two of them could have a real stare down competition, couldn't they?"

""Yeah, but his eyes aren't mean, are they? Just big and they kind of fit with his nose."

Tommy Swenson dropped off their drinks, and said, "It's Friday night so I'll be busy, but you need anything, just whistle."

"Tommy's a nice man. One of the few I've met. Hey, speaking of men, do you know that Thorogood guy? We hear he might take over when McArdle leaves and then Mackey and everyone else gets shut down. I think this town would fall apart if that happened, don't you?"

"Nah, I don't think much would change except our arrest rates. They'd go up. But, yeah, I know Thorogood. And if I read him right, he will shut stuff down . . . oh, wait a minute. Do you know who his best friend is?'

"I dunno, the mayor?"

"Delaney. I hear he's also Mackey's friend. Can that be right?"

"Well, Mackey and Evelyn work together and they are very different."

"Do you get along with her? She did pick you to show me around."

"I do what I'm told. I don't mess with her."

"What about her and Mackey? They're different, how?"

Swenson waved across the room. When Puckett turned she saw Butchie. He nodded and she knew it was time to leave the comfort of the bar and go back upstairs.

37

EVERYTHING WAS BLACK
IN THE BLUE ROOM

Butchie led Puckett down a short, well-lit hallway. There were small, antique landscape paintings along the way. As soon as they entered the Blue Room one of Voronova's big henchmen blocked her view of Delaney and told Puckett she would have to come with him to wait in the Club Room until Delaney was ready to leave.

"I think I'd better confer with Delaney about that," she said while wishing that Delaney would turn away from those damn posters and look across the room.

Evelyn stepped in and, looking directly into her eyes, said, "Really, it's OK, Ms. Puckett. There are things in this room we just can't have a police person looking at. I'm sure you understand."

Puckett suppressed a chill shudder and looked across the room.

Delaney and Voronova were moving now, but neither had turned their eyes to the scrum forming near the door. They were slowly strolling and Voronova was doing the talking. Delaney was listening intently. Watching him, Puckett wondered if he was now seriously considering whatever kind of deal Evelyn and the Russians were offering.

With Evelyn and one of Voronova's bodyguards trying to block her view of him she finally raised her voice, "Delaney! Would you . . . "

"Enough, you come now." The exasperated Russian grabbed her arm and started to force her back out the door. Butchie was on him immediately, swatting him across the head and sending him to the floor. He caught the other Russian with a backswing of his huge arm as the man tried to help his partner. Evelyn scurried to rejoin Delaney and Voronova just as the first Russian was getting up from the floor. In one motion Butchie grabbed and tossed him against the wall. As he moved to pick him up again, his partner roared, "Butchie!" and as soon as Mackey's man turned, shot him in the chest.

With the sound of the pistol shot reverberating like thunder off the room's four walls, Butchie's angry eyes glared at the shooter just before they went blank. He went down and the floor shuddered with the impact.

The shooter holstered his nine-millimeter and started toward Puckett. Evelyn reached into her purse as she circled behind Delaney. Voronova shouted at her bodyguards but they were now motionless, made still by surprise and curiosity. Voronova and Delaney also stopped, mesmerized by the same sight – Natalie Puckett performing a pirouette with all the confidence and control of a Bolshoi prima ballerina, spinning on her left foot once, twice, six times, smiling at the startled onlookers. Only Evelyn was not transfixed by the sight.

She whispered to Delaney in a contorted, but controlled, deep voice, "Conor, why did you have to ruin everything?" Delaney felt a needle plunge into the back of his neck. The room began turning a deeper shade of blue

Puckett's pirouette ended abruptly when her right foot struck like an asp, the steel toe biting deep into the Russian's groin. Evelyn tapped his mate on the shoulder and whispered in his ear.

Puckett's opponent was doubled over in shock and pain, when a second kick caught him squarely on the chin. He spewed blood and teeth across the carpet and was falling when a side-saddle kick smashed into his temple. He was motionless and silent as he hit the blue floor.

His partner moved quickly, his arm encircling Delaney's neck in a vise-like chokehold, using him as a human shield. Delaney, struggling for consciousness from Evelyn's injection, weakly twisted and stomped, all the while grabbing the Russian's extended arm. The fading Delaney had just enough strength to keeping him from steadying his pistol long enough to pull off an accurate shot at Natalie Puckett. For her part Puckett, now holding his partner's pistol, was in perpetual motion, shifting right, circling left, stooping, leaping and looking for her own shot. For as long as he was conscious, Delaney would be protecting both of them. But if this standoff went much longer he knew the chokehold would kill him.

The Russian's first shot was wide to the right, shattering a Tiffany vase. Delaney lifted his feet and tried to pull on the Russian's arm with his full weight. The Russian was as strong as he looked, but Delaney kept him from steadying his pistol.

He kept his eyes on Natalie Puckett and felt his exertions, against his will, becoming weaker. Then time began to expand and she was moving slower. The Russian's breathing slowed and Delaney could feel his heart slowly banging on his ribcage. As everyone in the room became more and more indistinct, he could still see Puckett, crouched like a big cat, coolly watching for a weakness in her prey's defense. His second shot was as wildly inaccurate as the first and left a hole in a Beardsley print.

Delaney never saw it, but he sensed it, spinning and unerring; then felt the bullet smash through his assailant's skull. Blood and grey matter smeared over his head and shoulders as the man slid to the floor.

Delaney barely made out a slow-motion Aloysius Higgs striding into the room, a wisp of smoke drifting lazily from his .38. Delaney thought he saw Higgs drag Evelyn out of the room and wondered vaguely about where Voronova was. An indistinct Mackey was hurrying toward him, several feet behind a much quicker Natalie Puckett. Delaney thought it strange that, while everyone else was fading into shadows, Puckett was as bright as a full moon on a cool August night. Then everything turned to black in the Blue Room.

38

BEING AND NOTHINGNESS

The sun was a hot brass disc glowing faintly through a heavy fog, settling behind the old fort and casting a long shadow on the far shore, where I stood watching, as five happy white-onyx Indians, brandishing a drum and pipe, waved to me as they galumphed down to the shore, to sit in a semicircle at the edge of the great muddy river, the Father of Waters. There they banged on the drum, the heartbeat of their nation. And, as they sang their ancient songs, spread an offering of sacred tobacco on the current, creating a small ripple that grew into a wild boil. The deep Mississippi River parted and a tip of bright white stone broke through, rising, with the dark liquid cascading off the massive white onyx figure until he reached his full height, with one arm still enfolding a pipe of peace and the other lifted in greeting, while all around him swirled clouds of white-headed eagles screaming, "Move, move them, move those slow thighs, dammit, move them." But the Great Spirit, unperturbed, gazed kindly upon the firmament and, speaking in a soft rumble, declared, "I am Gichi-Ziibi, Father of Waters and only Parrant of The City, behold the works of my centuries and eons, ye temporal powers, and despair."

As silence fell across the shadowland the Great Mystery smiled and winked down at me. Without his lips moving, he whispered, in that silent language that goes directly to the heart, "Why are you here, Owl Eyes?"

"I need to know what I should know and how I should act." I felt a sense of shame at the inadequacy of my answer.

With his eye still fixed on me, he continued his interrogation, "Since you have the gift for seeing into this darkness, have you learned the differences between and within human tribes?"

"Every tribe seems to wrongly believe that gender, race, color, wealth and class are important distinctions."

I thought I saw his eyes roll toward the heavens before he silently replied, "These divisions are the children born of narcissism and fear. They are the kind of small differences that have led to patriotism, bigotry, cruelty and war."

Feeling like I was getting close to something, I said,. "If these are small differences, what does a big one look like?"

He stared at me for a long time before answering. "The big difference, the one that matters, lies in the choice between Being and Nothingness. Every self, every community, must choose one or the other. What will your city choose, Owl Eyes?" He saw my discomfort and a small grin tugged at the corners of his mouth. "The answer should come easy. Why doesn't it?"

The God then began a smooth descent back into the paternal waters. But as he did, the plunge of his powerful frame created a massive vortex that pulled everything in after him – the fog, the fort, screaming eagles, drummers and, finally, me.

SATURDAY

The missing link in cosmology is the nature of dark matter and dark energy.

—*Stephen Hawking*

The center that I cannot find is known to my unconscious mind.

—*W. H. Auden*

Operating in an unlit world, the unconscious mind is a brilliant detective.

—*Jo Coudert*

The deft hand of the collective consciousness rules humankind. The atavistic echo of ancestral voices guides us in ways that often escapes our conscious, rational minds.

—*Kilroy J. Oldster*

in my beginning is my end....in my end is my beginning

—*T. S. Eliot*

39

THE COSMOLOGICAL INCONSTANT

In the river I found myself drifting happily in an amnion of dark matter until, caught in an upward current, I emerged into the fog-dimmed light of the hanging gardens of Babylon. Over there, stretched out among the black and white azaleas and zinnias, my owl eyes caught the merest flick of a tail before making out the full form of the white tiger, with its head on Plato's lap, luxuriating in the stroking of its skull and ears as a tiny walrus addressed it,

"Crabalocker fishwife, pornographic priestess;
Boy, you've been a naughty girl, you let your knickers down."

The tiger's head shifted slightly and the cruelly disinterested yellow eyes lasered pure malevolence at me. I slipped quickly and quietly back into the comfort of the dark matter.

Centuries later, or was it only minutes? I pushed through the darkness again and looked across a dimly lit room at the back of a tall, broad-shouldered figure outlined by a thin shaft of light squeezing through the barely opened door. The figure turned, slowly, and a gargoyle bearing a peculiar resemblance to Major Tom, swung his glowering red eyes across a hospital room and found me in bed, huddled and afraid. The thing opened its maw and issued a distant and muted Whumph! *as I slid back through the invincibility of the dark matter.*

Later I climbed out, this time into a classroom filled with endless copies of me, all seated in a boundless auditorium, watching and listening to the lecture. "I am

243

Alexander Vilenkin and what I am holding here," – he waved an infinite number of strings, each holding an uncountable number of universes – "are you and your homes, all your dreams and all your hopes. Here is every deed you ever did or thought to do. Every thought you have ever had, every ambition and, most assuredly, every single, every last, fear, I hold here draped across my arm. Would you like to hold one?" he asked. "These strings are very interesting; not really mathematically precise, at least not yet, but very interesting, don't you think?" I peered deep into one and, when I spied the black hole at the center of it, scuttled back into the comfort of my own primordial darkness.

Unaccountably, I struggled out yet another time and here found the dark goddess Kali on a high pedestal, her six arms waving to the rhythm of the drums of her dancing worshipers, all writhing in ecstasy. Kali, with a skirt of human arms, a belt of skulls and necklace of serene-faced rotting heads. I recognized Graham Byrd, Suzanne Porter, Danny Fortuno and Karleen Martin among them just as she reached down and plucked the infant Viktor Boris Volkov from a worshiper's breast. As she bit down on his skull, brains and blood spewed across her thin, grinning lips and down her chin. She stuffed the infant Viktor's body down her maw and reached for me, but I made a mad dive back into the comfort of my familiar darkness.

The light, dim though it was, beckoned again and when I emerged, I found a single figure sitting at a computer. "Hello there, I am Brahma and I'm fine-tuning this simulation of your world – well, actually, your whole universe. You always knew that you were only pixels in my simulation, didn't you? Well, I can assure you that Shem and Shaun know. You are just little ones and zeroes in my wonderful flowing river of ones and zeroes. Here's a quiz for you: Is this whole universe my simulation or did I just create a chip that's implanted in your comatose brain to give you the illusion of a life? It's multiple choice, pick one." I scrambled away from the horror and fell heavily back into the flow of my precious dark matter.

This was a place of comfort. Here there was no fear; it was calm and soothing, a balm of immaterial darkness. Easy, so easy, to just rest awhile, or even stay. Why was there guilt in wanting to? A strong but invisible undertow lofted me up once again despite my best efforts to resist it.

Peering out of the darkness, I saw McArdle and Mackey, seated in a dim light at a card table in Eddie's back room. McArdle looked at his cards and casually said, "Nope, can't let that happen. My job, after all, is to rein in this fuckin' lawlessness."

"But mine," said Mackey while laying down a something of spades, "is the capitalist imperative - expand, overcome, stretch beyond any gravitational limits. It is the constant you face, ya know, me and my kind never go away." McArdle laid down the black ace, "That's the big difference between you and me, m'boy. I am the limit, and you can't push beyond me, not without destroying yourself, so quit fuckin' around, I'm good for business and good for you." Mackey folded his cards.

McArdle glanced my way, "Well, well, if it ain't the cosmological inconstant. You know how much me and him need each other, don't you? So come to us, my boy." They held out their arms and smiled benevolently as a fox suddenly appeared, seated on the floor between them, and just as quickly disappeared, blinking in and blinking out of existence, again and again, all around them.

I drifted back into the comfort of my perfect darkness. As a feeling of contentment swelled, I spied a distant figure making its way toward me from the far reaches and as it drew closer it took shape. An otter.

It quickly circled and I was about to ask the animal what it was doing in my dark place, when it grabbed the front of my shirt and stared into me. All I could see were the deep brown eyes framed by a profound darkness, nothing else. I recognized the voice: "Time for you to go, owl eyes." She didn't speak, but the meaning was clear, even in the depths of the dark river.

Desperate with the need to stay, I said, "What are you doing here? And, by the way, where is here?"

"Child, you know this place. It is between."

"Between what, Grandmother?"

"Between the only difference that is not small and not of a kind."

"Being and nothingness?"

"Of course. And you have been here, dwelling between them, Owl Eyes. You know you have rested here enough. You have much to do before you can rest again."

"But I'm tired. So tired."

"*You should return under your own power. You will be stronger that way.*"

I felt like a petulant child when I replied, "OK, I will, but when can I come back?"

"*You will come back many times, as many times as you have been here before.*"

I remembered. Time ceased.

This was the dark river where time and space flow together, between the banks of Being and Nothingness, each held in abeyance by the other. I finally peered through the dim airy substance of the dark matter and could see that I was encircled by all my other lives. I heard my manifold other selves declare themselves to the multiverse:

> I am the hunter driving a stone tipped spear into the heart of the last mastodon.
> I am the mad priestess of Kali.
> I am a space ranger on a ship attempting to pass from one universe to another.
> I am a farmer, over and over again.
> I am a brilliant, but never published, poet.
> I am an attorney.
> I am a mother over and over again.
> I am a sophist in a Greek city-state.
> I am a soldier over and over again.
> I am a prostitute.
> I am a murderer.
> I am a slave in Egypt and Iceland and Mongolia.
> I am a shaman in the taiga.
> The otter laughed as I broke into the light. Or was it the Universe?

SUNDAY

If we should watch a city coming into being in speech... would we also see its justice coming into being, and its injustice?

—*Plato*

This thing that men call justice, this blind snake that strikes men down in the dark, mindless with fury, keep your hand back from it, pass by in silence.

—*Maxwell Anderson*

Justice cannot be exerted in a vacuum where there is neither good nor evil, right nor wrong.

—*Sabine Baring-Gould*

A society regulated by a public sense of justice is inherently stable.

—*John Rawls*

40

A SINGLE TEAR

Back in the semi-dark room with the same thin shaft of light squeezing through the barely opened door. He had an IV, but no catheter or endotracheal tube. There were the ever-present glowing machines of modern medicine and some other creature curled up on a chair next to his bed. It stirred and saw his open, apprehensive owl eyes. Natalie Puckett smiled briefly and said, "Welcome back."

He waited for a ghastly metamorphosis that never came. Delaney sighed with relief; the universe was watching with benign eyes today.

She waved to the other side of the bed as a single tear coursed down her cheek. Delaney continued to stare at her until Henri Bouchard said, "Yeah, welcome back. How did you like living in a coma-world? See anyone we know?" He grinned and pointed, "You ever gonna let that thing go?"

Delaney looked down and saw that he was clutching a furry pouch. He felt a rush of exhilaration. "Grandmother Raven?" His throat was a knot of pain and he hoped the Russian hadn't done permanent damage to his voice box. "You brought this, Henri?"

"Of course, as per our agreement." He grinned across the bed at his cousin. "Years ago, Natalie, we both pledged to the other that if things looked bad enough, we'd bring Grandmother's otter skin medicine bag."

"It's why I'm alive."

"Maybe. The nurses might argue with that. They almost kept me out until your official police escort waved me in.

"They said you would be dead before morning." Natalie said. "They may have exaggerated your condition. Or not.

"I saw an otter. It made me come back."

"Made you?" Natalie asked. "You didn't want to?"

"Not at first." He paused, surprised at the intensity in her voice. "Natalie, what happened to Marta Voronova?"

She winced before answering. "I don't know, Delaney. I haven't even thought of her with all that's been going on."

"What Natalie's not saying is that you were her responsibility and she was busy slapping your face and yelling to keep you from fading out before the paramedics arrived. Then she rode to the hospital with you and has been right next to you all night long. Have you slept at all, Natalie?"

She laughed. "What do you think I was doing in that chair? But to get to your question, Delaney, I don't think anyone was paying any attention to her. I would guess she slipped out unnoticed. Do you know where she might have gone?"

He shook his head.

"Why do you care? Henri asked.

"Did you know that her father was a shaman in the Siberian taiga? Stalin sent him to a gulag, hence Marta's ties to the Vory." Delaney silently vowed not to torture his voice box with that many syllables again.

"Marta? The two of you are using first names now?"

A nurse walked into the room. She frowned dubiously at Delaney and said, "Well, well, still alive, are you? How do you feel?"

"Putrid." He motioned for her to remove the IV and when she tut-tutted about the doctor having to order it, Delaney started to detach it himself, followed quickly by the nurse reluctantly taking the needle out of his arm.

She was troubled even more when he stood, staggered to the closet and began dressing himself. "Really," she clucked, "you can't do this, it's dangerous, you'll hurt yourself."

Two more nurses walked in as he turned back to Henri Bouchard. "Kyle?"

Bouchard nodded to the door and called, "Starbuck?"

Delaney croaked, "Starbuck?"

"Seems appropriate."

Kyle Lilly came into the now crowded room and almost before Delaney could get a word out said, "Are you sure this is a good idea, Conor? They said you had . . ."

The pain in his throat intensified as he rasped, "I'm fine. Anything happens, you bring me back, OK? Big day ahead. If you get the car, I'll meet you downstairs." Pausing to rest his throat, he continued, "Kyle, please take the rest of the day off after you get me to the office."

As Lilly made his way down the hallway to the elevators, Delaney gulped down a glass of water and asked Henri to make a call, check on Voronova and meet him at the office later. Natalie had apparently slipped out when the nurses came in. "Your cousin, Henri, you know about her?"

"Yeah, we took those classes together."

"You mean you can . . . ?"

"Kick the shit outta someone before they even know I'm kicking them? Yeah, I can, but I think Natalie's better at it."

Delaney thanked the nurses as he left. His appreciation was heartfelt. He'd loved nurses ever since his childhood separation procedures.

Kyle had the Prius waiting at the hospital entrance. As they pulled away Lilly asked, "Where to , Boss?"

"Mackey's."

"Really? For your first stop?"

Delaney ignored the implications of the question. "Any news from the office or elsewhere?"

"A couple things. Yesterday Shem said there was something about all those financial reports you had the police department send over. Said he just couldn't put his finger on it. Cy said the same thing. Early this morning Shem talked with Henri and now thinks he found it. He wants you to call him as soon as you can."

Delaney was making the call before Lilly finished his sentence.

41

FRIENDS FOREVER, MR. STATELY

"I just heard you were out," Mackey said as he put down his phone and Delaney walked into his club room. His big smile firmly in place, he looked at Delaney for several seconds. "It was only a few hours ago they decided you were gonna die. But here you are. You know, I was trying to imagine what life would be like without you, and I couldn't come up with anything. That's when I knew you'd make it. But I do have a question for you."

"Just one?" Delaney croaked.

"Yeah. What the fuck are you doing here when you should be in that hospital bed for at least another twenty-four hours? You sound like a frog with the dry heaves." He walked over to the bar and brought back a bottle of water.

Delaney nodded his thanks. "I'm here because your ass needs saving and I might be able to help."

No longer grinning, Mackey reacted. "Take your help someplace else. My organization has been compromised and I got a shitload of stuff to do to keep us in business."

"Let's not play the injured party, Malcolm. I'm the one who almost cashed in. 'It doesn't involve any real risk. You ain't gonna be in any real danger.' You want to explain what happened and why I should ever think of trusting you again?"

"Sure. You wanna tell me why Butchie went off like a maniac? Normally, he handles these kinds of events with greater control. You have a conversation with him?"

Delaney, needing to change the subject, shrugged. "Ok Malcolm, I know you're pissed and hurt, but I want to see if we can salvage something out of this." Mackey winced at the sound of his voice. Delaney took a drink from the bottle and asked, "You haven't heard from McArdle yet, have you? That means he's either undecided or is already exploring other options. My money has to be on the former."

"So what? So fuckin' what? Why are you still here?"

"Look, my friend, I told you McArdle was insanely pissed about these Riverrun murders. I think he must now suspect you knew about them all along. If he is convinced of that, you are done. And I mean dead done. Hell, if he even knew the truth he'd be pissed."

"Christ's sake, Delaney, stop talking. It hurts to listen to you. But the truth? You don't know what the truth is."

After taking a quick drink, Delaney replied, "I know the truth. Let me give you the condensed version. Years ago, you're on one of your jaunts to Kansas City and meet the woman who runs the Blue Light franchise there. With your natural nose for talent, you find out she's got a brain, a real good brain for business." He knew he shouldn't be talking at such length but went on anyway. "You bring her to St. Paul. She's agoraphobic so you put her up right here. You have to have her close. You don't really trust her. She was, after all, part of the cannibalistic Kansas City operation. "

Although he couldn't tell if Mackey's scowl was in reaction to his voice or what he was saying, Delaney continued , "A while ago she floats the Port Authority scheme to you. She's got a friend in Milwaukee that could be your insider in the front office, privy to all the financial plans and schemes of the Port Authority. You'll know the Port's plans before anyone else, thanks to Suzanne Porter. Do you know how she got Porter in there?"

Mackey, lips tightly pursed, shook his head and Delaney continued, "By either bribery or threatening to kill kids. That was Evelyn's modus operandi. It was easy. Offer big bucks. That usually worked. When it didn't, take pictures of their kids going to school, show them a picture of a bloody, dead child and tell them that's what happened when somebody didn't cooperate. People really do fold when facing that kind of cruel reality. She pulled that trick on the Milwaukee big businessmen who signed glowing letters of recommendation about Porter, whom none of them had ever met." Delaney began to sweat, but shook his head when Mackey started to talk.

"Evelyn sold you on the notion of a cute little sideline business where you'd be able to buy properties low and sell them high, thanks to another of her friends. Graham Byrd handled Port Authority properties all over the city and, most importantly, knew all the real estate appraisers in the county. When he helped bribe these guys, and they were so easily bribed, no need for threats of child murder, you were in business."

He took another drink of water before continuing, "But that was small stuff compared to the Port Authority bonds. What better way to launder Cayman Island funds? You already had Jacob Berkeland and his bank tied into your business, but, unbeknownst to you, Evelyn tied him down even tighter. Probably with threats of one kind or another, just because she was a psycho and liked watching people suffer."

Delaney stood and sauntered over to the bar. "Malcolm, Evelyn – Adam – had a dark and empty place where most of us have a heart, soul, something that gives us our humanity. She was a psychopath and didn't know how to appeal to any emotions other than greed or fear. She got to you through greed. She made those designer drugs that showed up on the streets of St. Paul, Kansas City and Cleveland, didn't she? She made you a lot of money with them, didn't she? Then came the intricate Port scheme, an idea you were ready to leave in her hands because she made you a big bundle with the drugs. How am I doing so far?"

Mackey glared at him.

"But why get into tearing out throats, creating a big stink you definitely did not need? She did it for some very good reasons beyond the sick, abject joy of it. It shifted suspicions away from you or anyone else in your organization. This just wasn't your style. The big thing was, it put this town on edge. McArdle and his police force were almost totally distracted and. the local media were featuring the story and posing those easy, frightening headlines like, 'Who's Next?' and 'Police Baffled by Serial Killer.' Lucky for you they missed all the Port Authority connections."

Delaney paused and slowly shook his head. "Beheading Karleen Martin and laying a tattoo on Shaun's neck? They led me and the St. Paul cops to chasing a bunch of abstract clues leading inevitably to her. She needed everyone, including you, to know just how damned clever and smart she was."

"She is the smartest person I ever knew, except maybe for you."

"She was clever because there was no way to find her culpable in any of these cases. She was agoraphobic and never left home. The word play on Ambrose Bierce was another clever distraction, one she knew I couldn't resist."

"She did all of this stuff so she could get rid of me and take over?"

"The short answer is yes. The longer one is that she needed to create a state of shock in the city that would enable her and the Russian Mob to move in and totally reorganize and dominate this city.

"But you knew, didn't you, that she was the Riverrun killer when Fortuno went down. Maybe even when Porter was killed. That's why we went upstairs to talk about the murders, where Evelyn could hear us. You thought you were tipping her off and offering up Pinckney as a fall guy. Didn't work out too well, did it? And if McArdle finds out, you're done."

"That's enough. I can't stand listening to you. What the hell do you want? In twenty-five words or less, please."

Delaney's throat felt raw and he began to wonder if the damage was permanent. "I'm meeting McArdle later and I think I can convince him to keep your 'partnership' in place. But I need to know something first - is she dead? If she isn't, McArdle won't go for it."

"She's disappeared."

"Higgs?"

"Yeah. What more do you need?"

"Now," Delaney paused, "about Butchie . . ."

"He's going to live, but he'll be laid up in the hospital for a few weeks. So, tell me, Delaney, why did Butchie do what you told him to do?"

"Trade secret, Mack, you know I can't tell you that."

"Who is Butchie working for, me or you?"

"The only time Butchie works for me is if my life is threatened. Otherwise, he's your man. Entirely."

"And you can guarantee McArdle?"

"I can let you know later."

"Thanks, I think."

"One other thing, and this is entirely for you and for the City of St. Paul. The Port Authority thing, you own a bunch of their bonds and if you do nothing with them, there's going to be a crash and you'll lose a lot of money, so will the city."

Mackey frowned. "I got accountants can take care of that."

"No, they can't. They can only tell you the numbers. On strategy, well, that's not part of their training. You're going to lose money, but I can help keep it to a minimum."

"So, what do I have to do?"

"Nothing, just approve those transactions that are referred to you."

"You'll be doing the referring?"

"No, Evelyn's lawyer will. She's the one who set up the accounts in the first place. But I do guarantee they'll be the best deal you can get. Deal?"

"Yeah, of course." Mackey paused before looking away from Delaney. "You remember when we were kids and nobody wanted us around? I was so lonely then; felt so alone that I got this empty feeling and got so I even didn't feel anything, not even how alone I was. Then Evelyn came along and I didn't feel alone any more. Her and me, it was like we were riding the same wavelength. And now, shit, now I find out I was more alone with her than I ever was before. That empty feeling, Delaney, that damned numb feeling, is back again. Know what I mean?"

Delaney, briefly remembering the years with Cody, nodded. Mackey stood, went to the bar and poured two shots of Jameson's. "Here's something to fix that frog in your throat." They drank and Mackey extended his hand. "I trust you. We got a deal."

A slight smile tugged at the corners of Delaney's lips as he took Mackey's hand in both of his and said, "Friends forever, Mr. Stately, till death do us part."

Mackey's broad smile reasserted itself. Delaney had a way of making him feel that all was well in the world. An outsider viewing the two of them would have seen Delaney sipping several times from a tall bottle of water while talking for several minutes straight, and Mackey nodding in agreement to all that he heard.

42

DISQUIET

Thorogood's scowl was firmly in place as Delaney walked into Delphi's sun-flooded conference room. "Conor, this is crazy. Nobody expected you back this soon. Docs said you have a decent constitution, but you're not supposed to be walking around." Dalton Gettler, Ann O'Leary and Natalie Puckett were with Thorogood.

"Nice to see you again, Detective Puckett and, by the way, thanks for saving my life." He took a drink from a tall glass of water.

Thorogood hesitated. "Listen to you. It sounds like somebody tried to rip your throat out. Before we begin, there is a six-hundred-pound gorilla in the room that we should discuss right now. I think our rookie detective was kind of an FBI mole and turned them on to this case. That's why she may have to leave the force."

A surprised Delaney spoke carefully and slowly: "So? She didn't really do anything wrong. We are on the same side, after all. It's my guess that the FBI called her. They need Native American agents. She'd be a prize recruit." He took another drink.

A loud clap filled the air. "Do you mind? I'm right here, you two; please don't talk about me as if I weren't. Delaney, the Chief's right, you sound awful."

O'Leary broke in, sounding hurt, "OK, Puckett, there's a trust issue here. Don't you think you should have told us you were talking to the suits? You should be gargling salt water, Delaney."

"How did you all come to learn of my *perfidy*? And does anyone want to know how this happened?" Puckett was clearly offended by their conclusions.

Thorogood paused before replying. "Hanson told us."

"What precisely did snake eyes tell you?"

"That you accepted their offer and then changed your mind, changed it because of this case."

"So, Hanson seeks a little revenge when I decide the St. Paul PD is a superior experience to being an FBI agent and you two decide I should be, what? Punished somehow?"

"You were the one who told them about the Riverrun cases and, you may remember, I said I'd cashier anyone who talked about it to anyone outside our team. Remember? What am I supposed to do now, pretend I never said it?"

The door opened and Henri Bouchard came in and quietly sat next to Thorogood.

Delaney nodded to Bouchard and turned to O'Leary. "Puckett has the makings of a good detective? Great instincts?"

"Best I've ever seen. Yeah, Puckett you're good, very good." O'Leary couldn't suppress a grin. "And brave enough to go on a dinner date with Delaney."

Thorogood smiled at the dig at his friend. "Well, look, Natalie, I can't afford to be jettisoning good people. There are just too few of you. I actually believe that old saw about the department only being as good as the people we have working in it. You know that. I am not about to make a Greek tragedy out of this incident. At the same time, don't ever make me face another situation like this." He threw a sideways wink at Bouchard before concluding, "If there is a next time, I can assure you that I won't be nearly as much fun to deal with. Even if your cousin threatens to disown me."

Two hours later Thorogood would call Puckett with another warning and the offer to permanently assign her to the detective squad.

But now he looked over at Delaney with a grin, "What's he doing here?" and clamped a big hand on Bouchard's shoulder.

"Thought you might want to thank him." Delaney swallowed some more water. "Always been a shadow member of this group and I asked him to come in out of the cold."

"Well, thank you, Henri. I haven't thanked anyone else, yet, but thank you anyway." Turning back to Delaney, he said, "You want to know how things went down?"

O'Leary pushed her chair back and crossed her legs as Delaney nodded. Thorogood went over how he and a team of officers arrived less than ten minutes from the time of Delaney's collapse. Paramedics quickly moved the injured out of the building and into Phelan Hospital. Thorogood's crew stayed to search through every room of the building.

"You might be surprised at what's in there," Thorogood said. "One room has several large wall safes and another looks like a chem lab. There's also two bedrooms and three meeting rooms, complete with mahogany tables and comfortable chairs. Quite the digs. Just like here. We got a search warrant later, but didn't really find out anything we didn't already know."

O'Leary asked, "Did you know about that elevator in the back that went down to a tunnel going from the basement to that parking ramp up the block?"

"No," Delaney lied. "It explains how she got out. No one saw her leave."

Bouchard, frowning, raised his hand and said, "I thought she had agoraphobia? What was she doing going in and out of the building?"

"We think she may have had an accomplice. An Igor to her Frankenstein, as Dr. Phil put it." Thorogood smiled again, and continued, "There's a limited number of suspects and we have all sorts of files and papers from scouring Mackey's place. We should be able to run him down pretty quickly. Right, Detectives?"

O'Leary gave a quick thumbs-up, while Puckett shrugged and flashed a nervous grin.

Delaney asked, "Did McArdle know you were going to toss the place?"

Thorogood grinned. "Things were moving a little too fast for me to check in with him. He was not pleased, but he understood."

"Mackey?"

"He was at the hospital looking after you and Butchie. He was really pissed about our tossing his place. Of course, he was probably more pissed about some other things, don't you think?"

Puckett broke in, "By the way, Higgs said something that sounded like he was taking Evelyn to Caracas? It sounded like Caracas, but Higgs has a strange accent."

"Carcosa, land of the dead in an Ambrose Bierce short story. We've seen the last of Evelyn."

The news was greeted with an apprehensive silence. O'Leary cleared her throat. "Are you sure about that? Higgs actually said 'Carcosa?' He doesn't have a reputation as a particularly literate guy."

"It is what he said and what he meant." Turning to Thorogood Delaney asked, "You have a big dragnet and you got nothing so far?"

Thorogood winced at the soreness in Delaney's voice. "That's about it. But we've got every flight out of the airports covered. Same with the trains, buses, cabs, Uber, Lyft and rental cars. Every car registered to Mackey is accounted for in that ramp and no reports of stolen vehicles from there. We have bulletins out to Caracas and across this country. Special notices went to Tulsa, Kansas City, Milwaukee and the border patrol. I think we'll leave those in place for another week or so, just in case."

"Gunnar?"

"Not well. His brother's death hit him hard and he blames himself for it."

Delaney raised an eyebrow. "How so?"

"It ties back to Fortuno. Your suspicions were right about Gunnar covering for him. According to Gunnar, nearly all of Fortuno's kills were shot in the back at close range. Gunnar doctored the autopsies to make them look more legit. We're going to go back and look at those cases again, but we're pretty sure some of them will loop back to Evelyn or Mackey, and maybe even involve his brother's bank somehow. He is, by the way, retiring immediately, which will probably save his ass from a criminal trial. The county doesn't need the publicity that would come from that."

"What do the media know about last night?"

"That there were two cases of food poisoning and an accidental, self-inflicted gunshot wound. It was buried in the newspaper, never made it on TV.

"And another thing, Megan Hartley was right about distracting the media. I don't know how long it will hold, but there's been little attention paid to the Riverrun cases in the last few days."

Delaney glanced at Puckett, O'Leary and Gettler before turning to Thorogood again. "What's next? Investigation being shut down?"

Smiling broadly, Thorogood said, "Disband this band of warriors? Not yet. Igor is still out there so we'll meet tomorrow morning again. I want each of us to go back over our assignments and notes and see if there's any stones we've left unturned. Henri, if you're available, I'd appreciate your joining us. By the way, I don't have the authority to shut us down until the chief gives the order.

"Speaking of the old demon, Conor, I understand you and I will be meeting with him in a little while."

Thorogood shook his head. "He'll want to talk with us about closure on these cases and how to handle the public announcements. He's just happy this whole dismal affair is over and that his force got it done in such short order."

Delaney wondered if Thorogood could believe it was all that simple. It seemed to him that the three cops were too anxious to declare victory. Looking at the other faces in the room, he was certain that Henri Bouchard and, perhaps, Dalton Gettler, shared his unease.

Gettler finally stirred and said, "Can I get back to the lab? I have something that I really need to get to. Oh, for your throat Mr. Delaney, I would suggest gargling with a good quality mouth wash."

Delaney noted Gettler's disquiet but thought little more of it.

43

A STORY TO TELL AND TO SELL

"Phineas and Samoan, ever hear of 'em, boys?" The Big Chief was seated comfortably behind his broad desk, hands folded over his ample midsection.

"No?" McArdle snapped, "I didn't think so and I am not surprised. For your information, they were spies, the earliest spies we know of by name. But there had to be a lot before them. They spied in Jericho before the walls came tumbling down and hid out in a whorehouse. If either of you ever read your Holy Bibles you'd know these things.

"Spies," he continued, "have been essential to every military force since the beginning of time. Sometimes we give them new fancy names, like confidential informant, source, whistle-blower, or snitch. But it all boils down to the same thing, doesn't it?"

When neither Thorogood nor Delaney answered, McArdle continued, "The correct answer would be yes. Now tell me, young gentlemen, why do you think I am delivering this little homily unto you?"

Thorogood replied, "You're going to tell us, aren't you, Chief?"

McArdle's one eye danced back and forth between them. "Yes, I am going to tell you something that should have been obvious to the two of you a long time ago. Mackey ain't the only one in this town who's got spies and leakers in his employ. I have them everywhere," he gave Delaney a prolonged glance. "And I do mean everywhere. And they are as invisible as ravens at midnight. A mouse doesn't fart in this town without me knowing about it."

Delaney refrained from correcting McArdle on the spies' names – he suspected that the man wasn't really confused about them - and from telling him that Marguerite and Kyle were both double agents – they only gave McArdle Delaney-approved information or lies.

McArdle leaned forward, elbows on his desk. "All this is by way of telling you that I, too, now know the identity of the Riverrun killer. And I, too, know that this freak of nature is almost certainly dead. An added bonus comes with that. The Russians are done, they are so done, in our fair city. Right? So, boyos, time to celebrate, no?"

Delaney smiled. He'd had Henri Bouchard phone McArdle just an hour ago. "We only confirmed it today," Delaney said. "Today, because we only got solid information today, after I escaped from the hospital."

McArdle frowned. "You swallow a hacksaw or something? It pains me to listen to you, so whatever you have to say, keep it short. About this *solid information*. Oh, that's good, and what is *solid information*?"

"It comes from an unimpeachable source. One that is absolutely trustworthy."

"Who?"

"You know I can't, and won't, tell you that."

McArdle belched. "That's what I think of your *unimpeachable source*."

Thorogood waved his hand. "Does this mean you want us to close the case?"

"That's what I want to discuss with you gentlemen. That and the future, or lack thereof, of one Mackey Stately. The media weasels will want a body. As I see it we have three options for that. We make Mackey dig up the freak and give the body to us, we shoot Mackey and call him the killer, or we make him give up one of his guys, dead of course."

Delaney and Thorogood looked at each other for two seconds before laughing out loud. "When you two hyenas are done giggling maybe you'll tell me what's so damned funny?"

"That's crazy, Chief." Delaney said, still smiling. "Just shoot Mackey or one of his men? You do know murder is against the law, don't you?"

"OK, smartass, how about this – it'll make for a great headline – we know that our killer is dead because Foxy Higgs dragged her away. Is that our story, huh, is that it? And what do we say to their next question – do we have Higgs under arrest? And the next one, why not? So, smart boys, what do you want to do?"

"We wouldn't have this problem, any of it . . ." Thorogood began before McArdle cut him off.

"Save your moralizing for someone who gives a shit. And who, incidentally, hasn't given it decades of thought, because anyone who has will agree with me and tell you to hurry up and graduate from Sunday School."

Thorogood sighed. "OK, I think I know what will work. The ethics, to say nothing of the legality of it, are highly dubious and I don't much care for it, but it will work." McArdle looked at him, skeptically, but expectantly. "Adam Bierce. You say we have a DNA match to Adam Bierce and have it on good authority that he has fled Minnesota. We believe he is heading back to Kansas City or Tulsa, his previous residences, but we've released a national bulletin and alerted the FBI. We release that drawing we have of him to the press, along with the story."

"Shit, I was hoping to shoot Mackey. But your story could actually work," McArdle said before punching a button on his phone. "Megan, come in here, darlin', we have something for you." His one eye flashed at them. "That is unless either of you have some objection?"

"Of course, I don't like it. I'd rather be in a position to tell the truth," Thorogood replied.

"Truth," McArdle sneered. "The truth is written by the winners, my good man, remember that. The winners. All else is dross."

"Would you ask Ms. Hartley to wait for just a few minutes, Chief?" Delaney said. "There's one other thing we need to talk about, privately."

"It's about your buddy Mackey, isn't it? And in answer to your question, no, I haven't decided what to do with him. I already know what you want, but please, tell me why I should be in agreement with you. In twenty-five words or less, please."

"Two words will suffice – Port Authority.

"The value of Port Authority bonds, and properties, are going to take a dive. But how fast and how deep that dive is, can be controlled. It will be better for everyone if it's gradual and steps can be taken to mitigate its losses. Better for the Port and better for the city."

"What has Mackey to do with this?"

"His funds from the Cayman Islands, and elsewhere, have kept the Port solvent for the last couple of years."

"You mean his ill-gotten gain inflated the value of these things to begin with and now we need him to . . . Christ, what tangled webs we weave."

"You have it, Chief. You need Mackey to manage the underground economy and an important part of the city's so-called legitimate economy."

"OK, Mackey stays, but he fucks up and there will be no further discussion. Period, end of story. Now can I call in the ice goddess, please? I'm sick of looking at you two. Tired of listening to you, too." McArdle flipped a switch, and as Megan Hartley entered the room he said, "Megan my dear, please sit. We have a story for you. A fabulous story for Assistant Chief Thorogood to tell and you to sell."

44

A WHOLE LONG LIST OF CONNECTIONS

Thorogood and the two detectives left two hours ago and now Delaney and Henri Bouchard were in the Delphi conference room listening to Sheshdhar Shivaji. "You know how we all have a number of professionals providing some specialized services to us? I mean doctors, dentists, insurance agents, bankers, and so on.? When Henri posed the idea of putting together a list of service people each victim hired over the last five years I thought we might find several individuals or companies that were connected to all three." He paused for a moment, looking at the two of them expectantly. Delaney silently thanked the universe once again for guiding Shem to Delphi.

"Instead, I found that Byrd and Fortuno had used the same plumber, but only once for each of them. Hard to make anything out of that. But as it turned out there was one name that did pop up for all of our victims." He frowned and looked at Delaney. "It was a lawyer. Care to guess who?"

Delaney shifted uncomfortably. His voice reduced to a harsh whisper, he recited:

> "Crabalocker fishwife, pornographic priestess
> Boy, you've been a naughty girl, you let your knickers down."

Shem and Henri looked at each other before turning back to Delaney. Still unable to talk above a whisper, he continued:

> "I am the egg man, they are the egg men

I am the walrus, goo goo g'joob".

Henri shook his head. "I don't get it."

"You would if you saw a picture of this guy. He's got this moustache, takes up a lot of acreage on his face." Shem replied.

"Mark Minim," Delaney said.

Henri wanted to know, "He's connected to the victims and Evelyn? And the Beatles?"

"Yeah, there's a whole long list of connections, except for the Beatles. How did you know, Boss?"

Delaney waved him off and made a rolling motion with his hand.

"Right, OK. He was Porter's attorney when she bought a condo in a Port Authority development. It would have been unusual if he hadn't run into Byrd at some point. Both were heavily involved in dealing with Port Properties. But it's when we get to Fortuno that it gets interesting. Dollar Danny's phone bill shows a bunch of calls between the two of them in the days leading up to Fortuno's death. There's also a slew of calls between Evelyn and Minim.

"Then there's the Port Authority. He handled the legal work for a lot of commercial projects both for the Port and for other parties in Port sales or purchases."

"Another connection: Pinnacle City Bank and Trust. He did all his business there, both legal and, uhm, questionable."

"Questionable?" Bouchard asked.

"The questionable part is the legal work he did for Evelyn in purchasing Port bonds with Cayman Island funds. He was also the attorney when Evelyn was tipped off about the Port's plans and she bought up properties the Port would later be purchasing. Whenever the Port Authority or property was involved, he was Evelyn's attorney."

"Thoro and I interrogated the bastard two years ago. The only thing I remember about him is that big walrus mustache and a truly malevolent stare. He got really pissed off at the questions I asked."

Delaney thought back to the ways the Riverrun killer had drawn him in when Bouchard said, "He was pissed at you, not the questions. This raises another question, is it possible that Evelyn didn't know? That she wasn't even involved?"

"No," Delaney said. "Just a moment. . ." He was making a call. After a few seconds he spoke into his phone: "Thoro, remember that attorney we questioned in the murder of Kyle's wife? Yeah, Mark Minim. He looks like our Igor. More likely than any of Mackey's men. How soon can you get eyes on him?"

"Wait," Shem said, "I'm tracking his credit cards. I'll be right back." Less than a minute later he returned with the news, "He checked into the Grand Portage Hotel this afternoon."

"Did you hear that . . .? Just a minute."

He looked at Bouchard who was already calling the hotel to ask the staff for a description of the person checking in as Mark Minim. In less than five minutes he said, "It ain't him, unless he's in his twenties with long blond hair."

Delaney was back on the phone with Thorogood and finished the call almost immediately. He called another number and after a short delay said, "Kyle, sorry to interrupt your off time, but it's important. Can you check our cars right away, check them for IEDs? . . . Yeah, I think there's a very good chance we'll have a bomb planted on one or more of our cars. Let me know what you find. Thanks, Kyle.

"Thorogood is sending cops out to scout Minim's residence and office and any other place we might suggest. Cops are also going to play bodyguard for Delphi staff again. Shem, he needs your data. Trusting that much of it is protected by privacy laws, he's sending a detective over to get your leads and see if he can find a clean route to them. Should be here within the hour. OK?"

As the tech wizard started back to his office, Delaney's hoarse whisper stopped him. "Shem, good work. What's the latest on Shaun?"

"He's getting cabin fever, but looking forward to the painful operations that will remove his tattoo. Boss? I have to ask, how did you know?"

"Lucky guess."

"Car bombs?"

"Same."

Shem waggled his finger at Delaney, "Shame on you bald-facedly lying like that."

With Shem out the door, Bouchard frowned. "Grand Portage, a car bomb?"

"A coincidence?"

"We both know better, don't we?"

45

CAN YOU SEE ME NOW?

Having seen Henri off at the elevator, Delaney stumbled into his condo, one floor up from Delphi's offices. Every cell in his body was weeping for sleep. They were right, all of them, he should have stayed longer in the hospital. Even now he could feel the pain in his throat evolving into something that spawned microbes. He hoped it wouldn't be pneumonia.

He stepped into his open-space condo with a feeling of relief. On a sunny day the big windows gave him a view of nearly all of the city and flooded his home with light. The view on a clear night almost made him feel like he was among the stars.

The condo had nearly 3,000 square feet. Bedrooms and baths took up nearly 1,000 feet. Delaney, having told himself for the last twelve years that he was going to learn how to cook, had a 400 square foot kitchen. Its placement next to the entryway was an almost daily reminder of his procrastination skills.

But he wasn't thinking about any of this as he flicked a light switch and walked into the kitchen for a glass of cold water. The day had been full of wind, rain and black clouds. Nightfall only deepened the daytime darkness. He was just dragging himself around the counter that separated the kitchen from the rest of the area when he jerked to a stop. A lamp came on and he was now fully awake.

Seated uncomfortably on the couch not a dozen feet away, Mark Minim looked exactly as Delaney remembered him, except for the red plush box at his side and the .45 he was pointing at Delaney's chest.

Minim grinned like a pig-eyed Cheshire cat. "My, my, Conor Delaney. I guess we know who's the winner in this game now, don't we? Sit down, right there." He pointed the pistol at a straight-backed chair near the kitchen area. "Evelyn and I have you now, don't we? She always said I'd be able to corner you. She's one smart lady, don't you agree?"

Minim held the pistol with both hands, arms stiffly extended in front of him. Delaney didn't think he'd be able to hold it like that for very long. A .45, fully loaded, can weigh over five pounds.

"I guess so. Mackey says she was."

"What do you mean *was*?"

"Haven't you heard? She's dead."

Minim didn't look to be either strong enough to hold it like that for very long, or comfortable enough to hold it casually in his lap. "You're a liar. She said I shouldn't waste time listening to you."

With the pistol still trained on Delaney he nodded at the red box and said, "Guess what's in here? The question is, do I use it on you sooner or later? What do you think, Delaney? I think I'll follow Evelyn's advice and do it sooner

"And that reminds me, *Delaney*, Evelyn doesn't think that's your real name."

He's delaying, drawing it out, Delaney thought. He's afraid and unsure; his psyche will have to dredge up a barrel full of resentment rage before he can pull this off. That is, if nothing scares him.

"You know, the two of us researched all kinds of public records and there's no evidence of a Delaney birth in any state the month you were supposedly born. No record of a Delaney birth anywhere in this country except for an obviously phony birth certificate in this state. It's not a real record – it refers to a hospital birth, but the hospital has no record of it. Very sloppy work.

"She found something there, but it's strange. A kid named Delaney is listed in the child welfare records of the Grand Portage Indian Reservation, but the record stops cold right there. There's no record of school, parents, foster parents, nothing. It's as if a kid showed up and disappeared.

"So, who are you, *Delaney*? I hoped to have the answer before we got to this little impasse, but, you know, I can't really wait any longer, can I?" He glared at Delaney. "Here I am, you jerk."

And here's where the anger build-up begins, Delaney told himself.

"You thought you were so superior when you talked down to me and Pastor Diffley. You acted like we were hardly worth the time it took to talk to us. There we were; me a successful and highly respected attorney. Did you know I was even nominated to be President of the County Bar Association? No, of course you didn't. And Pastor Diffley, a real man of God. And you practically accused him of having an affair with Jennifer Lilly. If you ever heard him preach you'd know he was really filled with the Spirit. You, you treated us like dirt."

His nostrils flared and Delaney knew that under the moustache his lips curled into a sneer. "Now look at me. I am . . . " He laughed. "I am in control of your life and death. Can you see me now? Can you hear me now, you arrogant fool?"

Delaney saw the first quiver of Minim's arms. The adrenalin rush that enabled him to hold his pose for this long was beginning to wash away.

"Evelyn respects me, you know. She appreciates my business acumen. We have made a lot of money for each other. We'll make lots more when you and Mackey are finally gone."

"Mr. Minim, please listen to me. Evelyn is dead and Mackey is very much alive and in charge."

"The gall of you," Minim spat, "Trying to weasel your way out. Who do you think you're dealing with? You are just like the other three. They just wouldn't be satisfied with what Evelyn gave them. They had to have more, always more, so, time for punishment.

"You never guessed that I was her punisher, did you? I am the one she chose. Speaking of which, she chose me to take care of you, too."

He was now holding the pistol in one hand, resting it on his knee. As he lifted the tiger's claw out of the box Delaney said, "Do you know that you are on camera and every move you've made and every word you've spoken has been recorded? See that camera up there?"

He stared at Delaney for a brief moment before awkwardly twisting, pistol in one hand, tiger's claw in the other, to look up and back, eyes quickly searching an empty ceiling. As he did, Delaney dove behind the kitchen counter. With a glance over his shoulder, he saw Minim spin around, dropping the tiger's claw and, while trying to get the pistol up into a shooting position, knock over the nearby lamp. Minim, now operating in semi-darkness, screamed, and Delaney guessed the razor-sharp claw tips had bit into his thigh.

Distracted and slow, Minim was unable to even get into his shooting position before Delaney hit the kitchen light switch.

Minim tried to hurry after him but was stymied by his weight and by trying to hold the pistol in that same awkward position he had seen them use on dozens of TV cop shows. And now it was dark. From a nearly closed pantry door Delaney watched as Minim fumbled along the wall searching for a light switch. Peering into the kitchen, he aimlessly pointed the pistol into the darkness.

Seeing Minim aim his pistol across the room, Delaney tossed a cast iron skillet behind him. It made a loud metallic thud and Minim quickly turned. He shot and the bullet cut into a wall, nowhere near the pan Delaney had tossed.

A sudden loud and insistent pounding on the entry door would, Delaney knew, compound within Minim's mind, a growing sense of disorientation that had to be heightened by the roar of the .45.

"Open up, now. St. Paul Police," a woman's voice shouted. The pounding became louder. Delaney knew she must be striking it with something metallic, not her hands. Delaney watched a confused Minim take two steps toward the door and begin pouring rounds through it. With the volleys and their echoes rolling like thunder off the walls, Delaney knew that Minim never heard him move in from behind to knock the panicked killer unconscious with the cast iron skillet.

Delaney ripped the pistol from Minim's grip and dashed for the door. He threw it open to find his police bodyguard, unharmed and pointing her revolver straight at his chest. Natalie Puckett took two quick steps and circled her arms around Delaney's neck as he pulled her close. They held each other like that for a long time while their fear, each for the other, slowly melted away.

MONDAY
MONDAY

A people without the knowledge of their past history, origin and culture is like a tree without roots.

—*Marcus Garvey*

Society or culture or whatever you might want to call it, has created us all solely and wholly for the purpose of maintaining its continuity and status quo.

—*U. G. Krishnamurti*

We are all hypnotized, aren't we? Don't we all live in a particular culture in a particular historical era? That is the inescapable experience that finally directs our every thought, our every action."

—*Dante Connacht*

46

REDEMPTION

Conor Delaney, always punctual, walked into Matteo's ten minutes late. She was seated at a table near what had been their booth, close to the front of the restaurant.

"Conor," Camille Bennett said as he sat. "It's so good to see you again, but I have to apologize in advance. You said this was important, but I'm really pressed for time. I have a deposition tomorrow and still need to do more preparation. I hope I don't sound too rude."

"I understand. That's billable time and this isn't."

"Conor, you sound awful. Have you been to a doctor? It sounds like it could be strep throat. You know, Ida has a wonderful cough syrup that's just the thing for a bad throat."

Delaney's eyeballs rolled toward the ceiling before he said, "Apologies to Ida but I have a very good doctor and nurses to look after me."

"But you sound so . . . raspy."

"It's temporary," he replied, taking a long draught from the water glass set in front of him. "But, sore throat and all, I come bringing you an offer of a great deal of new business – business that will keep you busy and challenged."

"Really? That's very nice of you." She smiled. "You have my attention."

"Actually, Camille, it's a major mop-up job, cleaning up a mess you, unfortunately, helped to create. But it will have lots of billable hours."

"What are you talking about?"

"KaliRose Investment Corporation. Ring a bell?" He could feel his voice growing fainter.

She visibly stiffened. "You know I can't discuss that with you, not any of it. Client confidentiality. You understand, don't you?"

"Sure. I'm even called upon to exercise it myself once in a while. But that's all right; I don't think you can tell me much I don't already know. And you should know, Evelyn Rose is dead."

Her facial expression was surprise, her body language, relief. "Are you sure? I mean, what do you . . . How do you know this?"

After signaling the waiter for another glass of water, he said, "I know because I was there when she was hauled off to her well-deserved fate. So she's gone, but KaliRose Investments is still a fund that needs looking after."

The waiter came over with a pitcher and another glass to take their order; Caesar salad for both.

When he left, Camille, in a low voice, asked, "How do you know about this?"

"Trade secret, of course. But it's my business to find out about these things, isn't it? And here's what I found out: Neat, little-known investment fund out of the Cayman Islands buys and sells St Paul Port Authority properties *and* bonds to launder funds that are, not to put too fine a point on it, illicit." He paused for another drink. "These kinds of transactions, like all big money deals, require an attorney to navigate all the curves and hazards that other lawyers have built into the system. You, my dear, are the attorney for this enterprise. You were the facilitator for most, if not all, of KaliRose's Port deals. Want to hear more?"

"Conor, please, please," she quietly stammered, glancing around the room. "It wasn't like that. You know it wasn't nearly that simple."

"I believe you. I'm guessing that when she first came to you, it was just as a rich woman needing some legal help with a simple little investment scheme. You only caught on to the real nature of the work after a while?"

"That's right, and when I did I tried to end the relationship. But my partners, they wouldn't do it. They saw the fees it was bringing in, and Pinnacle City

Bank was already a client. They thought we could really build solid and profitable relationships with the bank and Port Authority, to say nothing of the investment fund. They insisted I keep managing that account." She shook her head slowly. "Because of the terms of the partnership, I couldn't get out of it. So, I worked with her, hating every minute of it. Her eyes, I've never seen anything so frightening." She shuddered at the memory."

"Well, the wicked witch is now dead. From here on you'll work directly with Mackey."

"Conor, no! I can't do that." Her eyes were large and the fear was palpable.

"Relax, Camille. You're perfectly safe and your legal work will actually be for a good cause." He smiled in spite of the pain.

"Working for Mackey? How is that a 'good cause'?'"

Their salads came and they both took a few desultory bites before Delaney said, "As you well know, KaliRose has been propping up Port Authority bonds, buying and selling at strategic times. Without that opaque support, the value of the Port's bonds, and the commercial and residential properties they underwrite, would plummet. The city's economy would take a hit that would take years to overcome."

"I still don't see why..."

"Mackey has agreed to let KaliRose be managed in a manner that will allow that devaluation to take place over time and minimize the damage to the Port and the city, even if it hurts his bottom line."

"What does that have to do with me and more business for the firm?" The fear was still there, but her voice steady, now that business was on the table.

"You, my dear Camille" he stopped briefly to water his throat again. "You are to be the manager of that fund for all Port Authority matters. Mackey has agreed to let you handle it in whatever way you think best."

"But if he's my client...?"

"He wishes it managed in a way that will best benefit the City of St. Paul."

"You really do care about this City, don't you, Conor?"

"Yeah, I guess so." He hesitated, as if surprised by his answer.

Camille managed a small, unconvincing smile. "You have Mackey's agreement to this arrangement in writing?"

"Better. I have his word on it and you can draft up a representation agreement that will reflect the new purpose of the fund. He'll sign it."

"You do understand that my job is that of a managing attorney for this account. I supervise the work of several other attorneys. They are a combination of staff and outside contractors."

"Yes, of course, but you are the chief strategist. It's your name on all the legal papers and you're the only one who had direct contact with Evelyn. That will remain the modus operandi with Mackey."

"Conor, I don't like having to work for Mackey."

"Look on it as the price of redemption. You shouldn't have gotten involved in this whole mess to begin with." His hoarse voice made him sound more judgmental than he wanted.

She frowned and said, "It's all so simple for you, isn't it? You, who so easily gave up your insurance company's client, giving Gene Swearingen all he needed to drive that drug company into bankruptcy. The people in that company trusted you, Delaney, and you betrayed them."

"Those trusting people committed fraud, sold illegal Chinese drugs, said they were American-made and ended up killing somewhere between twenty-five and fifty of their customers - customers who trusted them. Should I have let them kill more?" Now he wished he could talk more forcefully. "Let me tell you a story . . ."

She pushed her chair back. "I really should go. My client is trusting me to be prepared for that deposition."

Delaney waved his hand, "Indulge me, Camille," he whispered. "I won't take more than five minutes or so. The story concerns two lawyers in one of the southern states. They had a client who confessed to them that another man was serving a life sentence for a murder that he, their client, had committed. Being good lawyers, they told no one until nineteen years later, immediately after their client died.

"The innocent party was then released, based on their information." As the pain intensified he wondered why he'd chosen to tell such a long-winded story. "But the man lost nineteen years of his life and could have died in prison. Had one of the lawyers talked, what would have happened? The innocent man would have been released, the guilty one would have been punished and the attorney would have lost his license to practice law.

"It seems to me that was a trade-off the attorney should have made. I'm pretty sure he could have found another line of work."

"I disagree. He did exactly what the canon of legal ethics requires."

"What about justice? Isn't that a higher calling than the canon of legal so-called ethics?"

"Sorry, this is a fascinating topic, but I have to go."

"Just one more question," he whispered faintly, rocking back on his chair's rear legs. "When did you first know I was on Evelyn's hit list?"

Camille's whole body tensed again, and she looked around as if seeking an escape route. "Oh, God. I swear, Conor, please, please believe me. I never *knew* anything and I couldn't go to anyone just having suspicions. I would have been disbarred for that."

"And I was almost killed - just like Graham Byrd, Suzanne Porter, Danny Fortuno and Karleen Martin."

Camille's eyes began to tear up. "You still don't get it, do you, Conor?"

"Don't get what?"

"What drove us apart? You never even asked why I left you. And I loved you so much. Walking away from you was the hardest thing I have ever done. But I had to."

"Had to? I don't think anyone was holding a gun to your head. But as long as we're on the subject, why did you leave?"

"It was Mackey. When my Uncle Mel told me that you and Mackey were best friends, it felt like I had been stabbed. He laughed about it, said it was a thing left over from childhood and at least your criminal friends operated at a high level. But all I could think of was that Mackey was a murderer, a drug lord, a pimp and a thief. Just the sound of his name frightened me. And you were his friend? That's when I realized that I really didn't know you; didn't know anything about you. Goddamn it, Conor, you frightened me then. I couldn't stay with a man who was Mackey's best friend." Her gray eyes glistened.

He handed her the kerchief from his jacket. "But you knew that from the moment we met. You even mentioned it."

"That was before I met Evelyn and saw how Mackey and his people actually operated. It makes me sick to think about what him and his people do. And he's your friend?"

Delaney was about to reply when his cell rang. He saw who the caller was and said, "Dalton, can I call you back?"

"I just talked with Assistant Chief Thorogood and he said to talk with you right away."

"This has to do with whatever was making you so nervous yesterday, doesn't it?"

" Yes it does, Mr. Delaney. You see, there was a hand. It was found down by the river, where the three victims were found. You know we lifted prints and DNA from Mackey's apartment? Well, you see, the prints and DNA from the hand match those of Evelyn Rose, er, Adam Bierce."

Once again Delaney felt something black and foul rising in his throat. "Thank you, Dalton. I have some calls to make."

Camille looked up. "What's wrong? Are you OK?"

Delaney held up his hand to ask for silence and rang Mackey's number. "What's the matter, Delaney?" Mackey asked, definitely in a happier mood than he was yesterday.

"Malcolm, can you put me in touch with Higgs?"

"Yeah, he's right here, for a change, having lunch. I'll put him on." He was pleased that Mackey said nothing about his voice.

Higgs' naturally raspy voice came through the phone: "Mr. Delaney, you want Higgs?"

"Higgs, did you kill Evelyn?"

"Higgs don't kill nobody."

"That phone and this one are both encrypted, now tell me . . ."

"Yeah."

"How?"

"Gotta move away from Mr. Mackey here. Some things, he don't wanna know. Now, very simple. Her wrist I manacle to a block of cement, put her claw on that hand and into the river she go. Where other bodies were found, there she was dumped."

"Was she alive when you tossed her in?"

"Very much, of course."

"Higgs, one of her hands was found on the shore down there." There was a long moment of silence before Higgs hung up.

Delaney turned and looked at Camille's now wide eyes and, shaking his head slowly, said quietly, "Camille, your client is alive."